PRAISE FOR EDWIN HILL

Who to Believe

"A small town simmering with secrets and betrayals is the setting for this compelling and twisty story. Deeply layered characters and a master's touch in deploying point of view to subvert reader expectations make *Who to Believe* a read-in-one-sitting thriller. I loved it!"

—Liv Constantine, internationally bestselling author of *The Last Mrs. Parrish*

"Confounding twists and seismic reveals stud Edgar nominee Hill's meticulously crafted, diabolically plotted mystery . . . A devilishly clever delight."

—*Kirkus Reviews* (starred review)

"As soon as readers think they've found a safe landing place for their sympathies, Hill detonates one of the series of game-changing twists he's planted throughout the narrative. Fans of Riley Sager will want to check this out."

—*Publishers Weekly* (starred review)

"*Who to Believe* is an inventive and fiendishly layered suspense novel. The characters are compelling, the setting rich, and the tension electric. A first-rate exploration of secrets dark and deep."

—Lou Berney, Edgar Award–winning author of *November Road*

"*Who to Believe* is a powerful, twisty dose of suspense that will keep readers guessing. Edwin Hill navigates the dark corners and complicated relationships of a small, seaside town with precision and panache. The kind of novel that evokes its influences while ratcheting up the thrills."

—Alex Segura, bestselling author of *Secret Identity*

"Kudos to Edwin Hill for a book so sophisticated, suspenseful, and shocking . . . Mute that cell phone and curl up for several hours of great suspenseful reading."

—*firstCLUE*

The Secrets We Share

"Full of whiplash twists and dark family secrets, Edwin Hill's new stand-alone is clever and chilling. Be advised to not trust anyone."

—Peter Swanson, bestselling author of *Every Vow You Break* and *The Kind Worth Killing*

"This suspenseful story will have readers careening from one . . . conclusion to the next."

—*Library Journal* (starred review)

"Hill keeps the clock ticking and the twists coming right up to the shocking conclusion. Suburban thriller fans will be well satisfied."

—*Publishers Weekly*

"Shari Lapena meets Ruth Ware. A compulsively readable domestic thriller about two sisters and the secrets they share."

—Charlie Donlea, *USA Today* bestselling author of *The Suicide House*

"A superbly crafted thriller that delivers on every level. Hill is a master storyteller who leads the reader through a maze, expertly unveiling one twist after another."

—Femi Kayode, author of *Lightseekers*

"My first Edwin Hill book and definitely not my last. *The Secrets We Share* is chock-full of mystery, intrigue, and nail-biting suspense. Murder, long-buried but never forgotten family secrets, twisted relationships, and brilliantly drawn, rich characters make this a fast-paced and compelling read. Pop it on your bookshelf now."

—Hannah Mary McKinnon, internationally bestselling author of *You Will Remember Me*

"With a rich, dark backstory of childhood trauma reminiscent of Tana French's *In the Woods*, this mystery is Hill's best yet."

—Karen Odden, author of *Down a Dark River*

"A bold, ambitious novel with a big, multigenerational storyline and a smart balance between mystery and suspense . . . For fans of Robert Bryndza and Karin Slaughter."

—*firstCLUE* (starred review)

WHAT HAPPENED NEXT

OTHER TITLES BY EDWIN HILL

Who to Believe

The Secrets We Share

Watch Her

The Missing Ones

Little Comfort

WHAT HAPPENED NEXT

A NOVEL

EDWIN HILL

This is a work of fiction. Names, characters, organizations, places, events, and incidents are either products of the author's imagination or are used fictitiously. Otherwise, any resemblance to actual persons, living or dead, is purely coincidental.

Published by Thomas & Mercer, Seattle
www.apub.com

EU product safety contact:
Amazon Media EU S. à r.l.
38, avenue John F. Kennedy, L-1855 Luxembourg
amazonpublishing-gpsr@amazon.com

ISBN-13: 9781662536854 (paperback)
ISBN-13: 9781662536847 (digital)

Cover design by Jarrod Taylor
Cover image: © Steven Kornfeld / Getty

Printed in the United States of America

To Jack

What do I remember about the murder on the lake? Nothing, really, though Julian insists I know more than I realize. "Charlie, dude," he says. "You have to dig deep. Start with what's true, then ask what happened next. And keep asking until someone tells you the truth."

But what is the truth? I've pulled details from police reports and read through archives of local news coverage to establish a timeline of the murder and identify the key players—the cop who responded to the call; the detective who took the case; the infant, me, who survived; and the man who didn't—but the story didn't catch on or devolve into a media sensation. Once the police investigation ended, the whole thing petered out. Now, even though we live in a world where crimes get dissected and rehashed and retold, where strangers debate what might have happened, where the guilty live in a perpetual state of unease, I can't find a single online forum dedicated to uncovering *this* truth. My truth.

But Julian's right. I should dig deep. There has to be more to the story. And if I ask the right question, if I find out what happened next, maybe the whole thing will finally feel real. Maybe my father will stop existing as a monster who haunts the shadowy corners of my world.

Chapter One

There is one thing I know for sure about the day of the murder: My aunt Hadley wasn't at Idlewood.

The rest of us were, though—my mother Jane, my brother Reid. My father Mark, too. Even my father's old friend Paul Burke, up from New York for the long Memorial Day weekend, had paddled to our dock from the next cove. As the sun edged behind the foothills surrounding the lake, the adults toasted the start of summer with gin and tonics. "Where's the rest of the gang?" Paul asked. "Isaac? How about Andrea?"

My mother glanced at my father, who stared out over the water.

Paul must have sensed the underlying tension between my parents as he polished off his cocktail and swung into the red canoe to leave. "It's my fault they're keeping to themselves," he said. "I bailed Isaac out with the whole restaurant thing, and he's been avoiding me ever since. I told him that dump was a bad investment. Still is." He shoved away from the dock and paddled out of the cove.

"The restaurant *was* a bad idea," my father said to my mother. "You should know better than I."

He transferred the cocktail glasses to a tray and headed toward the house, avoiding stones and exposed tree roots along the path. My mother lingered on the dock, probably grateful for a respite from my father's brooding silence as she set up the paper lanterns for the festival that started at sunset.

Idlewood was an old family camp on Hero Lake in New Hampshire that my mother had inherited from her father two years earlier. It sat on an island connected to the mainland by a long, narrow footbridge. In those days, we used an outhouse and piped water from the lake. Even now, we cart what we need over in wheelbarrows.

Inside the cabin, my father finished making the Bolognese that had been simmering on the old gas stove all afternoon. Wearing a pink apron that read TWIN DELIGHTS, he chopped parsley into a fine mince. A copy of *Gourmet* magazine lay open in front of him. At the kitchen table, my twelve-year-old brother, Reid, labored over his math homework, mumbling under his breath as he struggled through an algebra proof.

My mother eventually left the dock and came up to the house, where she busied herself by setting the table on the porch for dinner. In the kitchen, she peered out a window, through the trees and across the water toward the parking area on shore, where my father's yellow Volvo sedan stood out among the birch trees. Late evening sun shone off the water while the first loon of the season cried. Since my parents had only opened the cabin that morning, fishing poles and the winter's cobwebs spanned the rafters over our heads. On the CD player, Janet Jackson sang.

I lay in a bassinet tucked in the corner of the kitchen, so most of these details come from what I've pieced together as I've researched the day's events. Some of them, I've filled in with my imagination.

My father blew on a spoonful of Bolognese and carried it to my mother, who still hovered by the kitchen window. "Taste," he said.

I wonder if he meant the small kindness as a peace offering.

My mother relented. "Delicious."

"Happy summer," my father said.

"Let's hope."

My father would have been thirty-four then, two years younger than my mother, whom he'd met at a Hero Lake Junior Association dance when they were both teenagers. He was an accountant at my mother's construction firm and wore glasses and had the slender build of a cyclist. He hiked and performed with the local summer stock theater, and was busy rehearsing to play the lead in *Pippin*. Unlike my mother, his image at that age is fixed in my mind. I have a photo of him pressed between the pages of a rarely used thesaurus, a photo that ran in the local papers afterward, one that stares back at me with my own blue eyes.

He returned to the stove, while my mother checked the landline for the beep of a voicemail, even though the phone hadn't rung since we'd opened the cabin. She distracted herself by lifting me from the bassinet, holding me over her head, and calling me "Charlie Bear" until I laughed.

Through the trees came the roar of an engine, followed by the pop of a stone beneath a tire. My mother returned me to the bassinet, then touched the curly blond hair that fell around her shoulders and checked her reflection in a mirror. A moment later, a black pickup truck slid in beside the Volvo. Isaac Haviland got out of the cab and came to the shoreline on the other side of the footbridge.

"I thought you told him to stay away," my father said.

"Mark, please," my mother said. "I'll take care of it."

My father kept the apron on and the chef's knife in hand as he went out onto the wraparound porch with my mother trailing behind. Isaac Haviland stood on the opposite shore with his fists on his hips. He was tall and sturdy, with dark hair and a heavy beard. He wore a flannel shirt open to a white T-shirt. He shielded the sun with a hand.

"Jane," Mr. Haviland called across the water, "talk to me."

My mother touched my father's arm, but he shrugged her off, and she watched from the porch as he headed down the path, disappearing into the trees and onto the footbridge. A moment later, he reappeared on the shoreline. The two men were far enough away that my mother couldn't make out their words, but not so far that their anger didn't permeate the evening air.

The hinges on the screen door groaned as Reid joined my mother. She ran her fingers through his silky blond hair.

On the shore, my father shoved Mr. Haviland.

"I thought they were friends," Reid said.

"They are," my mother said. "But even old friends have rough patches. And I should make sure they don't make things worse."

Reid clung to her as though he knew what would happen next. "Stay," he said.

My mother cupped his cheek in the palm of her hand. "There's nothing to worry about. I'll take care of this. You keep an eye on Charlie Bear."

She extricated herself from Reid's embrace. By then, the sun had begun to set behind the foothills surrounding the lake. She passed through a thicket of blueberry bushes and brambles, and when she emerged onto the shore, she kept her voice light. "What are you boys getting into?"

On the porch, Reid sensed both men had calmed in her presence, enough so that he went into the kitchen and lifted me from the bassinet. He balanced me on his shoulder and cooed in my ear as he returned to the porch and watched the three adults through the trees. My father's shoulders had softened as he and Mr. Haviland spoke for a few moments. Finally, Mr. Haviland opened the door to the pickup truck, as if to leave. Then he turned to my mother, eyes closed. Later, Reid would tell the police officer, "Mr. Haviland looked like he wanted to kiss my mother. I think he called her *my love*."

My father flicked his wrist, a move so subtle that Reid barely noticed the flash of steel in the fading light. My mother waved her arms and screamed in our direction. Red, lots of red, bloomed from Mr. Haviland's white T-shirt. He clutched at his stomach. My father held my mother by her curls with one fist, and the bloodstained knife with the other. She clawed at his face, twisting her foot around his until they collapsed to the ground, blood oozing from where my father had slashed at her face and hands with the knife.

The sun slid behind a hill. The whole world seemed to stop in that instant, as day turned to night and brilliant color faded to shades of gray. Reid's feet were rooted to the porch. I wonder what he might choose to do now if he could relive this moment. I wonder if he's spent a lifetime asking how this day could have turned out differently had he run toward danger.

I started to cry.

That sound—a baby's wail—bifurcated our world into a before, when we had a family, and an after, where our father's choices have haunted us.

Around the lake, lights flickered. One by one, paper lanterns illuminated the darkness and lifted up off docks and into the night like tiny hot-air balloons. On the shore, my mother fought to wrest control of the knife. Blood coated her hands. My father hurled her to the ground. She grappled for his leg as he lunged toward the island, those blue eyes burning with rage.

He was coming for us next.

"We should run," Reid said.

I suppose he was talking to me.

Chapter Two

Memorial Day weekend

"The intro's good," Julian says to me over the phone as I weave along the rural highway in New Hampshire. "I like how you reconstruct what you *believe* happened on the lake and question your own reliability."

"I'm not reliable at all," I say. "I was a baby."

"You've done your research, though. The rest of the podcast can be about deconstructing your assumptions, but you'll need to ask lots of questions to get to the core of what happened. Keep at it, especially when someone doesn't want to answer."

I pull off the highway and onto a long rural road. "No one will want to answer," I say. "My mother and brother . . . we never talk about what happened."

"Charlie, you can do this," Julian says. "Trust me. And if they don't get angry—enraged, even—there isn't a story worth telling. CrimeCon's in September. Let's aim to have a trailer ready by then."

I click off the call.

Julian was two years ahead of me at prep school. Now he's a producer at the public radio station in Boston where I've been stuck working as a production assistant since graduating college four years ago. Julian's career trajectory, unlike mine, took off recently, when he developed a six-part series on the Boston Strangler, one that focused less on the gruesome nature of the crimes or the man convicted of committing them, Albert DeSalvo, and more on the lives of his victims. The series did well and got picked up nationally, and when I told Julian about the murder on the lake, he proposed a podcast that I'd host and he'd produce. "What would it be about?" I asked. "My mother had an affair, and my father killed her lover. It's pretty clear who the good guys and bad guys were."

"There's always more to tell," Julian said. "It's a murder in a small town where everyone knows each other. Besides, no one is all good or all bad. You have to find the right angle. A story like this one can catch on in the true-crime world."

So, for the last few months, Julian's worked his network to build interest, while I've mapped out how much of my story I know and who to speak with to fill in the gaps. This morning, I left my apartment in Somerville outside Boston and headed north to New Hampshire, where the whole thing began. Now, a quarter of a century after my father killed Isaac Haviland and left my mother to die, I'll start asking questions. Maybe this project will jump-start my career, too, but what I really want is to learn who my father was before. That way, I'll understand who he became.

And why.

I arrive at the end of an overgrown driveway and check the GPS. I'm in the middle of nowhere. I drop a pin and text the location to Julian. If you don't hear from me in the next fifteen minutes, I write, call in reinforcements.

I hit send and hope the message goes through, then ease onto the driveway. Two enormous brown dogs trot out of the trees, following along until I reach a tidy farmhouse with pansies spilling from window boxes. A pair of motorcycles sits beside a shed. The dogs approach the car window, tails wagging, teeth bared. Sweet and salty. Which side will they opt for if I open the door?

I tap record on my phone. "Lisa Lawson's house, Enstone, New Hampshire, twenty miles from the site of Isaac Haviland's murder. Lisa is the surviving partner of Wendy Burrows, the lead detective in the homicide investigation. Detective Burrows died a few months after the trail went cold in the search for my father. I found Lisa's name listed in Wendy's obituary."

I crank down the car window an inch. Dog slobber coats the glass. "Are you friendly?" I ask.

One of the dogs whines.

Julian will appreciate the question and the response. It adds texture to the audio.

Behind me, someone taps the glass. I spin around. A woman stands on the other side of the car, pitchfork in hand. She must be well into her seventies, with a mound of silver hair piled on her head. I lean across the car and crack that window open. "Lisa Lawson?" I ask.

"Who's asking?" the woman says. "And you can't be lost, because this house is on the way to absolutely nowhere."

"Charles Kilgore," I say. "Charlie. I called a few times. No one answered."

"Do you pick up your phone when you don't recognize the number?"

I open the car door an inch. The dogs press forward. "Will they bite?" I ask.

"They won't, but I might."

I ease out of the car as both dogs leap up to lap me in the face. They're friendly, in an aggressive, nonconsensual way. "I wish I had treats," I say.

"You'd never get rid of them," Lisa says, snapping her fingers so the dogs come to her side. "This one's Lenny. The other one's Squiggy. You're too young to get the reference."

"*Laverne and Shirley*," I say.

"Score one point for the handsome stranger who rides into town. What do you want, anyway?"

"You were married to Wendy Burrows."

"In another lifetime," Lisa says. "And we weren't exactly married. Wendy and I were together long before any of that was legal. And she probably died before you were born."

"I'm looking into one of her cases. A cold case."

Lisa takes in my chartreuse cardigan and bowling shirt. "You can't possibly be a cop." Her eyes narrow. "Charlie Kilgore . . . You're that baby, Mark's kid. I should have known. You look exactly like him. Same floppy black hair. Same blue eyes. Same skinny ass." She glances toward my car. "Same yellow Volvo."

Yes, my yellow '83 Volvo sedan is the same car that was parked at Idlewood when my father killed Isaac Haviland. I found it stored in a shed a few years ago when I needed a free set of wheels, and it started on the first try. The car has a cassette tape deck, a functioning cigarette lighter, and an interior that reeks of tobacco and pot. Lately, the asphalt has started to show through the rusted-out holes in the floor. Now that I'm in New Hampshire and away from the busy streets of Somerville, I'll find the time to slide under the frame to see what I can patch.

I plan to keep the Volvo until it dies on the side of the road, or at least until I finish recording this podcast. Photos of me behind the wheel will play well in social media posts.

"Could I ask you some questions?" I ask. "It'll only take five minutes."

"How about thirty seconds," Lisa says, "and then you can get the hell out of here. I didn't know your dad well, but he was supposed to be in *Pippin* that summer. I played Berthe. Your father could sing. Tenor. Beautiful voice." She puts a hand to her hair, and I swear she blushes. "But once your father screwed everything up, I had to sing with Whit Entwhistle, who couldn't hit a single note."

Ruining the local musical was hardly my father's worst crime. "But Wendy, your wife—"

"I told you already, we weren't married. If we'd been married, I'd have her pension and could afford to get the roof on this house replaced."

"Wendy was the lead investigator on the Haviland murder."

"And we were supposed to go camping in Old Orchard Beach the day after Wendy got put on that investigation. I tried to rebook the site, but they were full, and Wendy wound up having to work around the clock anyway. The whole summer was ruined."

"Did Wendy ever mention my father, or why he did what he did?"

"Nothing worth sharing," Lisa says. "She was due to retire at the end of that year. Look what happened with that."

From what I've read, Wendy Burrows was either a good cop with a good close rate or a cop who did her best to close cases quickly—I'm not sure which. What I do know is that she was found in her car at the bottom of the lake. "She died in the middle of a homicide investigation," I say. "That's suspicious, right?"

Lisa swings the pitchfork over her shoulder. "Wendy was a state detective. She was always in the middle of an investigation. That was her job. What is there to say, anyway? She ended most shifts by drinking a fifth of vodka over on Foss Hill. That night, she hit the gas instead of the brake and drove off the ledge into the lake. It was before they put in the guardrail. With the way she drank, I'm surprised it didn't happen sooner. Why are you asking about the Haviland case, anyway? It's not like your father wasn't guilty."

"Could he have killed Wendy?" I ask.

"Your father?" Lisa asks. "Only if he came back as a ghost."

The door to the house opens and a woman steps onto the porch. "Lunch is ready, Lisa," she says.

"My minder," Lisa says under her breath. "This one keeps me on a short leash, but they don't last. I'll have her out of here within the week."

The woman approaches. She must be in her early forties, with dark hair tied in a ponytail and sensible shoes. "Can I help you?" she asks.

"We're fine, *Zoe*," Lisa says. "Charlie here's an old friend."

"I'm Karen, not Zoe," the woman says. "You ran Zoe off last month. Why don't we come inside? I made us some tomato soup."

"They don't let me have a grain of salt," Lisa says to me. "Not a single one. Nothing tastes like anything." Karen takes her arm, but Lisa shakes her off. "Wendy and I could have spent months camping at Old Orchard Beach without worrying about a thing. Instead, here I am. With *Zoe*."

"Karen," Karen says.

◆ ◆ ◆

Reception on my phone doesn't return until I've left Lisa Lawson's house and nearly made it back to the highway. Julian picks up on the first ring. "How'd it go?"

"Dead end," I say. "She didn't want to talk. At least, not about the right things."

"Did she sign a release?"

"I didn't get a chance."

"Head back in a few days. Keep working her and get her to sign. You never know where these things might lead. Meanwhile, upload the recording and I'll see what's there."

I click off the call, transfer the recording to my phone, then post the file to the Cloud for Julian. Ahead, a sign marking the town line for Hero, New Hampshire, appears at the side of the forested road. I tap record and set the digital recorder on the dashboard. "Friday, May 22," I say, practicing my narration. "Arriving in Hero, twenty-five years later, a tiny town nestled in the foothills of the White Mountains where nothing as spectacular as my father's epic collapse has ever happened, before or since. Tonight, we'll celebrate the start of summer—"

Behind me, blue lights flash as an SUV cruiser hugs my tail. I groan and pull to the side of the road as one of the local cops, Seton Haviland, takes her time exiting the cruiser and sauntering alongside the Volvo in her police uniform.

I should have expected this.

Chapter Three

Hero is too small of a town to arrive without being noticed, especially by a cop like Seton, who wears aviators and has dark hair cropped short. Her boxy uniform hangs off her as though she picked it up at a costume shop for a Halloween party and forgot to order the sexy version. She taps on the glass and waits for me to crank down the window before resting her tattooed—and jacked—forearms on the yellow door.

"Charlie Kilgore," she says. "Don't lose this beater. Otherwise, I won't know when you get to town. Glad you survived the winter."

"Good to see you, Seton," I say.

"You were speeding. It's Memorial Day weekend, and everyone's coming back to the lake for the summer. You have to watch out for kids."

We're in the middle of nowhere, on a road lined with thick forest and outcroppings of granite, but I've known Seton since we learned to swim together on the lake as kids. We still go swimming, and one of these days, maybe I'll work up the courage to confess I find her plenty sexy beneath that boxy uniform, in a tattooed, pierced, tough-as-nails kind of way. I suspect, though, that Seton wants to keep me safely friend-zoned.

"Does this car look like it can speed?" I ask. "I should report you for police harassment."

Seton shifts the aviators to look at me over the frames. "Report away. I'm the chief of police now—or acting chief, at least till they fill the vacancy. My mom's on the hiring committee. Think I'll get the job?"

Seton will get the job, and it won't be because her mother pulled strings. Seton's nothing if not competent.

She leans her back against the car and shimmies down until her legs form a right angle. "Missed my wall sits this morning," she says. "Gotta work the glutes. Did I tell you about the helicopter? The town bought one, and I'm getting my license. If you're nice, I'll take you for a ride."

The last thing in the world I want is to get in a helicopter with a novice pilot. "We'll see," I say.

"Sure, we will," Seton says. "How's the journalism career?"

"Good as can be," I say. "I like the radio station."

"You could move here and take over the *Kingston Gazette*. Ollie's ready to retire. We could work cases together, me the cop, you the reporter. *Haviland and Kilgore*. It'd be like one of those cheesy old TV shows, except nothing happens here besides the usual drug dens and hunting violations. And speeding."

"I wasn't speeding," I say.

"Speed limit's forty. You were going forty-two, but I'll let you off." She stands and shakes out her legs. "Here are some stories you could cover: The Randalls' rooster has been waking the whole neighborhood at the crack of dawn. And someone's stealing firewood from the Millers' house, but they refuse to put in a security camera. Autumn and Juna over on Sheridan Road are constantly getting out—they're dogs, by the way."

Before she can delve into minute details from the latest town meeting, I cut her off. "Do you ever run into Lisa Lawson?"

"That lady who used to be in local theater? Not really, but she lives in Enstone, not Hero. Why do you ask?"

"No reason," I say.

"Well, here's another thing going on around town," Seton says. "My mom has it in for Paul Burke. He tore down his old cabin at Burkehaven. Now he's putting in a whole development."

Seton's mother, in addition to being on the hiring committee for the new chief of police, is the unofficial mayor of Hero, a position she manages from the café she owns downtown. She's also the chair of the Hero Conservation Commission and opposes most new development, which usually involves attending public hearings and then getting drunk and rage-posting on the town listserv, the Hero Board. Unfortunately for her, the Burkehaven project was approved unanimously.

"I know all about Burkehaven," I say. "Reid's designing the development."

My family's construction firm won the bid, and Seton's mother's opposition probably has more to do with our involvement than anything else. Seton's mother, Andrea Haviland, is the widow of Isaac Haviland, the man my father killed, a topic Seton and I manage to avoid discussing however we can. It's the only way we've stayed friends.

"This is a part of the story you probably don't know," Seton says. "Someone took out the security cameras at the construction site yesterday morning with a spare sledgehammer. I'll give you one guess who the prime suspect is. My mom. I had to question her. She tried to blame it on teenagers who hang out there and drink."

"She could be right," I say. "We drank plenty of Bud Light at Burkehaven when we were that age."

"Well, now she's not speaking to me," Seton says. "But I finally moved out of her house. I got an apartment in town. It's over the café, so technically my mom's my landlord. And right now, I'm banned from the café."

With the sound of an approaching car, Seton stands straight, smile gone, her thumbs resting in her belt loops. The car slows as it passes, and the driver shouts Seton's name.

"Gotta look like I'm earning my keep," she says, dropping the act as soon as the car turns the next corner.

"Try arresting the Randalls' rooster," I say.

"Thanks, hack," Seton says. "That's a good line: *Thanks, hack.* I'll say it when we work together on *Haviland and Kilgore.* It'll be my signal to the audience that I know how annoying you are."

"There is no *Kilgore and Haviland*," I say.

"It's *Haviland and Kilgore*. Get it right. Alphabetical. I'm the main character. You're the sidekick . . ." Seton pauses, glancing past me. I follow her gaze to where the digital recorder sits on my dashboard, the red record light illuminated. "What are you doing?" she asks.

"Sorry, I forgot that was on."

She reaches over my shoulder and hits pause. "You can't record someone without consent. It's a felony. And erase what I said about my mom."

Another car turns the corner. Seton nods at the driver and touches the brim of her hat. When the car passes out of sight, she crouches. "Spill. What's the recording for?"

"A podcast."

"About *what*?"

"You can't tell anyone," I say.

Seton swears under her breath. "That's why you were asking about Lisa Lawson. She used to live with the lead detective on my dad's murder case. Is this some true-crime crap about our fathers?"

So much for the détente on that topic.

"Why would you dig all that up?" Seton asks. "We all know what happened, Charlie."

Damn. *We all know what happened, Charlie*—that would have been a good line to record.

"I'm trying to find out what *really* happened," I say.

Another good line.

"We all know what *really* happened, too," Seton says. "Your dad killed mine, and by some miracle, we're friends, though right now I'm not sure for how much longer."

"Will you say *We all know what happened, Charlie*, again for the recording?"

"No! I'm not saying anything for the recording. That story's been following me for my entire life. Keep me out of it."

"Okay, okay," I say. "I get it. You don't want to be interviewed. The podcast is mostly conceptual anyway, and it probably won't go anywhere."

"How about guaranteeing it doesn't go anywhere by not doing it?"

"Don't worry," I say. "I'm not great on follow-through."

"It's one of the things I like best about you." Seton kicks at the Volvo's front tire. "Are you coming to the café tonight?"

"I thought you were banned from the café."

"I don't listen to my mom."

"And that's one of the things I like best about *you*," I say. "But I won't be able to get there till tomorrow. We're opening the camp today. And there's the Lantern Festival."

Tonight, as on every Memorial Day weekend, paper lanterns will float over the lake—like they did twenty-five years ago.

"You lake people and your traditions," Seton says. "The Lantern Festival is a fire hazard. I should sic my mom on you and get it banned. Payback for your stupid podcast." A voice crackles over her radio, something about an incident at Burkehaven. "Speaking of my mom." Seton takes a deep, centering breath, one that she exhales for a full five-count. "I have to take care of another mess she's in the middle of. *You* stay out of it. Understand? And drop the podcast. It's a terrible idea. Like, the worst idea I've ever heard in my entire life."

She jogs to the cruiser and speeds past me toward town. When the sound of the siren fades, I start the recording again. As Julian told me earlier, if people don't get angry, there's no story to tell. And I have no intention of dropping the podcast, for Seton or anyone else.

"We all know what happened, Charlie," I say. "That's what Seton Haviland said to me. She doesn't want me to dig into the past. Her father died. My father killed him. We've carried the weight of that burden through our whole lives, of what happened, of what was taken, and what could have been."

I pause as another car passes, waiting until the sound of the engine has faded in the distance.

"Here's more of what I know," I say. "Seton's father, Isaac Haviland, hired Reid Construction to rehab an old train depot in town. My mother, Jane Reid, and Mr. Haviland began working closely together, which led to an affair. When Mr. Haviland showed up at Idlewood, he intended to convince my mother to leave with him."

I pause. The rest of the story is hard to say out loud.

"My father stabbed Isaac first, then my mom, then turned on my brother Reid and me, but Reid escaped with me in a rickety old rowboat. He pulled on the oars until we were a hundred yards from shore, drifting on the inky water, while paper lanterns floated overhead. It was early in the season. The docks hadn't yet gone in, and the other boats were in storage. That didn't keep my father from wading into the water and begging Reid to return to shore. Reid rowed farther into the lake to keep us safe, and my father eventually fled the scene.

"Hours later, a local cop found the two of us huddled on that boat. A massive manhunt began, with Wendy Burrows leading the investigation, and the next day, this yellow Volvo, the one I'm driving right now, was found at a trailhead in the White Mountains as a freak spring snowstorm hit the region and stranded hikers all over the range. Resources were diverted to search and rescue, and by the time the hunt for my father resumed, the trail had grown cold. The police claim my father died on that mountain, though his body was never found."

I tap my finger on the steering wheel.

"Isaac Haviland's murdered. My father disappears. The lead investigator drowns."

We all know what happened, Charlie.

We do know. Or we should know. My father died in those mountains. He must have. He was an accountant who wore glasses and sang in regional theater, not a mountain man, so if he didn't die, he should have been caught by now.

"But without a body," I say, "you can never truly know if someone's gone."

Chapter Four

The town of Hero spills over the foothills and clings to the lakeshore. Eagle's Nest Landing, the café Isaac Haviland built all those years ago—the one Seton's mother, Andrea Haviland, owns now—sits in an old train depot at the end of a long-defunct rail line. Out in the marina, piers have begun to fill with boats coming out of dry dock for the season. Quaint shops, a nineteenth-century hotel, a summer stock theater, and a grid of antique homes, one of which Seton's mother lives in, form the core of the town. On the southern side of the marina, brand-new condos rise from where a crumbling motel once sat, part of my brother Reid's plan to transform Hero and bring in more summer residents.

Beyond town, the street narrows as it curves through densely packed summer cabins dotting the shore. After a few miles, the houses grow sparse and then disappear as the road swerves away from the lake and past a cemetery with two dozen weatherworn headstones. A blue bungalow, my mother's winter home, sits at a T in the road.

I pull alongside a well-tended perennial garden, where my aunt Hadley's head of short dark hair bobs among daisies begging to bud. She holds up a hand to block the sun. "You're here," she says, her voice soft and girlish.

"Up for the weekend," I say. "Then it's back to the grind."

"At the radio station?"

"As long as they'll have me."

"I fly to Cairo Tuesday morning," Hadley says. "Maybe I can hitch a ride with you to the airport."

Hadley volunteers around the world as a trauma surgeon. When she's in Hero, she takes shifts at the Kingston Hospital ER on the other side of the lake. She's in her mid-fifties, her short hair cut more for practicality than fashion. Even when she's not at work, she usually wears scrubs, like this set, which is covered with what appear to be hand puppets.

"I'll be here most weekends this summer," I say. "I wish you were staying longer."

"I'm your favorite aunt."

"You're my only aunt."

"And your favorite aunt can only take so much lake time before going stir crazy," Hadley says, nodding down the dirt road. "Seton drove by like a bat out of hell. What's going on?"

"Her mother's up to something at Burkehaven," I say.

"Another sledgehammer?"

"Innocent until proven guilty."

"You always defend Andrea Haviland."

"She's nice to me," I say. "Same as you. And I'd defend you, too."

"Good to have an ally," Hadley says.

I wave as I pull away and into the forest. Here, a thick canopy of trees absorbs the sun, and the woods are damp and green with new growth. A lichen-covered boulder the size of a Volkswagen marks a fork in the road. A sign to the right points toward Burkehaven, while turning left takes me to my home, Idlewood.

Haviland and Kilgore.

Seton's the one who wants me to play sidekick. We won't have much narrative tension if I avoid interfering where I don't belong. Plus, I hear Julian coaching me to insert myself into the story, to be bold and ask uncomfortable questions. If he were here right now, he'd say, "It's the only way to get to the truth."

A moment later, the trees open on Burkehaven Cove, which sits on the southern shore of Hero Lake, five miles by boat from town, and a bit longer by car. Like Idlewood, Burkehaven is a family camp, one that used to have a small cabin on the shore and a much larger farmhouse out by the road at the base of the foothills. For years, Paul Burke's parents maintained the property's hiking trails and invited people in town to use the long shoreline. But Paul moved away to New York years ago, so when his mother died last year, he decided to sell out and develop the property. Now the cabin's been leveled, along with most of the trees, replaced by mounds of earth and construction equipment.

I park in a muddy clearing next to Seton's cruiser, get out of the car, and follow the sound of raised voices. At a bend in the shoreline, the entrance to the cove appears. Farther down, a nearly finished house sits on the point, surrounded by piles of earth ready for landscaping. As I get closer, the signature elements in Reid's green designs come into shape: rammed earth construction, glass walls, and public and private zones surrounding a central courtyard for intergenerational living—or for hosting parties on the lake.

Hardscape stretches from the courtyard to the shore, where a long dock extends into the water. There, I recognize Andrea Haviland's gray ponytail poking out from a green cap for the Boston Fleet hockey team. She's anchored her boat, a Bryant 219, a few yards from shore. It's the same model we have at Idlewood: nineteen feet long, eight-seater, right down to the maroon siding. My brother, Reid, and Paul Burke stand on the dock, along with Seton, who's positioned herself between the two men and the boat. Her police badge flashes in the sun each time she pivots.

"There's nothing *green* about this development," Mrs. Haviland says into a bullhorn, her voice echoing across the cove. "You cut down the entire shoreline."

"It's only us, Mom," Seton says. "You don't need that thing."

"Traitor," Mrs. Haviland says into the bullhorn.

"We're replacing the trees," Reid says, his blond hair poking from beneath a yellow hard hat. "We're putting in microforests of native plantings."

"Microforests?" Mrs. Haviland says. "What the hell is a microforest? And what's wrong with an old-fashioned macroforest? The one that's been here for the last hundred years?"

"Come on, Andrea," Paul says, holding his hands out in a kind of peace offering. "Can you cut me some slack?"

"Don't play victim, Paul," Mrs. Haviland says. "You abandoned Hero years ago, when you took off for New York."

Paul Burke is in his late fifties, the same age my father would be now, with a slim runner's build and thick salt-and-pepper hair. "I can't keep the property," he says. "The taxes are killing me."

"Burkehaven is worth millions," Mrs. Haviland says. "You could sell one lot, live off the profit, and donate the rest to the conservation commission."

"This is about access," Reid says. "You're desperate to keep things the way they were. I want to open the lake so people can live here."

Mrs. Haviland scoffs. "You're building eight houses that only the one percent can afford on land the whole town used to use. Now no one but your rich friends will have *access*, and they'll set up their security cameras and make sure no one else can come here even though they'll probably use the houses for a week or two a year, tops. But guess who *will* be here. Me and my trusty bullhorn. I call her Heidi."

"I bet you'll be here," Reid says. "Like you were when you smashed the security cameras."

"I had nothing to do with that," Mrs. Haviland says.

"Mom, take it down a notch," Seton says. "Please."

"You, Seton Haviland, are officially banned for life from the Landing," Mrs. Haviland says. "Don't even think about showing up for dinner tonight."

"We're replacing the cameras," Reid says. "I'll send you the bill. And the building permits are signed. You won't screw me like you did with Rocky Nook. You made your case with the zoning board and lost. There's nothing else to do."

"Oh, there's plenty to do," Mrs. Haviland says. "And don't worry. I'll find another violation to keep you from working. I'll put you out of business if I have to."

Reid moves toward her, his hands clenched, but Seton blocks his path. "Keep it civil, Reid," she says.

"Do something, then," Reid says. "Your mother's trespassing."

"I'm in *my* boat, on the *people's* lake," Mrs. Haviland says. "Public access. No one owns the waterways—not you or your rich friends."

Seton takes a deep breath. "She can be anywhere she wants on the water."

The conversation is getting heated, too heated. I announce my presence by catching a stone with the toe of my shoe and letting it skitter across the dock and into the water. I add a little stumble for effect as Seton spins to face me. "I told you to stay out of this," she says.

"*Kilgore and Haviland*?" I say.

"Thanks, hack," she says. "And it's *Haviland and Kilgore*."

"Charlie Bear!" Reid says, his shoulders relaxing. "Nice cardigan. You're rocking the geezer look."

While I dress like an old man, my brother opts for a carefully cultivated aesthetic of expensive thick-rimmed glasses and the plaid flannel that helps him blend in on a construction site.

"Don't listen to him," Paul says, pulling me in for a hug.

I nod toward Mrs. Haviland's hockey cap. "We did a story at the station on the women's hockey league last month. Have you been to any of the games?"

"A few," she says.

"You and I should go together sometime. It's easy enough for me to get to Lowell. We could meet there."

One of my strengths is that no one takes me seriously, so I can defuse almost any situation.

Mrs. Haviland offers a hint of a smile. "The season's over, but maybe next year," she says. "If I'm still talking to you."

She flips on the boat's blower and turns the key. The engine chugs and then roars to life as she hauls the anchor on board. "Good to see you, Charlie," she says. "I'll catch you on the lake this summer. We can go water-skiing. The rest of you can go to hell. And don't think about starting up construction, Reid. Not a single nail."

As she speeds away, Reid turns on Seton. "She reported an OSHA violation and got us shut down. That's the third time she's done this. I'm bleeding money, and if we can't start up by Tuesday, I'll lose my crew."

Seton raises her hands. "If you want to keep from getting shut down, Reid, play by the rules."

"Tell your mother to stay away from us."

"The water *is* public access," Seton says. "My mom can take her boat wherever she wants, even right up to the end of your dock, and there's nothing I can do about it."

A voice behind me says, "Let it alone, Reid. Seton's doing her job."

I turn to see my mother, Jane, emerge from the half-constructed home, her silver-kissed curls spilling from beneath a hard hat, a scarf tied around her neck, tan work boots poking from under the hem of her blue summer dress.

"Hi, Jane," I say.

My mother kisses my cheek. "Thanks for coming, Seton," she says, "but the situation's under control."

Seton's resolve melts a bit. "I'm sorry about all this, Mrs. Reid."

"Call me Jane. Charlie does," my mother says, scowling at me. "And 'Mrs. Reid' makes me feel old."

Once Seton leaves in her cruiser, my mother glares after Andrea Haviland's retreating boat, now a dot on the horizon. Nothing pisses my mother off more than an idle construction site. "One of these days," she says, "Andrea Haviland will get herself killed."

Chapter Five

Reid and my mother confer by the construction site, while Paul Burke stands with me on the end of the dock. He adjusts his wire-rimmed glasses. In the last few years, gray has crept into his hair and eyebrows, but he maintains the slender physique and effortless style of someone used to walking the streets of Manhattan. Today, he wears a gauzy white shirt open at the neck and tailored pants. "I left Burkehaven behind a long time ago," he says. "I'm ready to move on, though try telling that to Andrea Haviland. Somehow, she's morphed into a crazy old lady."

"You've known Mrs. Haviland your whole life," I say, without noting that Paul and Andrea are about the same age. If he wants to call her old, he can say the same of himself. "Can't you get her to chill out?"

"Andrea hasn't chilled out since she emerged from the womb. And the two of us haven't been close for a long time. But the trick is to redirect her focus. She has a soft spot for you, Charlie. Get her to try banning Jet Skis on the lake or something similar."

Paul, Mrs. Haviland, and my father were all friends growing up. As the three of them approached adulthood, each chose a different path: Andrea married Seton's father, Isaac, another local, and stayed in Hero. My father met my mother, and even though they lived in the bungalow during the winter, in a way, he became one of the lake people, rich and privileged, or seemingly so. Paul fled town as soon as he could. He went to college and law school in New York and hit up the well-heeled families he'd met on the lake to find new clients. For the last decade, his most important client has been an actress who lives in New York, too, and who he works for as a lawyer and manager.

To Paul's credit, ever since my father disappeared—I can't bring myself to say *died*—he's done what he could to serve as a sort of surrogate father, especially to Reid. He encouraged Reid to go to NYU and helped him navigate his transition into the professional world as an architect.

"I listened to your radio show," Paul says to me now. "The one about the Boston Strangler. It helped with the trip here from New York."

"That's our goal," I say. "To get you through those long drives."

"What's next?" he asks.

Now would be the time to confess to making a podcast about what happened on the lake, but if Seton's reaction to the news is indicative of how others might respond, I'll hold off. "My producer and I are batting around ideas," I say as my mother and Reid join us. "I'll tell you about them later."

"What will you tell us about later?" my mother asks.

"Charlie has a new project," Paul says. "Top secret, apparently."

Reid gooses my arm. "No secrets. Not at the lake."

I shove his hand away. My brother is thirty-seven now, nearly twelve years older than I am, and his role in my life sits somewhere between brother and uncle. Protector, too. I suspect a part of him hasn't ever left that rowboat he used to save us from our father.

My mother snakes an arm around Reid's waist and pulls him close. The two of them have a bond, one they forged the night they managed to survive. It's a strong enough bond to keep others on the outside looking in, even me. I wonder if it's the reason my mother sent me to boarding school while Reid attended public school here in Hero, or why I often feel as if I'm visiting relatives when I come home.

"Charlie," my mother says, "don't think I didn't see what you did there with Andrea, sweet-talking with her about hockey and waterskiing."

"Mrs. Haviland's not so bad," I say.

"Try dealing with her at a zoning-board meeting," Reid says.

I glance toward the half-built structure on the point. "Lake houses are supposed to blend in with the shoreline," I say. "You could practically see this one from space."

"Anyone who can afford the lake wants a showpiece," my mother says.

"And Freya Faith's lined up to buy," Reid says.

Freya Faith is the actress Paul works for. I haven't met her in person, though Paul's talked about knowing her for as long as I can remember. She grew up summering on the lake, and nearly everyone in town has a story of meeting her or seeing her perform even though she hasn't stepped foot in Hero for decades.

Freya played Agent Gina Shock on a series called *Scene of the Crime*, a police procedural. The show ran for years, and reruns still air nearly twenty-four hours a day, including an episode from season 2 based on what happened to my family. It was set on a lake and begins with a father who tries to kill his entire family with a chef's knife when he learns his wife is having an affair. I've watched it about fifty times.

"You convinced Freya Faith to move to New Hampshire?" I say to Paul.

"I haven't convinced Freya to do anything," Paul says. "And Reid, stop with the hard sell. What would Freya do up here in the middle of nowhere? She's a city girl."

Reid takes off his hard hat and runs a hand through his blond hair. I have a sudden flashback to being young, five or six, and sneaking into Reid's bedroom at the bungalow, where the walls were covered with images of Freya he'd torn from magazines and tabloids. Most were publicity stills from *Scene of the Crime*, but a signed headshot, one that Paul probably got for him, sat in a frame on his bedside table. I'd overheard my mother whispering with Hadley about the photos. "Freya plays a cop," my mother had said. "The photos . . . they probably make Reid feel safe after what happened."

I look at Reid now and wonder what he remembers about his teenage bedroom, whether he really believed a fictional TV cop could protect him from the terrors of the world. Maybe I can get him to sit down with Freya for the podcast and talk about the intersection of fiction and true crime, or what it's like to see his teenage fantasy in the flesh. Those are angles Julian would appreciate.

"You talk to Freya about the house, then," Reid says to Paul. "We need the sale."

"We need to line up *other* buyers," Paul says. "Freya will think nothing of stringing you along before leaving you high and dry."

Right then, a hundred yards down the shore, a truck pulls into the parking area beside my Volvo.

"Vance Moodey," Reid says. "What do you bet a little bird named Andrea Haviland told Vance the construction site has been shut down and he's here to make us settle our tab? The vultures'll be out in droves soon enough."

"I'll deal with Vance," my mother says. "Reid, Paul, stay here and don't make trouble. Charlie, walk with me." She pulls me with her off the dock and onto the shoreline path. "We have other projects in the works," she says, "including a lease for an outdoor mall in Finstock that Reid's managing, but losing Burkehaven would be a setback." We pass the remnants of the rustic cabin that once was the only structure in the cove. "Every time we build one of these monstrosities, the lake changes," my mother says with an air of remorse that surprises me.

"You didn't have to bid on the project," I say.

"Spoken like someone who's never run a business. People depend on me. I don't have the luxury of walking away from cash, Charlie. Especially not right now. Besides, if I didn't win the bid, someone else would have. And I mitigate what I can."

Vance Moodey stands by a truck with DON'T GET MAD, GET MOODEY stenciled on the door above MOODEY LUMBER. He wears a Red Sox cap and a blue flannel shirt and is doughy and tall with the red nose of someone who drinks too much.

My mother introduces us. “Come back after the weekend, Vance,” she adds, her words clipped. “Right now, I can’t tell you what you want to hear.”

“Jane,” Vance says, “you’ll have to deal with me eventually.”

“I need time,” my mother says. “I mean it.”

Vance turns his cap around. “I suppose we’ll touch base on Tuesday, then.” He gets into the truck and rolls down the window. “I won’t wait around forever. It’s not fair.” He backs the truck out and guns the engine as he takes off through the trees.

“He’s salty,” I say. “How much “” do you owe him, anyway?”

“More than I want to,” my mother says, “but it’s nothing for you to worry about. And everything isn’t about money. Get settled at the house. The boys from the marina will be by soon to install the docks. Make sure they have what they need.”

The scarf around my mother’s neck flutters in the breeze, lifting to reveal one of the scars from when my father slashed at her with a chef’s knife. My mother fought him off and then dragged herself a half mile through the woods to the bungalow, where she passed out in a pool of her own blood.

She’s been fighting ever since.

◆ ◆ ◆

I take the Volvo to the fork in the road, then drive to another parking area on the shore. Across this cove, golden light bathes the trees around Idlewood, our summer cottage. I toss a suitcase into one of the wheelbarrows and cross the footbridge, a narrow set of planks about fifty yards long connecting the mainland to the three-acre island.

The camp consists of a cottage, a second sleeping cabin, and three docks positioned around the island to catch the sun at different times in the day. We have the Bryant 219 motorboat, four kayaks, two canoes, and a hammock. We don’t have Wi-Fi or television. This is a place built to touch grass and relax.

The cottage appears through the trees, with its granite foundation, wraparound porch, and shingles stained brown. Unlike that new house at Burkehaven, this cottage blends in with the shoreline. Between bunkrooms and sleeping porches, the house accommodates twenty people. My mother finally installed a septic system fifteen years ago, but our proximity to the lake necessitates selective flushing.

Inside, sheets have been pulled from furniture, and shutters have been removed and stowed in the crawlspace beneath the house. Despite the open windows, the air in the vast great room retains a musty smell from being closed off for the winter. I roll the suitcase across the warped floorboards and up the narrow back stairs to my room, where a twin bed covered in a green-and-blue quilt I most recently tucked in last October greets me. Rickety secondhand furniture fills every corner of the room, and the crooked windows offer views of the lake.

Downstairs, I retrieve the old issue of *Gourmet* from a row of cookbooks covered in cobwebs. I turn to the recipe for Bolognese, where a splatter of tomato sauce dots the magazine's well-worn pages. I start the digital recorder, moving the mic close to the cutting board to capture the knife slicing through onions. I light the stove with a match and put an orange Dutch oven over the flame to heat.

"I don't question enough," I say. "So much of what happens at Idlewood is tradition. Five minutes ago, I parked my car in the same lot where my father stabbed Isaac Haviland. Right now, I'm making Bolognese using the same recipe from the same magazine my father used on the day he disappeared. There's a stain across the page I *hope* is from a tomato. Later, we'll watch paper lanterns floating over the lake. Afterward, we'll have this Bolognese for dinner and play cards on the screened-in porch, and we'll do it all as though nothing ever happened here, as though this recipe, this magazine with its tomato stains, those white orbs floating overhead, don't have meaning."

I add the onions to the Dutch oven, where they sizzle in the hot oil.

"I know how effed up this is," I say.

Through the window, I see a barge-like boat turn around the point and chug toward the island. A bevy of young men sit atop a pile of docks and rafts that they'll spend the next week installing at camps along the shoreline.

A moment later, two red kayaks edge around the point, following the same path as the barge—my mother in one, Reid in the other.

A voice sounds from behind me. "Reid better hurry. He never misses the show."

My aunt Hadley has materialized in the kitchen, still wearing those pink scrubs with the hand puppets on them. Another tradition at Idlewood is that Reid supervises the men in their skintight wetsuits as they install the docks. He used to believe no one noticed him watching. Now I doubt he cares.

"You were talking to yourself," Hadley says.

I nod to where the digital recorder captures our words.

"A new project?" Hadley asks.

I unwrap ground beef and add it to the pot to brown. "Where were you when my father killed Isaac Haviland?"

Hadley glances at the recorder. "That kind of project," she says. "Is it for the radio station?"

"Maybe."

"Are you sure you want to do this?"

"Mostly."

Hadley watches me cook for a moment before saying, "You remind me of your father. But only the good parts. You're not a rampaging murderer. And you already know where I was that day."

"Tell me again so I have it on tape."

"I was in Kosovo. At a reception. I have a photo of me dancing with the Swiss ambassador."

Hadley flew out of Kosovo the morning after the murder, as soon as she heard what had happened at the lake. She watched over Reid and me for the rest of the summer while our mother recuperated from her injuries.

I retrieve a can of whole tomatoes from the pantry. "I'm making a podcast," I say. "You're the only one who knows. You and Seton."

"If you told Seton, her mother will know soon enough, and then everyone in town will find out, so get ready to fess up." Hadley nods out the window, toward the kayaks. "The two of them will be pissed off. Practice on me. Why do this? And why at this moment?"

"They never found my father's body."

"They won't find it now," Hadley says. "Not after twenty-five years."

"Why not?"

"Because a bear probably ate him."

"Be serious," I say. "We all pretend that day never happened. Most of what I know I learned from reading police reports or old newspapers. I've barely spoken about it with Reid or Jane."

"You still call your mother Jane?"

"It's her name," I say.

"Well, she hates when you call her that," Hadley says. "Butter her up by calling her Mom. You may need to when she finds out about this project."

"I want the whole story, and to understand why my father did what he did. He was a monster."

"Mark wasn't a monster."

"But he is to me," I say. "And I want to know who he was, because that's who I might be."

"*You* are definitely not a monster, Charlie Kilgore, no matter who Mark became. But if you want to know more, here are some things to start with: Mark was a good skier, but not as good as he wanted to be. He played ukulele and sang 'Tiny Bubbles' at the firepit each summer. It drove me crazy, but I'd give anything to hear him sing it again. And he wasn't happy in New Hampshire, doing the books for the construction firm. He wanted something else, something bigger."

Hadley steps to the window. My mother and Reid have paddled halfway across the cove. "What do those two talk about when they're alone?" she asks. "Do they ever mention that day?"

That's the kind of question Julian wants me to ask.

Hadley leans toward the digital recorder. The red record button flashes. "Don't look too close," she says. "You might not like what you find." She pauses. "How's that for a sound bite?"

"You're a natural," I say.

Chapter Six

The docks are in, and the motorboat delivered from the marina. Paul arrives at Idlewood and joins Hadley, Reid, my mother, and me on the dock, where we light candles at the base of paper lanterns as the sun dips below the foothills. Around the lake, flames flicker, and white orbs rise into the air for the Lantern Festival, filling the night sky and reflecting their light in the inky water.

Afterward, on the screened porch, we uncork bottles of Chianti and fill our plates with Bolognese. Then the cards and the scorepad come out for a game of Oh Hell!

"What happened at Burkehaven this afternoon, anyway?" Hadley asks, as I deal.

Paul runs through the highlights of the confrontation with Andrea Haviland.

"Tempest in a teapot," Hadley says. "I'd expect nothing less from a visit to Hero." She points at my mother, who sits on my left. "Jane, what's your bid?"

"Two," my mother says. "But Andrea has a point, Paul. You don't need to sell the whole property. There are other options."

Paul bids zero. "Not ones that would line both of our pockets with cash," he says. "I barely come here anymore. Keeping that property isn't worth the tax burden. Besides, I won't let Andrea pull what she did at Rocky Nook. She blocked that whole development."

"What's your bid, Reid?" Hadley asks.

"One," Reid says, "and there's something to be said for not getting hit with a tax bill for thirty grand every year."

My mother rearranges the cards in her hand. "Don't start, Reid. It's my tax bill. My thirty grand, too."

Every year, families around the lake sell properties because of the taxes, but this is the first I've heard mention of that happening to Idlewood. "Would you sell?" I ask my mother.

"Not in a million years," she says.

"Take a guess at what a place like this one costs to maintain, Charlie," Reid says.

My mother shoots Reid a glare. "Your grandfather entrusted me with Idlewood, and I'll make sure it's protected."

Reid slouches in his chair, as I get the distinct impression this isn't the first time he and my mother have had this conversation. Again, I'm left wondering what they might have discussed without me. "How old were you when Grandpa bought Idlewood?" I ask.

"You call him *Grandpa* but call me *Jane*?" my mother says. "You never met Tony Reid."

"Tony, then," I say. "When did Tony buy Idlewood?"

"It was the early eighties," Hadley says. "I was twelve. Jane was sixteen. Our father liked that we lived on an island, especially after our mother died. He thought the island would keep us contained."

"He thought it would keep *you* contained," my mother says. "Hadley was wild. I was responsible."

"And it paid off in the end," Hadley says, studying her cards. "Nice house, here."

"Seems like an even trade," my mother says.

This time, there's no mystery to the barbs. My grandfather died from a heart attack right before his sixtieth birthday. He and Hadley had been estranged, and he left Idlewood to my mother and cut Hadley out of the estate. Most of the time Hadley seems to take what happened in stride, though once in a while she lets her guard down. "He didn't have much success containing us," Hadley says. "We met Paul right away. I mean, he lived next door."

"Not that the Burkes invited us for cocktails," my mother says. "They'd been coming to the lake for generations, and Burkehaven was for the docksider crowd. Paul's parents had their unwritten rules: who knows who, Princeton eating clubs, stock market tips, visits to Nantucket. If you didn't know how to play, they didn't ask you back."

"My parents weren't that bad," Paul says.

My mother slaps his arm playfully. "Your parents were snobs and so are you."

Hadley chimes in. "Our father opted for the dog races at Suffolk Downs, not the polo grounds in Newport. But we managed to find Paul and become friends. We met the others then, too."

My mother catches Hadley's eye, a signal not to go further, an interaction I'm so used to happening whenever we get remotely close to mentioning my father that the exchange nearly passes me by. Instead, I grab on and press further. "The others," I say. "You mean Dad."

"Let's not talk about that," my mother says.

These are the moments I need to lean into if I want to learn more about what happened. "Why not?" I ask. "Dad's part of who we are. I mean, look at tonight. The Bolognese, the Lantern Festival, the yellow Volvo. It's like we're reliving that night."

"You weren't there," Reid says.

"I *was* there."

"Not really," Reid says. "You were an infant."

Beside me, Hadley rearranges her cards. "I'll bid two," she says, steering the conversation away from my father. "That's five tricks so far, Charlie. You have to bid at least one."

I glance at my hand. Hearts are trump and I have a two of clubs, a four and six of diamonds, and an eight of spades. I won't take a single trick unless I get lucky. "One," I say, letting the topic of my father drop for now.

"Screw the dealer," Hadley says as she lays down the ace of hearts.

◆ ◆ ◆

Hadley wins the game, and I come in last. She folds the score sheet in half. "I may frame this one," she says, but an unsettled quiet has descended over the evening since I mentioned my father.

My mother shuffles the cards and deals a hand of solitaire. Paul and Hadley bring dishes and glasses to the kitchen, while Reid stares over the darkened lake. "I'll be at the firepit," he says. "Don't bother finding me."

He slams the screen door behind him. My mother watches as he melts into the darkness. A moment later, the smell of burning logs wafts through the trees. "Today is hard enough," my mother says. "It's the twenty-fifth anniversary of what happened. Reid doesn't need you to make it worse, Charlie. Frankly, neither do I."

It doesn't feel good when Reid and I argue, even silently, and I know it's my fault he's upset. Still, I'm not ready to let the conversation go. "Sometimes it seems as though none of it happened," I say.

My mother touches a scar on her neck. "Not to me. Or Reid. It's with us every day."

It takes all I have not to apologize and let the conversation fade away. Instead, I ask, "How did you and Dad meet?" and sit in silence, waiting for a response.

My mother continues her game, the snap of each card resonating through the night as she works through the deck. When I've almost given up on getting an answer, she says, "Mark and I met at Burkehaven. Paul's parents hosted a party at the start of the season for the kids from town, plus the kids from around the lake. It must have been 1981, and I was in high school. Hadley would have been going into the seventh grade." My mother stops playing solitaire, caught for a moment in the memory. "We listened to Rick Springfield and Blondie. Your father hovered at the edge of the party, hanging out with Andrea

Haviland, though she was Andrea Powell then. The two of them, they were inseparable. I assumed they were sweethearts."

Hadley appears at the doorway, wine in hand. "Lucky you had me," she says. "Don't forget Isaac and Paul. They were the other pair, always sneaking off, concocting some secret plan. Your mother and I showed up, these two awkward girls from the next cove. We didn't know anyone."

My mother smiles. "But I had my fearless sister at my side. She stepped right into the fray, and soon enough everyone knew who we were. After that night the six of us formed a little gang, Hadley and me, Paul and Isaac, and Andrea and your father. We did everything together."

I picture them, the summer air close, the music playing, the beginning of something unknown. Not one of them could have guessed where these new friendships would lead.

Paul comes to Hadley's shoulder, wiping his hands with a dish towel. "You're talking about Mark again?" he says. "Now I really need to head home."

"Let's stay on memory lane," Hadley says. "We can fill in details, see what Jane forgets. Mark—your father—he was cute. We forget that about him. I was the one who wanted to say hello."

"You were a kid," Paul says.

"I'd have been twelve that summer," Hadley says. "Paul, you and Mark would have been fourteen. And you'd have been sixteen, Jane. You all seemed old, but I think I was the one who chugged a Schlitz!"

"I *know* you smoked a cigarette," my mother says. "Because Dad smelled it on you when we got home, and guess who had to hear about it for the rest of the summer."

Hadley waves a dismissive hand. "It was a good night."

"It was," my mother says. "One I'd live all over again in a heartbeat."

Hadley catches my eye. "That would be a good line for the podcast."

And with that, it's as though my aunt pulls the needle from the nostalgia turntable and the music comes to a screeching halt.

My mother slams down the deck of cards. "A podcast, Charlie? Like the ones you make for the radio station? That's why you're asking all these questions."

Hadley gulps her wine. "Oops," she says, in a way that makes me wonder if she blew my cover on purpose.

"Thanks a lot," I say.

My mother's eyes flare as she turns on her sister. "How long have you known about this?"

Hadley holds up her hands in surrender. "This isn't about me, Jane."

"Hadley didn't know till right before dinner," I say. "She heard me recording. And I was planning to tell the rest of you."

Paul steps into the room. "Did you record us tonight?"

"You'd have to sign consent forms first," I say.

"No one's signing anything," my mother says, turning on me as I catch a glimpse of how she must react on a construction site when someone on the crew forgets who's boss.

I wish I could go back a few hours in time and confess to my plan, though if I had, I doubt I'd have learned even the small details that came out tonight. "I should have told you what I was doing," I say.

"You should have," my mother says. "Now I don't know if I can trust you."

She storms into the house and disappears upstairs. I feel awful, sick to my stomach from seeing my mother so betrayed, and at being the source of her betrayal.

"Well, that's that," Paul says, gathering his things to leave. "Nice job there, Charlie."

Paul has a way of making you feel worse when you know you're in the wrong.

After he leaves, Hadley gathers the cards and returns them to the box. "You knew they wouldn't be happy, but they'll come around. Or they won't. If this is important, it's up to you whether you want to keep going, whatever the consequences. You get to decide."

I doubt Hadley's apologized for much in life and wish I could match her self-confidence. She kisses my cheek and makes her way through the house and outside. I slump into a chair, not sure what to do next. Above me, my mother moves through the house, getting ready for bed, while out on the point, smoke billows against the moon.

I rest my hands on my knees and steel myself before stepping into the cool night air and following the path to the firepit, where Reid huddles beside the lake, the embers from the fire casting an eerie glow. I stop in the shadows. Reid's normally angular face has grown slack, his eyes shining as he stares across the inky lake surface, and I wonder if I've transported him to another night like this one, if he's thinking of our father, too. How often do these moments overcome my brother when no one's watching? What terrors does he suffer in silence?

He takes a deep breath, seeming to return to the present, his face sharp, his eyes alert. "I can hear you," he says.

I step out of the shadows and settle onto one of the boulders surrounding the pit. After a moment, I say, "I'm telling our story. Nothing more. I may tell the story for a podcast, and I may tell it for myself, but I want the whole story, not the pieces I've managed to cobble together."

Reid stares into the fire's embers. Where our mother seemed enraged, he simply seems sad. "I know you were there that day, too, Charlie," he says, "but I was *actually* there, in the boat, trying to survive while my own father waved a bloody knife at me, praying the whole time he couldn't swim that far. Praying the boat wouldn't spring a leak and sink with both of us in it."

I imagine my father's shouts, and Reid at the oars, breathing heavily with each pull. I imagine him cradling my tiny body between his knees.

"Dad was an angry, angry man," Reid says. "There's your whole story. Now find another one to tell, because this one isn't yours. It's mine." He stands and puts a hand to my shoulder. "I don't ask much of you, but leave this alone."

He heads into the dark. He must bypass the cabin and cross the footbridge, because a moment later, his car starts and roars off into the night.

I owe Reid my life. It's the one thing I know is true, and I could do what he asks and let this story go. If our situations were reversed, wouldn't I want the same from him?

I send a text to Julian. They know. They're angry. Sad, too.

It's nearly midnight, but Julian responds at once. Anger's good. Keep it going. There could be a story there, maybe even something to hide.

That's what I'm afraid of.

Chapter Seven

The embers in the fire have nearly burned out when, behind me, a twig snaps, and Paul Burke emerges from the trees. "All by yourself?" he asks.

"Me and the loons," I say.

He settles onto one of the boulders and rests a foot on the edge of the firepit. He wears a light wool coat and a striped scarf tied in a loop knot as if he's prepped for a walk in Central Park. He tosses a canvas bag onto the ground beside me. A bag of marshmallows falls out. "I found those in the kitchen," he says, handing me a metal skewer and keeping one for himself. "God knows how old they are."

We both push two marshmallows onto the end of our skewers and rest them over the embers, rotating them as the exterior turns golden and the scent of caramelized sugar fills the night air.

Paul holds a special place in my life. Growing up, he visited me on parents' weekend at prep school and took me to Yankees games in the summers. He drove me around New England on my college tour and used some connections to help me get into Newburg College in Connecticut. He's someone I trust.

"I didn't mean for you to find out about the podcast that way," I say.

"Well, your mom knows about it now. So does Reid."

I pull the marshmallows from the fire and slip off the crisp outer shell to savor the sweetness as it melts on my tongue. "Do you think about that night? About my father?"

Paul's marshmallows catch fire. He lets them burn until they fall from the skewer and smolder in the embers.

"This is off the record," I say, "if that's what you're worried about."

"I'm a lawyer. I worry about everything."

"And I wouldn't be doing my job if I didn't ask questions."

"What exactly is your job, Charlie?"

"I'm a journalist," I say, though I can hear the question mark at the end of the sentence, because mostly what I do is edit audio.

"If you're playing journalist, I'll play lawyer. Who else knows about this project besides us?"

"Only a few people."

"Who?"

"My producer at the station," I say. "Seton."

"Anyone else?"

"I talked to Lisa Lawson on my way to town. She was married to the lead investigator, Wendy Burrows. The one who died later that summer."

"How did you find Lisa Lawson?"

"Wendy's name was on the police reports," I say, "and then it wasn't. It didn't take much of a leap to figure out something had happened to her. I found Lisa's name listed in the obituary."

"Wendy Burrows was a drunk six months from retirement," Paul says. "She drove her car into the lake, and that was that. By then, the investigation had stalled anyway, and it never picked up again."

Or maybe Wendy Burrows got too close to solving the case.

"I get it, Charlie," Paul says, staring into the fire. "You have questions, and you want answers. I'd feel the same way if I were in your place. I'll tell you this much: Your father was a friend. A good friend. And what happened here on the lake, it doesn't leave you. Ever. Especially at night, when you can't sleep."

I wait for Paul to continue.

"I think about what I could have done differently," he says, eventually. "How another choice could have altered our fates. I'd come in from New York that morning and hadn't heard the local gossip about your mother's affair with Isaac Haviland. All I knew was that Andrea and Isaac didn't show up on the dock here at Idlewood, and the tension between your parents was palpable. But instead of sticking around, I paddled away."

"Would my father have listened to you?"

"Who knows? But with anything like this, the trick is to cut out the evil before it takes root, to eliminate the darkest parts. Your father showed his dark side that night, but what if I'd brought him toward the light. Or what if I'd convinced Isaac to leave. Or what if I'd stuffed a dozen deviled eggs into my mouth, tripped off the dock, and let everyone forget how angry they were at each other. Or what if—" Paul stops. "See how this works? I won't get much sleep tonight. Probably none of us will."

I know I won't.

"What does Seton say about your project?" Paul asks. "Is she working with you?"

"God, no," I say. "She tore me a new one when she found out what I was doing. And we don't discuss her father, or mine. It's our unspoken agreement."

"Not a bad strategy. The less said about some things, the better. Learn from that friendship." Paul stands and brushes pine needles from his jeans. "Are you going to ask Seton on a date this summer?"

I'm surprised Paul knows to ask, since I'm not sure myself what's going on between the two of us. "There's nothing between Seton and me."

"Keep telling yourself that."

Paul's footsteps fade into the night, but his words linger—the possibilities, the alternate paths our lives could have taken if one small thing had gone differently that day. Maybe my father would be here right now. Maybe Seton and I would have gone on that date. Or maybe our lives would have diverged long ago, as though we'd never met.

When I return to the cottage, I make my way through the house as quietly as I can, moving across the warped wooden floors and up the narrow stairs to the long corridor lined with bedrooms. As I pass my mother's darkened room, a faint, skunky odor lingers in the air, and a light clicks on. "Charlie?" my mother says.

I freeze like a teenager sneaking in after a night of drinking at Burkehaven.

"I hear you breathing," my mother says.

I'll have to face her eventually.

I tap open the door. She sits up, her back resting against the brass bed frame, her curls cascading around her shoulders.

"Are you talking to me?" I ask.

She lights a bud. "I've mellowed out," she says, offering me the pipe.

"Not tonight. I'm running in the morning. And what would Grandpa Tony say?"

She laughs, coughing on the exhale. "He'd find a way to blame Hadley."

I perch on the edge of the mattress.

"When you were young," she says, "you used to sneak in here and get under the covers with me. I'd be so tired, and half the time I was stoned and hoping you wouldn't get stoned from secondhand smoke. Now here I am wishing I'd appreciated it at the time."

"You're getting weepy on me," I say.

"Nostalgic. Thinking about what could have been."

Like Paul, out by the firepit. And, if I had to guess, like Reid, wherever he's gone. The only one of us sleeping soundly is probably Hadley, dreaming of dancing with the Swiss ambassador in Kosovo.

"I talked to Reid," I say. "I'll talk to him again in the morning. What was that about property taxes earlier, anyway?"

"Nothing to worry about," my mother says. "Reid has another life away from us. Sometimes I think he'd rather spend his summers in Provincetown or Fire Island, but he comes around eventually." She tucks her hair behind her ears, revealing the scars along her chest. "Tell me about your project. And I want details. Don't hold back."

I trace the stitching in her quilt, not sure where to begin.

"We got upset tonight," my mother adds. "*I* got upset, but emotions are overrated. I'd have been out of business decades ago if I'd let emotions rule my decisions."

"You're not as stoic as you let on," I say. "You're the one who hid from Mrs. Haviland this afternoon when she brought her bullhorn to Burkehaven."

"I wasn't hiding."

"What was keeping you occupied inside an idle construction site?"

"Okay, maybe I did hide. This town is too small to have enemies, so Andrea and I avoid each other when we can. But I mean . . . she is *so* annoying."

"She's not that bad."

"She's terrible."

I swing my legs onto the bed and lie next to my mother, eyes closed. If I want honesty, if I want vulnerability, I'll have to offer it, too. "Sometimes I feel as though I'm stepping into the middle of a conversation. I was always away at school. You and Reid, you had a life here in town, one that didn't involve me."

"Those years . . ." my mother begins. "They were hard. I made choices, and there were reasons, but it doesn't mean I wouldn't make other choices now if I could." She shifts beside me. "How does the podcast work? Do you record on your phone?"

"Or on a digital recorder."

"I won't sign a release. Not yet, but let's see where the conversations go."

"Are you sure?" I ask.

"Not at all, but I'll give it a try."

I run down the hall, grab the digital recorder from my room, mark the time and place, and return to my mother's room, where I lay the recorder on her bedside table next to the pipe. Maybe my mother will find it easier to tell her story on the record.

"Do I just talk?" she asks.

"Or I can ask questions. Whatever's easier. You were telling me about choices."

"You were making me feel guilty."

"Do you feel guilty?"

"All the time. I probably shouldn't have sent you to boarding school, but Reid . . . he was traumatized, and getting him through that took any energy I had. You were a happy kid. I wanted to give you some distance. Besides, you reminded me of Hadley: independent, fearless, ready to do whatever you wanted. She made friends and traveled the world, and I wanted that for you, too. That's what I meant earlier when I told her things had worked out for her in the end. Sometimes I'm jealous of the life she's led, untethered, free to do whatever she wants."

"Tell her tomorrow," I say. "Or I can play her the tape."

"You can broker all our secrets soon if you keep this up." My mother settles into the bed, closing her eyes, and for a moment, I think she might be nodding off. But then she says, "I'd broken things off with Isaac Haviland by the time he came to the lake, but he didn't want to hear it. He tried to convince me to leave with him."

"Were you tempted?"

"I'd made my choices by then."

"Why did you have the affair?" I ask.

"You have to ease into these interviews, Charlie. That's a big question, and not one I can answer at midnight."

"How about one clue," I say.

"Good marriages don't end. And bad marriages don't have a good guy and a bad guy. We all play our parts. I played mine, and so did your father."

"You make it sound like Dad had an affair, too," I say.

My mother rolls on her side and looks as if she might say more but stops herself. "Enough memory lane for one night," she says.

This was a good start, better than I'd hoped for after what happened earlier. "You'll get used to the recorder after we've talked a few times," I say. "Eventually, you'll forget it's there."

"I doubt that."

"Paul came to the firepit tonight. He talked about those moments before, when the world was one way, and all the choices he could have made."

"You can't change the past," my mother says. "No matter how much you wish you could. We walked through a door that night. What came before was a different lifetime. And what's followed, we've muddled through."

I stand to leave. "At the firepit, Paul told me to cut out the evil before it takes root, to eliminate the darkest parts. That's what this project's about for me, eliminating the dark so I can come toward the light."

I turn to say good night. My mother stares after me, as if she's seen a ghost, or as though I've spent the evening making her relive her worst moment. "I'm sorry," I say.

She shakes her head. "For what?" she asks. "You have a right to know your story and to understand who your father was. I should have told you about him a long time ago. You can ask me anything, Charlie. I'll tell you what I can. Get some sleep. I'll be gone in the morning at a site visit near Finstock, but we can talk when I'm back. There's something important I want to tell you."

I could press her to tell me now, but I get the sense if I push too hard, my mother will shut down. She'll tell her story at her own pace. I stop in the doorway, not ready to leave. "Why did he do it?" I ask.

My mother flicks off her bedside lamp. "When you find the answer, let me know."

If I've learned anything tonight, it's that we've each been asking the same questions for years. Maybe we can find the answers together.

A moment later, I lie in bed, staring at the ceiling, replaying tonight's conversations. When I finally sleep, I dream of rocking in a rowboat, of paper lanterns floating against a darkened sky, and of my brother's frightened heart beating against mine.

Chapter Eight

I wake with the sun. In the light of day, last night's events—the questions I asked, the secrets I kept, the relationships I risked—feel reckless, as though I approached a truth I'm not sure I want to find. I remember my brother sitting by the fire, transported to his worst night. I think about my mother and the secret she promised to reveal. I'm not sure I'm ready to hear whatever she has to say. I slip out of bed and creep down the hallway to where her room is empty, her bed unmade. She must have already left for the site visit in Finstock.

Back in my room, I stare at my phone. The podcast had seemed like a good idea in theory when Julian proposed it. I'd gotten a thrill from the advice to dig deep, to follow the emotion, and believed exposing my family's hidden truths would make me feel whole. I'd also hoped the podcast would take off and be good for my career in the way Julian's series about the Boston Strangler had jump-started his own.

But this morning, I'm not so sure anymore.

I type a text to Julian—I may scrap the podcast. Sorry—and stare at the screen, my thumb hovering over the send button. Despite my misgivings, I'm not actually ready to abort the project, though I'll see how I feel later, after I speak with my mother. I keep the unsent message on the screen, turn the phone face down, and leave it behind as I change into my running gear and make my way down the stairs and through the Ping-Pong room. When I get outside, my breath freezes in the cold air. Spring in New Hampshire can be fickle, and the long, lazy days of summer are a month off.

After stretching, I take off at a slow pace, across the island, over the footbridge to the parking area, where I notice Reid's Audi hasn't returned from wherever he escaped to last night. I'll text him an apology when I get back to the cottage. I jog along the shore and onto a path through the woods. A half mile later, I emerge at Burkehaven in the next cove, with its idle construction equipment and half-built house.

Heading inland, I run by the VW-size boulder marking the fork in the road, then past the bungalow where Hadley's staying. Eventually, I cut onto a dirt road by a white farmhouse set back among maple trees, where Paul's car is parked outside a red sugarhouse. This is Burkehaven Farm, where Paul grew up, living here in the farmhouse during the offseason, and at the cabin on Burkehaven Cove during the summer. Fieldstone walls and hiking paths crisscross the farm, including a trailhead I come upon that follows a swollen brook up into the foothills.

I run most mornings. It's the one thing I'm good at. I competed on a national level in prep school and kept at it through college. Now I push myself as the trail steepens and my breathing grows heavy. Sweat pours from my face and my thighs burn. I reach a fork in the trail, one way leading to Miller Pond, two miles off, and the other to the Ridge Trail, which I follow until the path levels out on a field dotted with wooden posts. This is a remnant of an old firing range where parents would send their kids to shoot at aluminum cans with BB guns. ("Different times," Hadley would say if she were here now.)

My breathing steadies. I increase my speed, sprinting the last mile, until I emerge at an overlook perched above Hero Lake.

Here, an abandoned hunting cabin with broken windows and a caved-in roof has begun to return to nature. Below, the lake spans almost to the horizon, the coves and inlets forming a kind of inkblot among the trees. I catch my breath, then stretch toward the sky before working my way through a routine of push-ups and squats. This is my special place, one I look forward to visiting for the first time each year.

I take another cleansing breath and settle further into myself.

Today I'll make things right. I'll meet Seton at the Landing for a drink. I'll apologize to Reid. I'll listen to whatever my mother has to tell me, and if I decide to scrap the podcast, I'll explain the decision to Julian in a way he'll understand. Maybe he'll be relieved not to have to serve as a mentor.

I finish the workout and perch on an outcropping of granite. My legs dangle over a sheer drop to a rocky surface fifty yards below. Here, it feels as though I'm the only person in the entire world, even as, out on the water, a single motorboat speeds across the surface, leaving a wake in its trail. I close my eyes and allow the sounds of nature—the breeze, the birds, the rustling of leaves—to fill in the quiet, as I contemplate what I learned yesterday.

For me, my father's been a blank slate waiting to be filled in. Some of his story I found in newspaper articles and police reports during my research—his job, his reputation, his motive for murder—but yesterday added shading to that image. He sang tenor and had a beautiful voice. He played ukulele and dreamed of a world away from Hero. He was Paul's friend. He danced to Blondie on a night my mother would yearn to relive decades later.

The edges of his character have begun to soften. He wasn't the monster I grew up believing he was, but a person, one who made terrible mistakes. And maybe this story is worth pursuing, whether I turn it into a podcast or not.

A scent brings me back to the present.

Smoke.

I pull my legs from over the cliff and scan the clearing and the crumbling cabin for another hiker. "Hello?" I call out.

No one answers, but the scent is stronger now, too strong to be from a cigarette. I search the horizon. Below, on the lakeshore, a plume of smoke rises from Burkehaven. Then a burst of flames erupts through the trees.

Fire.

I instinctively reach for my phone only to remember leaving it behind at Idlewood. I take off along the ridge, my feet pounding as I leave the summit, pass the shooting range, and scramble sideways down the steep trail, grasping at tree roots and granite to keep from falling until I emerge on the street below. At the turnoff to Burkehaven, I thump my fist on the bungalow's kitchen door. When Hadley doesn't answer, I test the knob. The door's unlocked. I shout Hadley's name, then use the wall phone to dial 9-1-1, before sprinting the last half mile through the trees to Burkehaven.

Thick, black smoke fills the air.

The half-constructed house on the point is in flames. At the dock, a maroon Bryant 219, the same type of motorboat we have tied to our dock at home, the same type Andrea Haviland floated in yesterday afternoon as she yelled into her bullhorn, tugs at a single line.

Glass shatters. Flames shoot toward the sky.

I shout Reid's name, then Mrs. Haviland's, wondering who could be here, who might be trapped in the fire, as I jog along the muddy path, shielding my face from the intense heat. A shower of embers singes my skin, while smoke fills my lungs. I throw myself into the frigid lake water. As I emerge, someone stumbles from the house, silhouetted against the flames, and collapses in the courtyard.

"Who's there?" I shout, pressing forward. "I'm coming."

Behind me, something rustles. I turn. A tree limb swings. My head explodes with pain. And the world goes black.

Chapter Nine

Someone says my name, though it's easy enough to ignore as I slip through the hazy, kind world of unconsciousness. I want to stay here, far from the unthinkable, far from the violence that brought me to this place. But the voice returns, this time with urgency.

"Charlie!"

Fingertips dig into my shoulder as my body shakes and my senses come into focus one at a time. First, something cool and wet runs along my face. The sun glows behind my eyelids, and the taste of copper fills my mouth. With the strong scent of smoke, I'm yanked into the real world as the back of my head begins to throb.

"Charlie Kilgore, if you don't wake up, I'll kill you."

I open one eye, then the other. Seton kneels over me in her police uniform, her face etched with concern. My thoughts are muddled as I try to remember what brought me here and touch the tattoos running up her forearm. "Did these hurt when you got them?" I ask, my voice rough.

"Not as much as your head hurts right now. Glad you're back."

"How did I get here?" I ask.

"You tell me."

Above her, thick smoke billows into the sky, nearly blocking the sun. The radio on her shoulder chirps an update I can't quite follow. She dips into it, saying something about an ambulance as I struggle to sit. "Don't move," she says. "The EMTs are on their way."

I try to speak, but my mouth is coated in ash. Seton pulls a bottle of water from a bag and holds it to my lips. I suck at the liquid, attempting to wash away the foul taste as she runs her hands through my hair. "You scared the shit out of me," she says. "What happened, anyway? Did you run into a tree?"

I touch my head. My fingers come away covered in blood. "I don't know," I say as images creep into my memory like forgotten dreams: an explosion, a fire, someone fighting to escape.

Concern flashes in Seton's eyes. "You'll remember soon enough. And head wounds bleed a lot. It's probably nothing, but we'll want to be sure you don't have a concussion or smoke inhalation or a fractured skull. Do you think you can stand? We should move away from the smoke."

Nothing happening right now makes sense. Fifty yards down the shore, a fire rages, and yet there's no urgency to Seton's actions. "We have to get to the house," I say.

"And do what?" Seton asks. "I alerted the fire department. They're on their way. My job is to contain the scene and make sure no one does anything stupid, and the only person to contain right now is you, so sit tight and don't make trouble. I told you yesterday the Lantern Festival was a fire hazard. Guess who's right again."

"The boat," I say. "It's tied to the dock."

Seton follows my gaze to where the motorboat tugs at its line. "What about it? That's *your* boat. Didn't you bring it over from your place?"

"I wasn't the one who came in the boat," I say as the events of the morning begin to take shape in my mind. "Reid . . . your mother . . . I don't know who's here."

A shadow crosses Seton's face. She stands and faces the flames, shielding her eyes as she takes in the scene—the burning house, the bobbing boat—as though for the first time. She shouts into her radio and takes off down the shore toward the fire. My head spins as I struggle to stand and lean over my knees.

"Mom!" Seton shouts. "Reid! Where are you?"

I fight nausea as I stumble after her.

"Stay back," Seton says as she rips off her hat and coat and dives into the lake, emerging from the water with her uniform clinging to her body. "The water will protect me from the fire."

We both know that's not true.

"Someone made it out of the house and collapsed by the courtyard," I say. "We need to get them away from the smoke."

"*We* don't need to do anything." Seton snaps her fingers. "Except give me your shirt."

I pull the blue running jersey off and toss it to her. She douses it in the lake, too, and wraps it over her nose and mouth. "Move back to where we were. The fire department's coming in their boat."

Seton squeezes my hand, takes a deep breath, and runs forward until she's swallowed by smoke. I wait, ignoring her instructions and feeling useless as the heat of the fire sears my bare skin.

Off in the distance, a siren sounds. Thirty seconds later the local fire boat speeds into the cove. One volunteer firefighter tosses the anchor overboard while two others set up a hose that sucks water from the lake and sprays it toward shore. I wave both arms, directing the water toward the courtyard. Then I dash forward. Smoke burns my eyes. I keep low to the ground, crawling as heat and smoke and a lack of oxygen begin to overwhelm me. I nearly turn back before a torrent of water cascades from above, cooling my skin and forming a pocket of air close to the ground that I breathe in deeply.

Ahead, Seton stands against the fire. I crawl toward her. Her eyes are bloodshot, and she coughs through the running jersey.

"We're almost there," I say.

"Go back!" she shouts before succumbing to a fit of coughing.

A few yards farther, my hand lands on wet cloth. I recognize Andrea Haviland's hockey cap at once. "Mom!" Seton says, shaking her mother's shoulder and pressing her ear to her mouth. "She's breathing."

A wall collapses, showering us with heat. Another rush of water from the fire hose cools the air. "Get under one arm," Seton says. "Stay low. Keep moving."

Somehow, we drag Mrs. Haviland's limp body across the ground and away from the fire. Behind us, flames shoot in the air as the house falls in on itself. Fifty yards down the shore, Seton kneels over her mother, checks her vitals, then speaks into the radio. "Where's the ambulance?"

"Five minutes," the dispatcher says.

"Make it one," Seton snaps.

"She needs oxygen," I say.

Seton shoves me. "Are you a doctor now? Thanks for stating the obvious. And next time, do what I tell you. You could have gotten yourself killed."

"So could you," I say.

She yanks the running jersey from her face and flings it at me. "Getting killed is *my* job, not yours."

Behind us, footsteps approach as my aunt jogs along the shore, dressed for the part in scrubs. "Give me an update," Hadley says as she kneels beside us and takes over the scene.

"Smoke inhalation," Seton says. "Maybe some burns."

Hadley puts an ear to Mrs. Haviland's chest and uses the flashlight on Seton's phone to check her breathing passage. "Vitals seem okay, as far as I can tell. Her skin's turning pink from the smoke, but no burns, thank God. She'll need oxygen as soon as possible."

Unlike me, Hadley doesn't get admonished for stating the obvious. In fact, Seton seems perfectly comfortable deferring to her. I slide away to give them room, leaning my back against a tree and slipping the jersey on as a coughing fit racks my body.

A few moments later, the ambulance arrives, sirens blaring. The EMTs hurry along the shore with a gurney, then follow Hadley's direction as they strap an oxygen mask over Mrs. Haviland's nose and mouth. Eventually Hadley leaves them and crouches beside me. "You scared the bejeezus out of Seton," she says as she checks my pulse, her bony fingers resting on my wrist. My lungs tickle, and I suppress another nagging cough.

"I do my best," I say.

"Open up," she says, shining the light into my throat. "You need to get to the ER."

I have an $8,000 deductible on my insurance. I'm not going anywhere near the ER. "I'll be fine."

"Your face is covered with blood. You have an open contusion on your forehead. And your lungs are filled with smoke. Two choices: You can ride in the ambulance or come with me. The ambulance costs extra, though."

"I'll go with you."

"Good call."

One of the EMTs waves to Hadley. "Sit tight and breathe deeply," she says, leaving me by the tree.

A fire truck pulls in behind the ambulance, and another team of firefighters uncoils a hose along the shore. Seton joins me and slides onto the ground. "They think my mom'll make it through this," she says, closing her eyes. "How did you wind up here, anyway?"

Some of the events of the morning are still hazy, but they begin to return to me as I tell her about leaving Idlewood and jogging to the Ridge Trail, pointing to where the rock face spills from the peaks above us. "I was at the overlook and thought I smelled a cigarette until smoke started billowing from the shore. By the time I got here, the whole house was in flames."

Seton swears under her breath and moves a lock of hair from my forehead. "That's a nasty cut."

The wound throbs the moment she mentions it, but I don't mind, especially if it means having Seton this close. These moments between us pop up when I least expect them, offering fleeting glimpses of possibility. I lay my hand over hers. Seton closes her eyes. "I don't want to make a mistake," she says.

"I know," I say.

She rests her forehead against mine. Pain shoots through my temples.

"Ow!" I say.

"Sorry," Seton says, shifting away to signify a return to the friend zone, a dance we've mastered. I wonder what would happen if one of us chose to seize one of these moments, if we followed our feelings wherever they might lead us. I wonder if our relationship would survive.

"My mom's done it this time," Seton says. "First, she took a sledgehammer to those cameras. And today, with the security system gone, she started a fire." She catches herself. "Are you recording this?"

I shake my head. "I don't have my phone," I say as the final memories of this morning snap into place: the noise behind me, the swing of a tree branch. I glance around the cove, trying to make sense of it.

"What?" Seton asks.

"The boat was already here," I say. "It was tied to the dock."

"Yeah," Seton says. "Because my mom was here."

But Mrs. Haviland was in the burning house, not on the shore with me. "Your mother stumbled out of the house and collapsed in the courtyard," I say. "Then I heard a noise and saw a tree limb swinging toward me. Someone attacked me, but it wasn't your mother."

Seton stands and faces the fire. "That means someone else was here," she says. "But who?"

Chapter Ten

As each sweep of the fire hose washes more of the crime scene into the lake, Seton snaps photos of what evidence she can, including her mother's boat. When she returns to where I slump against the tree trunk, she faces the bare rock face above us. "You had a view of the whole lake from up there, Charlie," she says. "What did you see?"

"There *was* a boat on the water." I take a moment to reconstruct the scene in my mind, still not trusting my memory. "It was heading toward the cove."

"Maybe you saw my mom driving *toward* the fire. Maybe one of those lanterns drifted into the house and smoldered all night."

That could be true, but it wouldn't explain who walloped me in the head.

Seton asks, "Is there anyone who has a score to settle with your family? Or with Paul?" She pauses. "Besides my mom, that is."

"You'd know better than I. You're the one who lives here," I say as I remember the man who came by the site yesterday in the truck, the one my mother couldn't get rid of fast enough. "Don't get mad, get Moodey," I say.

"Vance Moodey," Seton says. "What about him?"

"He was here yesterday, after you left," I say, telling her about the conversation with my mother. "She said she'd touch base with him once the weekend was over."

"He's probably supplying lumber for this job," Seton says, "but duly noted."

She snaps another photo, this time of my bloody face.

"Am I evidence?" I ask.

"Everything's evidence."

"Do I need a lawyer?"

"Not yet."

So much for the flash of intimacy between us.

By the shoreline, the EMTs wheel Seton's mother toward the ambulance. Seton appears detached from this whole situation, though I wonder what that demeanor might be hiding. "Be with your mom," I say. "I'm fine on my own."

"Actually, I need to stay as far from her as possible till my deputy shows up and I can hand off the scene. I don't want accusations or innuendo about this investigation floating around."

The EMTs slide the gurney into the back of the ambulance, right as my brother's Audi speeds out of the trees and blocks the exit. Reid climbs from the car.

"Hey, buddy," one of the EMTs shouts. "You have to move."

Reid ignores him, dashing toward the point, his blond hair disheveled.

"Stay here," Seton mumbles, leaving me by the tree and stepping into my brother's path. "You can't get any closer, Reid," she says.

"This is my construction site," Reid says, trying to maneuver around her.

Seton pivots to block him. I like seeing her take charge. "And it's my crime scene," she says.

"Not for long," Reid says. "Everyone already knows what your crazy mother did—it's all over the Hero Board. She started a fire and nearly got herself killed."

I resist the temptation to step into the fray. Reid must have six inches and fifty pounds on Seton, but I suspect she could take us both down in a fight. "Don't do something you'll regret," she says to Reid.

A second cruiser pulls in behind Reid's car, and an officer gets out.

Seton holds her hands out where Reid can see them. "That's my backup," she says, "so my job is officially over. I'm very sorry for your loss, Mr. Kilgore. Why don't you move your car so we can do our jobs?"

Reid shoves an index finger in Seton's face. "If your mother isn't booked and in prison by the end of the day, you'll have more than me to answer to."

"Reid," I say, leaving my spot by the tree and joining them. "Chill, okay?"

My brother's face softens as he takes in my appearance. "Charlie, what happened to you? You're bleeding like a stuck pig."

"It looks worse than it is," I say.

Reid glances at Seton. "Did your mother do this, too?" he asks.

"She didn't do anything to me," I say.

The EMT shouts toward Reid again.

"Could you move your car, Mr. Kilgore," Seton says, her voice steady, her words clipped.

Reid stares her down, then turns away, phone in hand as he punches in a number and speaks to whoever picks up.

"Sorry about that," I say. "He has a lot wrapped up in this project."

"I've dealt with way more emotion than Reid Kilgore offered up," Seton says, maintaining a remarkable detachment. I wonder when she'll break, and who will be there to support her when she does. "Besides," she continues, "he has every right to be upset. This is way worse than the Randalls' rooster crowing too early in the morning."

Out on the lake, a speedboat arcs into the cove and around the fireboat.

"That's one of the state detectives," Seton says. "He lives in Kingston, on the other side of the lake."

The boat slows as it approaches the shore. A man with thick, dark hair tousled by the wind stands at the helm, steering with one hand. He calls to the deputy and tosses her a line. She pulls the boat as close to shore as she can, where the detective leaps off, missing by six inches and landing with a splash. He seems undeterred as he stumbles over the rocks and recovers his footing.

"Detective Gilcrest," Seton says to me.

The detective's name rings a distant bell, one I can't quite place. He wears a slim-cut houndstooth suit and a white shirt, open at the collar to reveal a bare chest. It's an outfit a financial consultant might wear on the town. "Did he roll out of bed looking like that?" I ask.

"He has his own sartorial style," Seton says.

The detective approaches, adjusting his jacket, his sodden leather sneakers squelching with each step as he takes in the burning house and the firefighters at work. By now, they've mostly contained the flames.

"Glad you're on this, Chief," the detective says. "We'll need your department's support." He extends a hand toward me. "Gilcrest."

I guess we use last names, like on TV. "Kilgore," I say.

"Charlie, right?" Gilcrest says. Up close, he seems older than he presented from a distance, maybe in his mid to late forties. "You got into it with someone. What's with all the blood?"

"Charlie was on the scene when I arrived," Seton says. "I'll get you up to speed."

To her credit, she hits most of the salient points without pause, ending with, "The likely suspect is Andrea Haviland. She's unconscious. They're transporting her to Kingston Hospital."

Gilcrest turns to where Reid has finally moved his car. The EMTs drive off, sirens blaring, leaving Hadley and my brother in the parking lot with the deputy. "Andrea Haviland," Gilcrest says. "As in your mother."

"One and the same," Seton says.

"Why don't we chat in private, Chief?"

They consult by the lakeshore, and I watch as Seton's shoulders slump and Gilcrest puts a hand to her back and whispers in her ear. I wish I could do more to help Seton right now, that I could find the words to make whatever she must be feeling go away. I should be well suited for the role since I've spent my whole life dealing with someone else's crimes.

When they finish their conversation, Seton leaves to talk to the deputy, while the detective joins me.

"Is she okay?" I ask.

"The chief's a pro," Gilcrest says. "She's handing off this case to the state. Gotta watch our step here. Be official. She told me you helped pull the victim from the fire. Pretty dumb move there."

"It all worked out," I say.

"It doesn't always. She also told me she assumed the boat tied to the dock was yours, right? You were lying on the shore unconscious. She sees you, sees a boat resembling yours, and assumes the two things go together. She also assumed the fire started because of the Lantern Festival, that one of the lanterns drifted into the house and smoldered all night. Was that what you thought happened?"

"At first," I say. "But I saw the boat tied to the dock and recognized it."

"And you knew Andrea Haviland had started the fire," Gilcrest says, a statement, not a question, and I nearly trip up and nod in agreement. Before I can respond, he adds, "But the boat's the same type you have over at your place, so it could have been your mother or your brother here, which would make sense since it's their construction site. Why did you assume it was Mrs. Haviland?"

"I didn't know who it was," I say. "But Mrs. Haviland's been trying to get this site shut down. Is this arson?"

Gilcrest makes a note on his phone, and when I try to read what he's typing, he shields the screen. "We'll see what the state fire marshal's team turns up. Right now, I'm concerned with the assault."

And we both know a paper lantern didn't hit me with a tree limb.

"You're Jane Reid's kid," the detective says. "Where is she?"

"On a site visit," I say. "Near Finstock."

"I'll need to speak with her sooner rather than later," Gilcrest says. "To the owner, too. Paul Burke."

"I left my phone at the house, but my brother can call them. He's right over there."

"I know your brother." The detective meets my eyes. "I was out on my own dock last night with my wife and kids. The lanterns made me think of you and your family. They do every year. It's nice to see you all grown up, Charlie."

From the parking lot, my aunt shouts, "Duncan, wrap it up. Charlie needs to see a doctor."

Duncan Gilcrest.

Now I recognize the detective's name. Officer Duncan Gilcrest was the first to respond to the call at Idlewood all those years ago. His name is in the police reports. He was the officer who'd started the job a week earlier, the one who waded into the lake and convinced Reid it was safe to return to shore.

Chapter Eleven

I spend the rest of the morning and early afternoon sucking down oxygen in the emergency room and reading old magazines while wishing I hadn't left my phone on my bedside table. Hadley stops by from working in the ER to check on me a few times. "Two more shifts, then I'm out of here for the next six weeks," she says, adjusting the oxygen tube around my ears.

I wish Hadley weren't leaving for Cairo. She's a reliable ally when tensions rise at Idlewood. "Are you sure you want to miss the summer?" I ask.

"I'll be back in July," she says. "And what do you care? You'll be at work in Boston on Tuesday. You know I can only take so much lake time. I get restless if I stay here more than a few days."

She places an oximeter on my index finger. "Oxygen levels are low," she says, "but better than they were. One of my colleagues will be by to suture up that head wound. She'll assess when you can leave."

"Do you charge by the minute?" I ask.

Hadley ruffles my hair. "Good health is priceless," she says.

Tell that to my bank account. "Back at Burkehaven, you called that detective by his first name," I say. "How do you know Duncan Gilcrest? He's the same cop who—"

"I work in the ER," Hadley says, cutting me off. "Even if it is part-time. I know all the cops in the area. All the detectives, too, and I pay close attention to handsome ones who rescue my nephews. By the way,

Duncan would be a great interview for the podcast. His favorite topic is himself. Haven't you seen him on TV? He pops up on those true-crime shows once in a while. Last I heard, he was shooting some pilot in New York. God knows what happened with that."

The curtain slides open and Gilcrest appears. "The pilot didn't get picked up," he says.

"Too bad," Hadley says. "And don't eavesdrop. Doctor-patient confidentiality."

"I'm checking on the patient," Gilcrest says. "Mind if I ask a few questions?"

Hadley catches my eye.

"I can handle myself," I say.

"If that changes, tell the nurse to come find me," Hadley says. "And page me when you're discharged. I sent your mother a text to let her know what happened and told her I'd drive you home."

After Hadley leaves, Gilcrest asks, "How's the head?"

"Throbbing," I say. "Nothing worse."

"Want to walk me through what happened again?"

I review the events of the morning. Each time I repeat myself, my memory seems to become clearer.

"The scene must have been overwhelming," Gilcrest says. "There was the fire, and the boat, and you saw someone struggling to escape. And that's when you were attacked. Am I getting the timeline right?"

"Just about."

"Just about, or yes? The details matter."

"That's what I remember."

"Fair enough. A head wound can play tricks with memory. Tell me about the attack."

"I heard rustling, then saw a tree limb swinging toward me."

"You didn't run into something on your own?"

"If I ran into a tree, you'd find blood on it."

"True. But we haven't found a bloody tree limb, either."

"There was an inferno raging fifty yards down the shore," I say. "And a lake right beside me. Two convenient places to dispose of a bloody tree limb. Someone else was there, someone besides Mrs. Haviland."

"I believe you," Gilcrest says. "And you should be a detective, Charlie. If you were, you'd know I have to follow the evidence. We'll figure out who did this to you soon enough."

A text beeps into his phone. He glances at the screen.

"Is that about Mrs. Haviland?" I ask.

"She's still unconscious," Gilcrest says, without answering the question. "I'll want to talk to you later. Till then, do me a favor: Don't play hero."

After he leaves, I sit with nothing to distract myself but the questions he asked, and the tiniest seed of paranoia beginning to take root that I might be a suspect in my own assault. I wonder what Gilcrest imagines my motive to be and how he'd shape the details to build a case. It's the same kind of work we do at the radio station when we create a narrative around a news story.

I imagine massaging this story and laying out the timeline, who I'd interview to fill in details, how I'd connect today's events to what happened at Idlewood twenty-five years ago. I could plant red herrings by playing up Gilcrest's suspicions of me.

I have questions for Gilcrest, too, ones about my father and Isaac Haviland's murder. I want him to describe arriving on the scene at Idlewood, finding the bloodstains in the parking area, and discovering the rowboat floating offshore. I want to know when exactly he realized he'd stumbled into a homicide and how he earned the trust of my brother, a terrified twelve-year-old boy.

The curtain slides aside. A doctor scans my wristband and listens to my lungs again. "No concussion or skull fractures," she says as she stitches up the wound on my forehead. "You're lucky."

"Will I have a scar?" I ask.

"Only in a good way. Adds character." She types on my chart. "Don't smoke for a week. It'll exacerbate the cough."

"What about weed?" I ask.

"Not even weed," she says with a smile. "And call 9-1-1 if you get lightheaded or disoriented."

I won't be adding a 9-1-1 call to my hospital bills anytime soon. I'm not sure how I'll pay for *this* visit. She walks me out of the ER and into the waiting room, where I spend a few moments signing forms. As we finish, I ask, "Could you give me a patient's room number?"

I'd assumed Mrs. Haviland would be under guard, handcuffed to the bed, waiting for the DA to press charges, but there isn't a single sign of law enforcement outside her hospital room. She lies in the bed, eyes closed, an oxygen line running beneath her nose. I settle into a chair beside her as my mother's words from last night return to me: *Bad marriages don't have a good guy and a bad guy. We all play our parts. I played mine, and so did your father.*

Something else my mother said last night also gives me pause. She'd assumed my father and Mrs. Haviland were high school sweethearts. Maybe they did have feelings for each other. Maybe the two friends had crossed the line.

"Did you love my father?" I ask, softly. "Have you missed him all these years?"

Mrs. Haviland stirs.

"You were at Burkehaven this morning," I say as she groans and touches her face, somewhere between sleep and consciousness. "Who were you there to meet? Who was hiding in the woods?"

In the hallway, footsteps approach.

"Wake up soon," I whisper. "I have some questions for you."

Seton steps into the room, holding a coffee cup. "Charlie," she says, "they told me you'd been discharged."

I stand, my face flushed, somehow feeling as though Seton's caught me in the middle of something I shouldn't be doing. I wonder what she'd say to me if she heard the questions I just asked. I look down and shift my weight.

"What?" Seton says.

"I came to see your mother."

"Well, she's sedated, but the doctors say she's out of the woods."

Now that we're alone, the detachment she maintained by the lake has been replaced by a kaleidoscope of emotion—concern and fear and apprehension for what the next few days might bring. "Do you mind a hug?" I ask.

"Yes," she says, but steps into my embrace anyway, her body rigid against mine.

"There's an explanation for this," I whisper.

"And it's not a good one," Seton says, softening into my arms.

"We don't know that."

"We do, though."

I cough.

"Are you okay?" Seton asks into my shoulder.

"Mostly."

"I'll give you a ride home."

"You should stay here. Hadley can take me."

"I could use a break." Seton pushes away from me. "And don't mess with my reputation, Charlie Kilgore. I can't get teary-eyed where the nurses might see. They'll never let me forget it."

She marches out of the room to the elevator, punching at the down button before giving up and taking the stairs. I trot after her as we make our way through the hospital and outside. Once Seton reaches her cruiser, she covers her face with her hands and sobs, and I know her well enough to let her be till she swipes at her eyes with a fist. "If you tell one person about this—"

"I know. You'll kill me," I say, glancing at the clock on the dashboard. It's after five. I was in the ER all day. "We could go to the Landing for a drink."

Seton blows her nose. "I can only be away for so long. Gilcrest must be ready to make an arrest."

"Gilcrest came by when I was in the ER. He asked me if I ran into a tree."

"He's covering his bases," Seton says as she starts the car and pulls into downtown Kingston. It's a bigger town than Hero, with a main street lined with restaurants and shops and an extensive marina. "If you ran into a tree," she adds, "then Gilcrest doesn't need to explain who else was at the scene, and there wouldn't be reasonable doubt over who started the fire. He could focus on building the case against my mom. But he's a good cop, I'll give him that. He won't go for the easy close. I told him he couldn't speak to my mom without a lawyer. And I don't know why you're being nice to me after what happened today."

Seton's been nice to me my whole life, despite the events we try not to discuss. I owe her more than she knows. "It's not like *you* started the fire," I say. "How well do you know Gilcrest, anyway?"

"Our paths have crossed a few times. My department works with the state cops pretty often, and this is his county. They handle major crimes." Seton steers around a pair of bikers pedaling in tandem. "My father's murder made Gilcrest's career. The state cops scooped him up right away and promoted him after that other detective drowned. And he's been prancing around in his fancy suits ever since."

A few moments later, she approaches the turnoff for Burkehaven, where the scent of smoke hangs in the air. She pulls to the side of the road and asks, "Hadley stays at that house there when she's here, right?"

"At the bungalow? Yeah. She takes care of the flower beds, and it gives her some space away from the rest of us."

"I listened to your 9-1-1 call. You were efficient, appropriately upset."

"Works in my favor?" I ask.

Seton glances toward the bungalow. "In *your* favor, yes," she says.

The 9-1-1 log would show that the call came in from the landline at the bungalow. And I suspect Seton's wondering now why it took Hadley so long to arrive at the scene, which I've wondered myself. There could be any number of explanations. Maybe Hadley sleeps in the nude. Or maybe she didn't want to talk to her annoying nephew at the crack of dawn. Or maybe she'd driven to the Landing for coffee. I won't offer a theory unless Seton asks. Thankfully, she pulls onto the lane, pressing the accelerator and mumbling, "Bungalow," under her breath. "That's not like any bungalow I've ever seen. It must have five bedrooms."

It has eight, but they're small. Plus, there's the little studio out back.

"I wouldn't mind living in that *bungalow*," Seton says as she jerks to a stop beside Reid's Audi. I follow her gaze to where Reid stretches on the dock before his afternoon swim.

"Does he always wear a Speedo?" she asks.

"He has one for every day of the month," I say.

"At least he wears it well. I've seen much worse giving tickets at the town beach." Seton closes her eyes. "I need to find a lawyer."

"Ask Paul," I say. "He doesn't do criminal law, but he must have someone to refer."

"Paul won't help me," Seton says. "My mom burned down his house, and they hate each other anyway. Besides, I need money for the retainer, and I don't have a clue where it will come from."

I would help Seton if I could, but most months I barely make my rent check. "I don't even know how I'll pay my hospital bill," I say.

Seton rubs the bridge of her nose. "I'm not asking for a handout, Charlie. And I don't know how to break this to you, but you're rich. Don't act as if you aren't. You live on the lake. You went to prep school and a fancy private college. And please stop calling that house a *bungalow*."

"I'm a production assistant at a public radio station and drive a forty-year-old car I fix myself. And I owe tens of thousands of dollars in student loans."

"Do you have any idea how much this island is worth?" Seton asks. "Or how much Reid Construction will pull in from building those houses at Burkehaven?"

None of that money's mine, though Seton doesn't want to hear that right now. "I could take a loan against my 401(k). I might have five thousand dollars there."

"I don't want a loan!" Seton says. "But don't talk about your hospital bills like we're in the same boat. I'm sure your mom will pay them for you."

I put a hand on her arm, but she shakes me off. On the dock, Reid dives into the lake and swims toward the opposite shore, his strokes strong and assured.

"Tell Reid he shouldn't swim alone," Seton says. "And you and I should keep our distance from each other till the state cops learn what happened. I have to watch out for myself. And my mom."

She grips the steering wheel and won't meet my eyes, and I can tell no matter what I say in this moment, it won't be the right thing. I get out of the car, and she backs away. "Take care, Charlie," she says through the open window, before speeding off into the trees.

Seton's been a friend—maybe a little more—for as long as I can remember, the two of us bonded by shared tragedy. We could have given up on each other years ago, but if we had, I'd have lost the one person who truly understands growing up under this particular shadow of grief. I can't imagine a life without her in it, or that these latest events might finally push us apart.

Chapter Twelve

I change out of the smoky running gear I've been wearing all day and check my phone. The unsent text to Julian about scrapping the podcast waits for me on the screen. I delete it for now, then wash my face, scrubbing at the last remnants of ash and blood. The wound on my forehead is tender and swollen, with a welt forming around the stitches that will probably take days to heal. I sweep dark hair from my forehead and sneer into the mirror, my blue eyes—my father's blue eyes—staring back at me. Maybe the doctor's right and the scar will add character.

And maybe Seton and I can talk tomorrow and leave what happened today behind us.

Outside, chilly air and thick clouds have rolled in with the promise of rain. Thc dock is empty, while out in the lake, Reid cuts a line through the water as he swims across the cove, breathing rhythmically to the left and then to the right. I perch on one of the Adirondack chairs as he reaches the opposite shore and begins the return.

My brother has another life away from Idlewood, one he doesn't share much with the rest of us. He keeps an apartment in Boston's South End, the penthouse in a building he developed. It's only a few miles from my place in Somerville, though we rarely see each other. I've found photos of him on social media with groups of handsome men on beaches or yachts in far-flung locales. Once in a while, he'll bring one of those men to Idlewood for the weekend, though they rarely make a return appearance.

He swims up to the dock, touching in with a flourish and shoving away. When he sees me, he says, "No permanent damage?"

"Maybe a scar," I say.

"You had us worried there."

He hauls himself out of the water, his body long and well muscled. He pulls the swim cap from his blond hair, tucks his goggles into the side of his red briefs, and lies on the dock to stretch.

"The water must be freezing," I say.

"I'm used to it," Reid says. "Was that Seton I saw out in the parking area? Watch what you say to her. She's a cop, and she has a personal interest in what her mother did. Don't be too trusting."

I won't mention our argument over money.

Reid slides his left leg under his right and leans across the dock. "Gilcrest had plenty of questions for me," he says. "Now I need to get the insurance company to sign off on the damages from the fire. Not the easiest thing with arson."

"Do they know it's arson?" I ask.

"They will soon enough," Reid says, turning onto his stomach and lifting his chest forward. "The state fire marshal's here. Let's hope he gets what he needs before the rain starts."

"When you talked to Gilcrest, did he mention Dad?" I ask.

Reid finishes the stretch, stands, and slides his feet into a pair of flip-flops. "Not once," he says. "And right now, Mom and I have enough to deal with without you opening up old wounds. Let this podcast thing go. And stop asking questions."

He leaves me on the dock and heads up the path toward the cabin.

Now I've managed to piss off Seton *and* Reid. I sit by the water until the first of the rain begins to fall, forming concentric circles as it patters onto the lake. I snap a selfie of the welt on my forehead and text it to Julian.

The phone rings thirty seconds after I hit send.

"Charlie," Julian says. In the background, a dog barks and a baby screams. "Nice setting in that photo. Where the hell are you?"

"On our dock," I say.

"*On our dock.* What I'd give to say that one of these days. What happened to you, dude? You look wrecked."

I hit the highlights of the day.

"Andrea Haviland, your mother, Paul Burke, the cop," Julian says. "The same players as the first case."

"Except for the dead ones," I say.

Julian whispers something. "Sorry," he says. "Dinner at the Allende household is chaos. And this arson case, this whole mess, could be the hottest story around."

"Or it could be a whole lot of nothing," I say.

"But you never know until you dig in and get dirty. That's what journalists do. Here you have the past folding in on the present. It would make for a good narrative, especially if the fire's connected to what your father did."

Julian's grasping for a story, but I need to focus on the truth, not constructing something sensational, especially not at the expense of my family and friends. I settle into the chair. "I'm not sure what I'm doing. I'm flailing around without knowing where to start."

"It's how you do the job. You flail—and fail—until you finally realize you've asked the right question."

"Well, right now, I could use some time away from the family."

The baby in the background screams again. "I could use some time away from the family, too," Julian whispers. "But don't tell anyone I said that." Glass breaks. "Oops. Yuck. Listen to me, I have to get off the phone, but letting this story go would be a huge mistake. Grab on to it and don't let go. Or someone else will tell the story for you."

He clicks off the call. The light rain has transformed to a cold drizzle, and the wind has increased. Up at the cottage, Reid stands at the stove in the kitchen. I don't want to face him right now.

I step onto the boat, unsnap the cover, and start the blower. A few moments later, I ease into the marina in downtown Hero, where I cut the engine to headway speed. The lights in the Landing blaze, and voices from the crowded pub reverberate across the water. I take the last spot at the town pier and cover the boat before hurrying through the rain, along a gangway to the street above, where a few smokers puff away while water pours off the eaves. I sidle in beside a woman huddled under an umbrella with a cigarette tucked into the side of her mouth and a German shepherd sitting at her feet. I've never smoked tobacco before, but tonight—with Reid and Seton and everyone else pissed off at me—seems like the night to start. "Could I bum one?" I ask.

The woman taps a cigarette from a pack, lights it between her own lips, and hands it to me. She seems familiar, though Hero is tiny, and I've seen most of the people who live here at one time or another. As I crouch to pet the German shepherd, a growl begins at the back of its throat.

"Ginger needs permission to be kind," the woman says, her voice low and throaty. "Should I give her permission?"

"I'm pretty harmless."

"Release," the woman says, and the dog transforms, melting against me. She wags her tail as I bury my face in her fur, letting all the stress of the day flow into her. I inhale on the cigarette. My body convulses with coughs, like the doctor said it would.

"First time?" the woman asks. "You must have had a worse day than I had."

"We'll have to compare notes."

I grind the cigarette out with the heel of my shoe.

"Hey," the woman says. "Those things cost about a buck apiece these days."

"I'll make it up to you. Let me buy you a drink."

She steps out of the shadows and eyes me up and down. She has the healthy, outdoorsy appearance of most of the people around here, and looks like she might be in her early forties—though, as I realize where I remember her from, I know for a fact she's older. She's changed since the last time I saw her on TV, playing Gina Shock on *Scene of the Crime*. Freya Faith, Paul Burke's TV star client, has swapped the brash red hair from the series for a more natural auburn, and replaced the tailored suit with a sparkly black blouse, capri pants, and stacked heels.

"What happened to your head?" she asks.

"I ran into a tree."

"Must have hurt."

"Still does."

"We'll see about that drink you owe me," she says. "My break's over, but I'll be at the bar later. Say hello."

She snaps the umbrella closed and disappears inside with the dog at her heels. I follow a moment later. The pub is packed, the air heavy with damp clothing and body heat. In the corner, at a makeshift stage, Freya perches on a stool, a guitar balanced on one knee, the dog at her feet.

Someone grips my shoulder. "I didn't expect to see you out and about tonight."

I turn to where Paul leans against the wall.

"I'm escaping Idlewood for a few hours," I say, realizing I haven't seen him since the fire. "Sorry about what happened today."

Paul nods toward Freya. "I'm distracting myself. These shows—" He clucks his tongue. "Do you know who convinced Freya to sing here a few nights a week? Andrea Haviland. So I have Andrea to thank for burning down my house *and* for ruining Freya's career."

Freya begins a slow rendition of Pat Benatar's "Love Is a Battlefield," her voice a throaty contralto. All around, phones snap photos for social media.

"She's good," I say.

"And if she performs a night here and there," Paul says, "we can spin that as spontaneous. A whole summer? It looks desperate." He finishes his drink. "Actually, I've had enough. Maybe I'll see you at Idlewood later," he says, stepping outside into the rain as Freya finishes the song.

Paul's been Freya's manager and lawyer since the nineties. He has a vested interest in what she does with her career, though from what I can see, Freya's soaking up the attention. I join in the applause, then grab a beer at the bar and head to the back porch. A group of women laugh at a table with a bottle of rosé between them. I must stare too long, because one of the women catches my eye and whispers to another. That one stares right back at me, until I retreat inside, pushing my way through the crowd to the bar, where a single seat has opened. Onstage, Freya sings Heart's "If Looks Could Kill," as though she was out on the deck with me and those women. A glass jar by the beer taps has a photo of Mrs. Haviland taped to it with DEFENSE FUND written in black Sharpie, along with a website to donate electronically. There must be a few hundred dollars in the jar already.

The bartender approaches. He's about ten years older than I am, with prematurely white hair and an angular face. He wears a tight concert T-shirt that shows his pecs. "Blancy, right?" I ask, remembering he and Reid used to hang out when they were in high school.

"Good memory," he says.

He pours me another IPA and slides the glass down the bar. "On the house," he says. "You were the hero today."

"Seton did most of the work."

"That's not what I heard."

"I'll donate to the defense fund, then," I say, pulling up the website and adding money to a growing pot of online cash.

"Every little bit helps," Blancy says. "It must have been a rough day all around. Tell your brother I'm thinking about him."

A middle-aged man slides onto the empty stool beside me. "Any news about the woman who was hurt?" he asks.

Blancy shakes his head. "We're all hoping. Andrea's the heart of this town, even if she is a little salty."

The man adds a twenty-dollar bill to the jar. "I'll take one of those," he says, pointing at my beer.

He wears thick glasses and has long gray hair tied in a ponytail, a look that signals he's either a biker or a multimillionaire, though my guess is probably both. "You up for the weekend?" he asks me.

"I'll be in and out for most of the summer, or I thought I would be."

"That welt on your head must hurt. You okay?"

"Nothing worth talking about," I say, taking a long quaff of the beer and letting the bitter liquid slide over my tongue. "How about you? What brings you to town?"

"Visiting an old friend," the man says. "Someone I'm worried about."

The door to the bar opens, and Seton enters. She's changed out of her uniform and into a pair of jeans and a formfitting fleece. Her spiky hair shines from the rain, and light glints off a stud in her lip. Even here, she moves like a cop, alert and scanning the room for trouble. She stops when she finds me. I wave as a kind of peace offering, but she doesn't approach.

"Is that your girlfriend?" the man asks.

"I'm not sure what we are," I say.

"Seton Haviland. I hear good things about her, that she's tough but fair. She's having quite a day, too. She must be worried about her mom."

The man's words are a good reminder that what Seton's facing right now has little to do with me and a lot to do with an uncertain future. "She is worried," I say. "Let's hope our friendship survives whatever the next few days bring."

"You have nothing but time, and a good friend is hard to find. Take it from someone who knows."

He finishes his beer and tosses two twenties on the bar. "I'm sorry about what happened, Charlie. But I'm glad to see you on your feet. You were all I could think about today. Let's hope tomorrow brings more light."

He lifts his thick glasses onto his hair, and my breath catches as he heads toward the door, past Seton, out into the rainy evening. I should run after him, but my body won't move, my limbs frozen in shock, because I'd recognize those blue eyes anywhere. They stare back at me every morning from my own mirror.

That was Mark Kilgore, my father, the man who disappeared into the White Mountains a quarter of a century ago.

Chapter Thirteen

Here's where I should confess that seeing my father isn't new. I've spotted him from time to time out of the corner of my eye, lingering on the edge of a crowd. When I've looked again, he's been gone, leaving me wondering whether he was ever there in the first place.

The first time I saw him was years ago, when he hovered on the periphery of a soccer game. I must have been six or seven and playing in the summer league in Hero, because Seton was on the team, too. I moved the ball down the field, in control, ready to strike, but spotting my father was enough of a distraction that I lost the ball and the other team scored. As kids ran onto the field to celebrate, I searched the sidelines, but my father was gone.

I can't remember whether Mrs. Haviland came to the game or if we met her at the Landing afterward, but I do know she bought us ice cream. "Sometimes you win," she told me as we sat outside on a wooden bench, "and sometimes you lose the ball and the other team scores. That doesn't matter in the end. Be kind, and focus on the positive."

By then, I'd pieced together some of my family's history. I knew Mrs. Haviland had grown up with my father. I also understood that my mother avoided her, but that Mrs. Haviland did things like taking me for ice cream. "You look just like him," she'd say sometimes, especially when we were alone.

Later that night, at Idlewood, I lay in bed while Reid read me a story. I yearned for the times when I was away from boarding school, together with my mother and brother, when Paul and Hadley would visit, when we felt like a family. "What would you do," I asked Reid, "if Dad came home?"

Reid put the book aside. "What do you know about Dad?" he asked.

"He went away."

Reid turned off the bedside lamp. "You should go to sleep."

"Dad came to my soccer game today," I said into the darkness, my voice barely a whisper.

Reid stood and retreated to the bedroom doorway. "You couldn't have seen Dad," he said. "And if you did, don't tell Mom, whatever you do. Dad was a bad man, and you'll upset her."

Chapter Fourteen

The crowd in the pub swirls around me as I stare at the empty stool where my father sat not thirty seconds ago. In the background, Freya Faith sings "Landslide," while Seton stands guard by the entrance. As if in slow motion, I get up and dash outside. On the street, a wave of people surges at me, shoving forward to escape the heavy rain. I force my way through them until I reach the middle of the road, asphalt shining under the streetlamps, and search every direction for that ponytail. Off in the distance, a motorcycle engine roars.

My father's gone.

I tap record on my phone. "I saw him," I say, my breathing heavy. "My father sat beside me at the bar. We talked for, I don't know, five minutes." As the words form, doubt creeps into my mind as it has before, eroding the certitude that propelled me out here to the street.

"It *was* him," I say.

I know it was him.

I step toward the pub and hold the phone close. I want to capture the patter of the rain and the music in the background. This time, I speak slowly and deliberately. "Mark Kilgore, my father, was at the Landing in downtown Hero, New Hampshire. He drank a beer. He talked to me about friendship. He called me by my name." I pause, trying to remember his exact words. "He said he was here visiting an old friend, someone he was worried about."

Someone such as Andrea Haviland, a friend who nearly died today. Could Julian have been onto something when he talked about the past folding in on the present? Because my father appearing out of nowhere on the day of the Burkehaven fire can't be a coincidence.

Back inside, Seton still stands guard by the doorway.

"You look like you saw a ghost," she says.

I search her face for a sign she saw what I saw, that she understands who was here tonight. But why would Seton recognize my father, especially when his appearance has changed so much? "That man sitting next to me at the bar—"

"Ponytail. Glasses."

"You saw him?"

"Of course I saw him. I'm trained to notice these things."

"Did you recognize him?" I ask.

"Never seen him before."

I nearly tell her who he was but stop myself. Seton would welcome a long-shot suspect to clear her mother of the arson charges, so I need to be one hundred percent certain before I say anything.

"What are you doing here anyway?" I ask. "I thought you'd be at the hospital."

"There's no change in Mom's condition," Seton says. "No arrest yet, either. I'll catch a few hours of sleep before heading back."

"Are we friends again?" I ask.

She folds her arms across her chest. "Check with me tomorrow."

"There's an empty seat at the bar. We don't need to talk, especially if we're not friends till tomorrow."

Seton barely shakes her head. "Let me stew in my own misery."

"You know where I am," I say.

At the bar, Blancy hasn't had a chance to clear the pint glass my father used. I wrap it in a paper napkin and slip it under my coat. There could be fingerprints on it. Or DNA. I doubt my father's fingerprints are on record, and I'm certain his DNA isn't, but I have my own DNA.

If I arrange a test of what's on the glass, there could be a parental match, and I'll finally know what's real and what isn't.

"Did your friend take off?" Blancy asks as he wipes down the counter.

"Does he come here much?"

"Not before tonight, though lots of people are passing through for the long weekend. If he's staying local, we're the only game in town. Come back tomorrow and bring your brother with you."

I'm not sure what Reid would do if he saw our father stroll into the Landing.

Blancy pours me another IPA, then moves down the bar, seeing to other customers. He grew up in this town but could only have been ten or twelve when the murder happened. In fact, most of the people at the Landing tonight are too young to remember Mark Kilgore even if they have heard about the murder, so my father could have come here without expecting to be recognized. Except . . . except Paul was at the Landing tonight, if only briefly. And Paul would recognize my father, no matter how much my father had changed.

Something cold and wet brushes along my hand. I jump, only to find Freya Faith's German shepherd sitting at attention beside me.

"Ginger likes you."

Freya slides onto the same stool where my father sat. It's only now I notice the music has ended and the crowd has begun to thin.

I hunch over my glass and take Freya in out of the corner of my eye. She has a way of carrying herself, cool and unattached, savvy enough to know a camera could capture her at any moment, and that all eyes in the room, including mine, are turned her way.

"Ginger's my emotional support," she says. "At least if they reprimand me for having her here."

I doubt Freya Faith gets reprimanded for much.

Blancy mixes her an old-fashioned while Freya chats with a couple who compliment her on the show. After they leave, she downs the drink in one gulp. "Sugar's good for the throat."

Blancy already has another cocktail ready.

"This one I'll sip," Freya says. "Did you enjoy the set? *Scene of the Crime* ended almost ten years ago now, and I'm trying to get back out there before the world forgets me for good. I may talk to my agent about booking some other clubs in the area, though my manager thinks it's a shitty idea. I'm testing material. I'm calling the show Rocker Chicks."

"Great name," I say.

"It's a terrible name. I'll come up with a new one, but I'm only playing songs from the eighties. Stevie. Chrissie. Cyndi. Maybe a little Madonna." She looks me up and down. "The eighties are ancient history to you."

"But I'm an old soul."

"If liking the eighties makes you an old soul, does that make me old because I *lived* in the eighties?"

"That's not what I meant," I say.

She taps a fingernail painted metallic blue against her glass. "Make it up to me. Order another beer and stick around. This town closes by nine, which isn't my style after all those years in New York."

She mentions New York like someone used to living in the public eye, someone used to having people she's never met know all sorts of private information about her. And I do know she lived in New York, while she doesn't know my name. I almost mention we're connected through Paul Burke, that same manager who thinks performing in tiny clubs is a bad idea, but I suspect bringing Paul's name into the conversation might spoil the mood.

"You have a good voice," I say.

"I went to Juilliard on an opera scholarship," she says. "No one knows that about me unless they read my Wikipedia page. I was one of those kids obsessed with my artistic principles until I got spat out into the world and learned wearing black and sneering didn't pay the rent."

She runs through this history like a stump speech, the kind of public-facing tale she's employed a thousand times to put strangers at ease. I enjoy listening, losing myself in her story, while forgetting my own for the moment.

"My first job was on a soap," she says. "*Eternal Flame.* Played Brenda Jackson, the town tramp with a heart of gold. I got to live in New York, and it paid the bills and taught me how to learn lines and hit my marks and deal with fans. Brenda was always getting in trouble—two-timing, embezzlement, hanging out with mobsters and spies. She came back from the dead twice!"

Like my father. So much for forgetting what's been going on in my own life.

"How'd that work?" I ask.

"She drove off a cliff and her car sank," Freya says, "but a month later, we learned her mobster boyfriend had a boat waiting to whisk her away. I had a summer share in Montauk that August, so the writers needed to explain her absence. The second time around, she disappeared during a Halloween party. She showed up two towns over with amnesia, working as a waitress with a new name and an awful wig."

"No body, no death," I say.

"At least in the soaps."

And sometimes in real life.

I scan the room to see if my father's returned. I feel the weight of the pint glass in my coat, something tangible, something that could provide definitive proof. "Where's Brenda Jackson now?" I ask.

"Probably sitting in a bar somewhere, stirring up trouble." Freya knocks my knee with hers. "Talking to an impossibly handsome young man."

That, I'm pretty certain, was flirting. And Freya Faith is smoking hot, and I don't care that she's twice my age, or that my brother had photos of her taped to his wall when I was barely out of diapers, because she probably has way better options than a production assistant at a public radio station who can barely pay his rent. "Maybe she's with a mobster," I say. "Or a spy."

"You can't be a spy. Spies need to blend in. You're too fine to blend in."

That was unmistakable flirting, and I can feel my face flush.

"Looks as though I have a shy one," Freya says. "Blancy, do you think this one's pretty?"

From behind the bar, Blancy raises a single eyebrow.

"If you swing that way," Freya says, "Blancy's your guy."

Blancy flexes a bicep. He isn't bad looking, but Freya's way more my type.

"I'm taken," Blancy says, checking his phone. "At least for the night."

"My type," I say, "wears black and insists on artistic principles."

"A man who listens when I tell a story," Freya says. "Not bad. What's your name anyway?"

"Charlie."

She fishes the cherry from her glass. "Tell me you don't have a wife and kids at home, Charlie."

"Not even a cat," I say.

"Good. Ginger hates cats. And I should pack up and call it a night. Help me with my equipment."

She played acoustic guitar tonight, so there isn't much "equipment" to help with. By now, the pub has cleared except for a few diehards and Seton, who continues to watch the room like a cop, but mostly watches me. "Give me a sec," I say.

Freya follows my gaze. "Whatever you need to do, but this train is leaving in two minutes, and it doesn't wait for anyone."

I grab my coat with the pint glass and approach Seton. "Tomorrow'll be here in a couple of hours," I say. "I'll swing by the hospital to see how your mother's doing."

"You have a new friend," Seton says.

"I'm about to find out," I say. "Does your department do DNA tests?"

"Are you testing to see if Freya's who she claims to be?"

"It's for something else," I say.

"We send samples to the state lab, but it's expensive and I don't normally have cause."

"What if I paid for it?"

"It doesn't work that way. We'd have to find a private lab." Seton's eyes narrow. "And why would you need a DNA test?"

"I'll tell you tomorrow when we're friends again."

By the door, Freya waits, guitar case in hand. "Tick, tick, tick," she says.

"Watch out for yourself," Seton says.

"Say the word and I'll stick around," I say. "We can go to the hospital together."

Seton bites her lip and shakes her head. "Go," she says. "I'll be fine."

I follow Freya into the rainy night. Across the street, she tosses the guitar into the covered bed of a gigantic pickup truck, while Ginger leaps into the back seat.

"What's the police chief's story, anyway?" Freya asks. "Is she your girlfriend?"

"I don't have a girlfriend."

"Are you sure?"

If Seton and I are on the "friends to lovers" train, we're clearly riding the local. "One hundred percent," I say.

Our hands brush, sending a chill up my back. Freya's sequined blouse sparkles under the streetlamp.

"You could do worse than Seton Haviland," Freya says. "She's as pretty as you, in a butch kind of way."

"You keep objectifying me," I say.

"I have plenty of experience. It happened to me for decades."

"Should I objectify you now?"

Freya glances to where Seton watches us from the doorway. "She seems awfully interested in you."

"What does it matter?"

"Because I don't like to be second best," Freya says as she pulls me in for a kiss.

Chapter Fifteen

I'm standing in the rain, under a streetlamp, and I'm not sure what to do, where to put my hands, or what they should touch, because I'm kissing a girl. But she's not a girl, she's very much a woman, and she's a good kisser—a very good kisser—and she's Freya Faith.

Freya fucking *Faith.*

"Relax," Freya says. "You're stiff as a board."

I pull back.

"I said relax, not stop. And chill out before you screw the mood."

From the back of the truck, Ginger barks and paws at the window, but not in a "Hey, guys, what about me?" kind of way. She'd probably rip my throat out if she could.

"Ginger can be protective," Freya says.

"I've noticed."

"She's gentle unless there's a reason for her not to be," Freya adds. "Anything I need to worry about?"

"This is a small town, and everyone knows who you are. They'll talk."

"I can handle gossip on the Hero Board. It's when I make the cover of the *National Enquirer* that I worry."

Unlike most of us, Freya's actually appeared in that tabloid. She steps back and opens the driver's-side door. She stands on the running board, her auburn hair falling from the knot at the back of her head. "Are you coming?"

I trip over my own feet as I scramble to the passenger's side door. Ginger bares her teeth, but when Freya tells her to sit, the dog transforms, woofing a welcome. I find myself sprawled across the front seat, kissing Freya all over again. This time, Ginger tries to nose her way into the action as Freya bats her away and mumbles, "Stop."

"Is that *stop* for me?" I ask.

"Not in any way."

By now, the town has mostly closed for the evening. Freya disentangles herself and swerves around the southern side of the marina and into the parking lot where the old motel used to be. A steel door opens beneath the new condos, and Freya pulls into an underground garage. Lights flood the empty space as she cuts the engine. Behind us, the steel garage door seals shut, and the kind of silence that comes from being locked in a soundproof room descends over us. "Should I let someone know I'm here?" I ask.

"Your girlfriend knows where you are. She'll take care of you."

"I told you Seton's not my girlfriend."

Freya kisses me. "I don't need to make enemies with the chief of police. I get enough speeding tickets as it is."

She jumps from the truck and opens the back so Ginger can leap to the cement floor. The dog puts her nose to the ground, sweeping the perimeter of the garage, her body low and agile. She pauses once, tilting her head, before sitting at attention, her ears pivoting. "All set," Freya says. "Grab the guitar."

I get out of the truck and pull the guitar case from the covered bed. At another steel door, Freya enters a code, and what sounds like the lock on a bank safe releases. Ginger trots ahead of us into a hallway, sniffing until she stops at an elevator door.

"Paranoid much?" I ask.

"Cautious."

"You just picked up a guy you've never met in a bar."

"You don't fit the profile of who I worry about."

"Thanks," I say. "I guess."

Inside, we take the elevator up two floors, where it opens onto a huge space of clean lines and glass that reminds me of Reid's apartment in the South End—as it should, since Reid designed this whole building. Freya hangs my coat in a closet, my father's pint glass tucked into the coat's front pocket.

"Bar's in the kitchen," she says. "Mix me an old-fashioned."

She whistles, and Ginger leads the way up a set of invisible stairs to the second floor.

The condo has soaring ceilings and inset lighting, with a vast open plan divided into separate seating areas. One area has a piano and a guitar stand. Another has a workspace with bookshelves that rise to the ceiling. A third has comfortable, overstuffed furniture and a huge television set. Modern art hangs on nearly every inch of wall space, including a portrait that takes me a moment to recognize as Freya. It's a nude.

A kitchen runs along one wall, with white cabinets, soapstone counters, and appliances that belong in a restaurant. I find a recipe for an old-fashioned on my phone and have doused sugar cubes with bitters by the time Ginger trots down the stairs. Freya follows, having swapped the glittery blouse for a flowing hostess dress straight from the sixties that somehow works in her favor.

I hand her the cocktail. She clinks her glass against mine. I take a sip and gag on the bourbon. "Lightweight," Freya says as she leads me through one of the sitting areas to a set of steel, floor-to-ceiling doors.

When Ginger gives the all clear, we join her on a deck that runs the length of the apartment and overlooks the harbor. The rain has stopped, and the skies have cleared, and a sliver of a moon shines down on the blackened surface of the lake. Freya shivers and steps a bit closer to me.

"What would bring someone like you to Hero?" I ask.

"The outdoors. The fresh air."

"The nonstop nightlife."

She inches closer. "Yeah, there's that."

I hear Julian in my head, coaching me to get to the heart of the story. "Didn't you grow up visiting the lake?" I ask.

Freya's shoulders stiffen under her hostess dress. "How would you know that?" she asks.

"You're the only TV star in town," I say. "Who else would we talk about?"

"I'm hardly a TV star. I've barely booked a gig in a decade. Honestly, I almost never leave my co-op anymore, but in Hero I'm famous. Everyone knows everything about me. Maybe that's why I enjoy it here." Freya leans on the railing, a breeze blowing through her hair. "But yes, my family came to the lake. We stayed at Burkehaven Cove in a little cabin."

"Paul Burke's place?" I say.

"You know him?"

"Everyone knows everyone here," I say.

"Well, Paul's mother and my mother went to Miss Porter's in Connecticut. We rented the cabin for two weeks every summer while the Burkes stayed at the farmhouse."

I sip the old-fashioned, this time allowing the bourbon to linger on my tongue to keep from choking. Freya knew Paul back then. She probably knew everyone involved in the murder: my mother, Paul, but also Isaac and Andrea Haviland. My father, too. "There was an episode of *Scene of the Crime* set on a lake," I say. "Was it based on the murder that happened here?"

Freya steps away from me. "Tell me you're not some true-crime freak."

"That murder is the most exciting thing that ever happened in Hero," I say, doing my best to feign casual interest. "People talk as if it happened yesterday. The guy who committed the murder, you must have met him."

"Mark Kilgore," Freya says. "Yeah, he was friends with Paul. He'd come to Burkehaven when we were staying there. Mark was nice. And I never believed what they said about him."

That's the last thing in the world I expected her to say, and I gulp the old-fashioned to mask my surprise, relieved by a fit of coughing that keeps me from spewing questions at her. She swears under her breath and retreats inside, returning with a glass of water. "You should stick to apple juice," she says.

I drink the water down.

We all know what happened, Charlie.

But do we? My father is missing and presumed dead, but tonight he walked into the Landing and drank a beer. I have his pint glass in my coat pocket. And until tonight, no one's ever suggested there could be another explanation for what happened on the lake. I wonder if I've been waiting my whole life to hear Freya's words.

"What didn't you believe?" I ask.

Freya tosses her hair as though she's on the set of *Scene of the Crime*, playing Special Agent Gina Shock. "Let's talk about something else. Or do something else." She runs her fingertips along my forearm. "Have any ideas?"

I've waited twenty-five years to find out what happened next, and I can wait a bit longer. Besides, I'm not about to miss this opportunity with Freya, and it won't present itself again.

"I suppose I do," I say, and then my fingers are in Freya's thick hair, and her hands are on my waist, on my belt, as she pulls me through the house, up those stairs to another steel door she unlocks with a code. She shoves me onto the mattress as doubts stop spinning through my mind and the steel door latches behind us.

"Are we in a safe room?" I ask.

"Off," Freya says, and the room goes black.

◆ ◆ ◆

I wake the next morning to something cold and wet in my ear. I shove Ginger's nose as she paws at my chest and then makes her way across the huge bed to where Freya lies beside me. Freya's voice, huskier than last night, sounds through the impenetrable dark. "Ginger likes you."

"All animals like me," I say.

"On," Freya says, and the recessed lighting slowly illuminates.

She props her head on a pillow, her hair tousled. She's wearing a vintage T-shirt from the Pat Benatar Tropico tour, and I wonder if she's wondering, as I am, how we wound up here, or when she might send me packing. I wonder if she'd be willing, as I am, to go at it again this morning. I move a lock of hair from her eyes, and she doesn't flinch. A good sign.

"Out," Freya says.

The muscles beneath Ginger's black-and-tan coat ripple as she transforms from pet to guard dog. She leaps from the bed and stands at attention by the door, eyes alert. "I had her trained by monks," Freya says, "but I drew the line at teaching her German. Too intimidating. She knows more commands than my ex-husband. But even the best guard dogs need to pee in the morning." She kisses me. It's a kiss I feel all the way down to my toes. "Did you know I was married?" she asks.

Freya eloped with an actor from *Scene of the Crime*, and they divorced a year later, when he had an affair with a reality star. His character got shot in the groin and was dismembered by a serial killer in the middle of that season. "Why would I know you were married?" I ask.

Freya slips out of bed, opens a wall safe, and retrieves a handgun. I scramble away from her. "Okay, I knew about your divorce. It was all over the internet!"

Freya slides a magazine into place. "That's better," she says, unsealing the door.

Sunlight streams into the room. Ginger trots out, nose to the ground, and my heart rate begins to return to normal. "Let me guess," I say. "A perimeter check?"

"Ginger keeps me safe," Freya says, nodding at the gun. "And so does this."

She patters after the dog, and I settle into the bed. As nervous as the gun makes me, Freya's as attractive as she was last night, and I'm thrilled to have woken up next to her. Plus, the bed is soft, and the sheets have a thread count I'll probably never experience again for the rest of my life.

When Freya returns, she closes the steel door to keep Ginger on the other side and lays the handgun on the bedside table.

"Get that thing away from me," I say.

"You must be a city boy."

"I grew up in Hero."

"Most people around here are used to guns."

Freya releases the magazine, returns the gun to the safe, slides into bed beside me, and lights a cigarette, exhaling toward the ceiling. I take the cigarette from her, inhale, and cough.

"It's a disgusting habit," Freya says.

"Then quit."

"I wish it were that easy. I do it to keep thin, to keep from completely disappearing now that I'm trying to get back in the game." She inhales and lays her head on my chest. "We could stay here all day."

I picture us lying together into the afternoon, working through the pack of cigarettes as though we're in some ancient movie. A scene flashes through my mind: a man and a woman in bed after a night of passion, the man delighted by the turn of events. "Have you seen *Harold and Maude*?" I ask.

Freya grinds out the cigarette. "Do you mean the movie where a teenager sleeps with a seventy-nine-year-old Holocaust survivor?" she asks.

That is the movie I meant. And I suppose, based on Freya's reaction and our age difference, I shouldn't have asked the question at this particular moment, especially when she hits me with a pillow. "*Harold and* fucking *Maude*?" she says. "Do I look seventy-nine years old to you?"

I cover my head, and she hits me again. I peek between my fingers as Ginger growls and tries to paw her way around the heavy steel door.

Freya straddles me, the pillow raised. And don't think I've forgotten the gun, either. She doesn't look anywhere close to seventy-nine years old.

"I take it back!" I say.

"You can't take it back. It's been said, and now I won't get the image out of my head. Ever! For the rest of my life."

"I'm sorry," I say.

Freya collapses onto the bed beside me and says, "Stay."

I'm not sure who she's talking to, but Ginger's growls stop at once. "I have a thick skin," Freya adds, getting out of bed, putting on a pink flannel robe, and tying her hair in a turquoise scrunchie. "But you spoiled the mood. Remember that the next time you say something dumb to a beautiful woman, Harold."

"My name's Charlie."

"Not to me, it isn't," she says. "And get up. I want something decadent for breakfast. Please tell me you know how to cook."

Chapter Sixteen

In the bathroom, I try my best to freshen up, smoothing my dark hair and brushing my teeth with an index finger. I'm taken aback by the purple welt on my forehead. I'd forgotten about the wound and the stitches, but seeing them returns me to yesterday's events. I check my phone for a message from Seton, but nothing's there. I'll drive to the hospital as soon as Freya sends me on my way.

I search the medicine cabinet for an aspirin, moving aside a bottle of metallic-blue nail polish before glancing behind me. With Freya's attention to security, my guess is that every room in this house has a camera—even the bathroom—and I bet she won't appreciate seeing me searching through her things.

Downstairs, the aroma of coffee fills the air. Freya adds four spoons of sugar and a glug of cream to her own mug and stirs. "How do you take your coffee, Harold?"

"Black is good. You want something decadent?" I say. "How about waffles?"

"Do I seem like someone who owns a waffle iron?"

Freya seems like someone who has anything she wants, though she clearly hasn't forgiven me for mentioning *Harold and Maude*.

"Pancakes, then," I say.

After I fumble through playing short-order cook, we head to the deck, carrying stacks of pancakes loaded with maple syrup and butter. In the marina, people have already begun to take their boats out for the day. We settle at a teak table beneath a pergola covered in budding rose vines.

"Not a bad way to greet the morning," I say.

"I kept my co-op in New York," Freya says. "I can go back when I'm ready. But this is a great escape for now."

"Is that what all the security is about? Escaping?"

"I have to be careful. I'm by myself. People know who I am."

"You sleep with steel grates over the windows and wake up with a gun. That's more than being careful."

Freya nestles the mug between her hands. "There are plenty of weirdos out there, fans who blur the line between fiction and reality. It gets scary, and for a while I let it get the better of me. Besides, we both know bad things can happen in small towns. You're the one who was asking about that case on the lake last night."

Now would be the time to come clean and tell Freya who I am. But I've already dodged the truth, and Freya, with her guns and safe room and guard dog, doesn't seem the type to forgive evasiveness. "People talk," I say, "and they were talking about the episode of your show set on the lake during your set last night."

"I worked over three hundred cases. They blend together."

"You didn't work *any* cases. You weren't a real cop."

Freya punches my arm. "Gina Shock wasn't a cop. She was a special agent with the CBI."

"Okay, what did Special Agent Gina Shock of the CBI make of the case on the lake? I mean, it was ripped from the headlines."

"*Ripped from the headlines* is from another show," Freya says. "But, yeah, I got a feel for storylines after a while. Some came together easily and felt organic. Others, not so much. Those ones, we'd have to massage to make them plausible, no matter how much we pulled from real life. That story, the one about the husband who snaps and kills his wife's lover and then goes after his own kids, it made no sense to me. Something about that case didn't add up."

Something about that case didn't add up.

That's a sound bite I should have captured.

I stand and shove my phone into my pocket. "Too much coffee," I say.

In the bathroom, I splash water on my face and take three deep breaths. Something I can't articulate is happening here; I feel it in my gut. I tap record on the phone. Whether I can use this audio or not, I need to capture it. Maybe I'll convince Freya to sign a release later.

Outside, my every movement feels deliberate and suspicious, especially as I lay the phone face down on the table between us. "Something about that case didn't add up?" I say, parroting Freya's words.

I'll have my own voice reflecting her earlier statement, even if that voice is shaking.

Freya sets her coffee aside. My heart pounds so loudly she must hear it.

"What's got you on edge?" she asks.

"I woke up next to Freya Faith. It may not be a big deal for Ginger, but it is for me."

"You're not the first to find me intimidating, Harold."

"I doubt I'll be the last," I say as I settle into the subterfuge of the situation. "But what didn't add up? Was it because you knew so many of the players? I mean, you work with Paul Burke. He's your manager. Wasn't he at the lake house right before the murder happened?"

Freya scrutinizes me one more time, then seems to shake away her doubts. "I knew those people as a kid," she says. "But the oddest thing was that I saw Isaac Haviland for the first time in years a few months before he was killed. He came to New York and was hanging around a shoot in the West Village. Security was tight on the set. He got roughed up a little bit, and I felt terrible about it, so I took him to a diner after we wrapped." She rolls her eyes. "He was looking for money. He wanted me to invest in the Landing."

"Did you give him any?"

"I gave him a hundred bucks and got rid of him as soon as I figured out what was going on." Freya shakes her head. "Isaac weirded me out, but that's not the part of the story I can't reconcile. When we shot *Scene of the Crime*, I used to hang out in the writers' room and drive them crazy questioning plots. There were so many holes in the Idlewood storyline—"

"Some guy's wife is having an affair," I say. "He finds out and loses it. That story's been told a thousand times."

Freya runs a hand along Ginger's back. "Sure, the setup was straightforward enough: Jane Reid has an affair with Isaac Haviland while they're working on rehabbing the Landing. Plenty of my cases involved someone sleeping with someone they shouldn't, and adultery's the oldest story there is."

"You don't have any cases," I remind her. "You're an actor."

"Good actors immerse themselves in their roles, and I played Gina Shock for thirteen years. I barely know where she ends and I begin. But what happened next?"

"Mark Kilgore killed Isaac Haviland and fled the scene once he realized what he'd done."

As soon as I hear myself say my father's name, I wish I hadn't. I should have called him *that guy* or *the husband*. I know way too much about this case for a casual twenty-six-year-old observer, but Freya seems to miss my fumble.

"Follow the evidence," she says. "That's what Gina Shock would tell you. Mark Kilgore was cooking dinner for his family. His older son was studying at the kitchen table. They were listening to Janet Jackson. Jane Reid had set up paper lanterns on the dock for the Lantern Festival. What happened next?"

I know exactly what happened next—Isaac Haviland showed up and called my mother's name across the cove—but I won't make the mistake of showing too much familiarity again. "I'm fuzzy on the details."

"Mark Kilgore leaves the house with a chef's knife and confronts his wife's lover."

I don't see the problem. "And?" I say.

Freya sits up. "When you're putting together a show, it has to hang together. If there's the tiniest blip in logic, the online lunatics rip the story to shreds. So, a character's having an affair with some guy's wife. He drives out to the house, and the guy—the one he's betrayed—charges out of the trees with a chef's knife. What should the character do?"

Nowadays, he'd dial 9-1-1, but there were no cell phones then, or not ones that got reception at Idlewood. "He could get in the car and lock the doors," I say. "Or maybe the guy held the knife behind his back. Or maybe Isaac Haviland was concerned about Jane and the kids."

"Let's say all that's true. We'd have to work the concern into dialogue, but what happened next?"

This time I don't fumble. "All I know is what I heard at the bar last night."

Freya waits for me to continue.

"Fine," I say. "Jane Reid left her kids on the island and tried defusing the situation. She asked Isaac Haviland to leave, and he was nearly in his car when he called her *my love*."

"That's when Mark lost it," Freya says. "He stabbed Isaac in the gut, and when Jane tried to intervene, he stabbed her, too."

Sounds like great TV. Drama. Intense emotion. Rash decisions. "Isn't this the kind of story your whole show was built on?"

"When things followed a certain logic."

"Murder doesn't follow logic."

"Each murder has its own logic. And here's something else we had to change for the show: Isaac Haviland crawled into the woods to escape. The police found him later, propped up against a tree, where he'd bled out, but if Mark was so intent on killing Isaac, why would he let him escape? On the show, we finished off the victim right away. And there's the whole thing with the preteen and the baby in the rowboat."

Now she's questioning *my* story. "That's the part everyone remembers," I say. "Two kids in a rowboat while paper lanterns lit up the sky. I mean, you used that image on the show."

"It couldn't have been more cinematic," Freya says. "But Mark stabbed his wife and left her to drag herself through the woods to her sister's house? Why would he let *her* go?"

"Because he realized what he'd done and was horrified with himself."

"But if you try your best to murder someone in cold blood, you don't feel bad about it and *then* threaten to also kill your *own children*. Once you find your conscience, it's there and you have to deal with it."

"Maybe he didn't realize his wife was still alive."

Freya waves a hand. "That could be the case, and all of these details are small, and one or two might have been fine in the final storyline, but not all. Audiences are smarter than you think they are. We had to kill off the boyfriend *and* the wife to make the story plausible. And let's not forget about the detective who died in the middle of the investigation. What's her name? Wendy something."

"She was in a car accident," I say.

"Yeah, drunk and alone. She passed out behind the wheel and drowned when her car rolled into the lake. That's an unattended death, not an accident."

I start to argue, but slump in my chair. This isn't fiction, and we're not in a writers' room.

"The end of that episode was a good one," Freya says. "The kids got kidnapped, and we found the husband hiding with them in a cabin in the woods. He hadn't died during the snowstorm at all. Gina exchanged herself for the children, and there was a terrific showdown. Tons of shooting."

I've watched segments of this episode before, but I've mostly focused on the beginning, the section about me. "There was a final twist," I say.

"Always," Freya says. "And guess who came up with it? Me! The writers were totally pissed off because as soon as they heard my idea, they knew the story *had* to end that way. The husband had been having his own affair. He tried to cut it off, and the woman framed him for murder. And do you know who he was having an affair with? The wife of the man who was killed by the lake."

My mother's words come to me again: *Good marriages don't end. And bad marriages don't have a good guy and a bad guy.*

"You're talking about Andrea Haviland," I say. Maybe Mrs. Haviland has something to hide, after all. With the podcast, I set out to learn more about who my father was, but Freya now has me questioning the very foundation of what happened on the lake. "Could she have been having an affair with Mark Kilgore?"

"I mean, I suppose," Freya says. "But this was a TV show. Not real life. If I were investigating this case, I'd start with the wife. Jane Reid. The wife should always be a prime suspect."

My mother did not stab herself so she could crawl through the woods and almost bleed out. "I don't think so," I say.

"If you say so, Harold. But give me a whiteboard, two pepperoni pizzas, and a team of sweaty writers, and I'll make it work. You can make any story work when you have a deadline."

I glance to where my phone lies on the table, recording our every word. It's time to be honest with Freya. "I should tell you something," I say.

"Don't bother baring your soul, Harold," Freya says. "We're almost done with breakfast. Who knows if we'll ever see each other again."

Her phone rings. She glances at the screen and clicks into the call. "What?" she says.

I hear a muffled voice on the other end. Freya nods and looks at me as she moves to the other side of the deck. Below us, a car pulls into the lot. Detective Gilcrest gets out wearing a black anorak and leather sneakers, a phone to his ear. He looks up to where I sit, as Freya clicks off her call. "I need to buzz him in," she says, her voice tight.

I'm pretty certain my game is up.

She slides open the glass door, and when she returns, she stands at the railing, looking out over the lake. I start to speak, but she cuts me off. "I don't appreciate being played."

Behind us, the detective steps onto the deck. I expect Ginger to growl. Instead, she twitches, as though desperate to greet him.

"Release," Freya says.

The dog dashes to the detective, tail wagging. Gilcrest crouches to pet her, then takes Freya's hand and kisses her cheek. "Charlie Kilgore," he says to me. "I heard a rumor I might find you here."

Chapter Seventeen

Freya extracts herself from the detective's clutches and stands with her back to the lake. "Don't get territorial, Duncan," she says. "Ginger doesn't like it."

On the contrary, the German shepherd seems perfectly content with the detective—certainly happier than she's been with me—especially when he takes a bag of treats from his pocket and doesn't make her sit before giving her one.

"You'll spoil her," Freya says.

"That's my job," Gilcrest says. "Save me any breakfast?"

"I could make you pancakes," I say quickly, too quickly, but the last thing I want is to be on the detective's bad side.

"Don't bother," Freya says. "The detective is leaving. And so are you."

"I can explain," I say.

"I doubt you can, Harold."

Gilcrest places himself between Freya and me, and I don't know if it's instinctual or deliberate, but it's definitely territorial. "You left your boat on the town dock," he says to me. "Blancy wants it moved."

"You're running errands for Blancy now, Duncan?" Freya asks.

"When it suits my purposes," Gilcrest says.

"*Charlie* was distracted," Freya says, drawing my name out.

"I can see that," Gilcrest says.

Freya piles the breakfast dishes onto a tray. "Bring these inside," she says to him.

For a moment, the detective seems as though he might push back. Instead, he says, "Let's go, girl," to Ginger and follows Freya's instructions, the dog prancing after him.

"You held back a bit too much of your story, *Charlie*," Freya says. "You were the baby in the boat. You're the guy who was assaulted at Burkehaven yesterday." Her eyes dart toward the stitches in my forehead. "I'm out of practice. Gina would have put this together in two seconds flat."

"I should have been more honest," I say.

"*More* honest? You weren't honest at all. What's your game anyway?"

"You know how the episode of your show ended," I say. "With the father being alive, after all. Could that be true? I mean, it happened to Brenda Jackson. Twice."

Freya starts to answer and stops as her expression softens. "You're a kid," she says.

"I'm twenty-six."

"And I'm *fifty*-six, so don't remind me. Your family's story made for good TV, but it's been a quarter century since that murder."

"They never found a body. My father could have gotten away."

"Listen," Freya says, "it's much harder to disappear nowadays than it was when Brenda Jackson came back from the dead on *Eternal Flame*. If your father were alive, Duncan would have found him."

"How do you know Gilcrest?" I ask.

"I told you I was dipping my toe back in and looking for work. I shot a pilot for a true-crime show earlier this year. I didn't tell Paul I went to the audition. The show wasn't picked up, but Duncan was one of the experts they brought in. He looks good on camera, and he looks good in person, too. We took it from there." She touches the stitches on my forehead. "He'll find whoever did this to you."

"I'm sorry I didn't tell you who I was last night," I say.

"In your defense, I didn't push you for it. But next time, I wouldn't hold back. And we had fun together, Harold."

"I'm Harold again?"

"You'll always be Harold to me."

Behind us, the glass door slides open. Ginger dashes out, followed by the detective.

"Charlie was leaving," Freya says. "He might show up in my next TV series. You both might."

I hope she won't have me shot in the groin and dismembered like she did with her ex-husband.

"I hear you've been asking around about your father," Gilcrest says. "Seton told me about the podcast."

My eyes dart to where my phone sits on the table recording our conversation. Before I can move, Freya snatches up the phone and glances at the screen.

I start to explain, but Freya cuts me off. "And there I was about to forgive you."

"Smooth move, buddy," Gilcrest says.

"Shut up, Duncan," Freya says, holding the phone toward me. "Delete every second of audio."

I search for an excuse, but this time I don't have one. I've managed to destroy any remnant of trust or good feeling between Freya and me with one boneheaded decision. I move the recording to the trash and delete it from there.

"Let me make something clear," Freya says. "Clear enough so a pretty blockhead like you can understand. If one word of what I said appears anywhere, ever, I'll sic a team of lawyers on you. And if you think your old family friend Paul Burke will come to your rescue, think twice. Paul works for me, and his loyalty lies with his paycheck. Understood?"

I stare at the deck and nod.

"Good. Now get out of my house."

My stomach is in knots as Ginger follows on my heels, a growl forming at the back of her throat. I find my coat in the front closet and make sure I have my father's pint glass from last night. Then I get in the elevator with the detective. Testosterone radiates off him as he lets me stew in my own silent misery. Outside, I take off toward the Landing.

"I'll drive you," Gilcrest says, in a way that doesn't give me much choice but to follow him to his SUV. He pulls away from the condo complex, waving a hand out the window toward Freya, who watches impassively from her deck. As we turn onto the street, Paul Burke swerves by in his own car and takes the spot Gilcrest vacated. I dread finding out what Freya will say to Paul about me, or how her choice words will get filtered and disseminated. No matter what, by the time we have dinner tonight, I'll be the butt of every joke.

"Here's a tip," Gilcrest says. "Be up front with people. It's one of the basic tenets of police work. If you'd asked, Freya would have given you an interview. She loves attention, like any actor, but she's not one to forgive, especially if you step on her privacy."

I don't need Duncan Gilcrest to tell me how much I messed up. All I want is to get out of this car and into my boat and away from this whole mess, but as he pulls around the marina and onto Main Street, he passes right by the Landing.

"Blancy can wait another half hour for you to move the boat," Gilcrest says. "I want to make sure I understand what happened yesterday."

He speeds along the lake, eventually turning into the woods at the bungalow. When he comes to the fork in the road, he stops the SUV and swivels toward me. Here, we're alone, and the sun barely penetrates the thick canopy of trees. Maybe the detective wants to give me a reason to stay away from his woman. I press my back to the door, ready to tumble out and run for my life.

Instead, Gilcrest says, "I wish I was meeting you under different circumstances, Charlie. It must have been tough to grow up with all this baggage hanging over your head. Trauma can follow you, whether you know it or not. I get why you're working on this podcast. Who have you talked to so far?"

"Freya, mostly," I say. "But you saw what happened there. I doubt she'll let me talk to her again."

"You can record me," Gilcrest says.

"Really?" I say.

"I've done hundreds of podcasts. And let me know what else I can do to help. Maybe we could get a book deal or a TV series. It's a pretty compelling story."

What would Julian say if I wound up beating him to a book deal? I lay my phone on the SUV's console. "Detective Duncan Gilcrest," I say. "Responding officer to the Idlewood Murders."

Gilcrest leans over the phone. "Hi, guys," he says.

"I've read about what happened," I say. "But you were there. An eyewitness to the aftermath."

"I'd been on the job for a week," Gilcrest says. "I'd graduated from Columbia the previous fall and moved back here from New York."

"You went to Columbia?"

"Try not to sound so surprised." Gilcrest touches pause on the screen. "I'll need a copy of the recording when we finish. And no funny business in the editing room. You have to make me sound good."

"I will," I say, and hit record again. "Tell me what you remember. You responded to the call. Where were you when it came in?"

"On Red Hill Road," Gilcrest says, without pause. "A few miles from your place. At first, all we knew was your mother had been hurt. I found her at that house by the graveyard. She was on the kitchen floor, barely breathing. I did what I could to stabilize her until the EMTs arrived, and then I took off for the island. You can verify this in my report, but I'd say I got to the island a half hour after the call first came in. Maybe forty-five minutes."

"You must have seen blood in the parking area," I say.

Gilcrest shakes his head. "It was dark. No moon. I couldn't see much. I ran through the blood and tracked it across the footbridge. It messed up the forensics later on."

"You didn't wait for backup?" I ask.

"Rookie mistake," Gilcrest says. "And the kind of mistake that can get a cop killed, but no, I didn't wait. I was much more concerned with seeing if anyone else had been hurt or killed. There was one light on in the kitchen, a pot of Bolognese burned on the stove, and your brother's half-finished math homework on the kitchen table, but otherwise, the place was quiet. Eerily so. I almost left when I heard a baby crying." He catches my eye. "You."

I imagine a younger version of Gilcrest standing on the shoreline, searching the dark until he found the rowboat far off in the water, silhouetted against a starry sky.

"It took ten minutes of cajoling to get your brother to row to shore," Gilcrest says. "Otherwise, we'd have had to send the police boat out to get you. Reid was freezing. Both of you were. I got blankets from the house, and Reid barely spoke." He pauses. "Once he told us what had happened, the state detective started the search for your father."

"Wendy Burrows," I say.

"You've done your research."

I take a deep breath and let the next question spill out. "What if I asked whether my father was alive?"

To his credit, Gilcrest doesn't dismiss the query offhand. He takes his time answering, and when he does, he seems to choose his words carefully. "Burrows was a good detective. She didn't find your father's body, but tried, and she didn't give up. By the time she died later that summer, she'd exhausted every avenue. Still, I can't say I haven't asked myself the same thing over the years. So, *if* you asked me if I thought your father was alive, I'd play cop and reflect the question back to you. Do you think your father is alive?"

"I know he wouldn't have wanted to be found."

"If you have anything beyond hope or a gut feeling, now's the time to share it."

I have the pint glass wrapped in a napkin, ready to be tested for fingerprints and DNA, but the detective hasn't earned my trust, not yet. "Maybe I'm looking for more than hope," I say.

Gilcrest nods as though he may have another question to ask. Instead, he puts the SUV in gear. "*The search for my father.* There's the logline for your podcast. You can find him for real, or you can find him metaphorically." He drives the rest of the way to Burkehaven, where yellow tape marks the crime scene. "You'll need to avoid an unsolved mystery, though. Audiences hate open endings."

Chapter Eighteen

I expect to find an army of CSIs in white Tyvek suits collecting evidence at the crime scene along the lakeshore. Instead, a lone, bored state deputy keeps guard in a cruiser. Gilcrest consults with him before sending him off for a break, then leads me along a narrow access alley lined with yellow crime tape to where the house's burned-out shell is covered in plastic tarps and surrounded by an orange barrier. "The fire marshal's team collected evidence before the rain came," Gilcrest says. "They'll be back today. They found evidence of accelerant, so this is officially an arson investigation."

Offshore, a boat floats on the calm blue water. The driver points a camera toward us. "Did Andrea Haviland start the fire?" Gilcrest asks, as though talking to himself.

"That's for you to determine," I say.

"It doesn't look good for her, though I can see what she's fighting for. Once these old camps are gone, they're gone."

Gilcrest is a cop. He's trying to disarm me, but I won't fall for whatever game he's playing. "You grew up on the lake," I say. "Did you know my mother?"

"The lake's big," Gilcrest says. "And I'm only forty-eight. Your mother had practically graduated high school by the time I was out of diapers." He musses his hair and opens the front of his coat. "You should get some photos. The light's good right now. I scanned your online profiles last night, and you hardly ever post. You'll need to do more social media if you want this podcast to go anywhere."

I wonder whether Gilcrest checked me out for professional or personal reasons. When did he find out his girlfriend left the Landing with another man, and who the man was? "I'm not interesting," I say. "I go to work, hang out with friends, play video games. Not much else."

"No one's all that interesting," Gilcrest says. "It's the packaging. You're young and good-looking. That sells. And you have a compelling story." He stops at a set of granite steps. "I like the gray stone. Foot up or down?" He poses both ways.

"Down. Arms folded."

He sets an expression of stony resolve as I snap a string of photos. "Try one with a smile," he says, his eyes creasing into a sly, practiced grin.

Afterward, he scrolls through the images, deleting as he goes until only two remain. "One serious. One smiling. You decide. But don't post either without approval. Now, show me where you were when the attack happened."

We retrace our steps to a spot by the shore next to a grove of trees. "I was beside those birch trees, there," I say.

"Thick underbrush, and plenty of places to hide," Gilcrest says. "Have you remembered anything new since yesterday? Sometimes things are clearer a day or so later."

I search my memory for a flash of color or a familiar voice. "Movement and sound," I say. "It happened fast, and with the fire, there were distractions, and then the branch swung toward me."

"How long were you out? From the moment you were attacked to when Chief Haviland arrived on scene."

"It could have been thirty seconds, or much longer. I didn't mark the time." I think for a moment. "But the fire hadn't progressed much when I came to. And Mrs. Haviland had collapsed in the courtyard. If she'd been there very long, she wouldn't have survived with all that smoke."

Gilcrest shoves his hands into his pockets. "Stop the recording."

I hit pause, and he makes me show him the screen before saying, "Seton Haviland asked you to lend her money yesterday."

"She didn't ask," I say. "I made an assumption."

"But she hinted at it. And she was mad at you when you said you didn't have any."

"Maybe."

"Haviland's a good cop," Gilcrest says. "She'll tell me anything that touches on the case, whether it's relevant or not. And I have to rule out every possibility."

He had me stop the recording because he's testing Seton as a suspect. "The conversation about money wasn't relevant at all," I say. "It happened as a result of the fire. We wouldn't have had the conversation unless her mother needed a lawyer, so there's no motive."

"Seton was the first on the scene. Maybe she was here before you and knew what her mother had done. Maybe she panicked when she saw you arrive."

I picture Seton kneeling over me when I came to. "She couldn't have attacked me because it contradicts the timeline. I was on the ground here. The house was engulfed in flames, but Seton's whole focus was on me. She didn't know her mother was in danger until I told her. That was when she went into action-hero mode and ran into the inferno."

"Pretty solid deduction," Gilcrest says. He had to have worked most of this out on his own, and I wonder about the motivation behind this line of questioning. Maybe he's testing my loyalties.

"Any hanky-panky between you and the chief?" he asks.

"Are we in kindergarten?"

"Sex. Have you had sex, or anything close to it?"

Nothing beyond a few lingering touches over the years. "Neither of us would make that mistake," I say. "Too much baggage. And if the chief's such a good cop, wouldn't she have disclosed a sexual relationship?"

"Let's hope," Gilcrest says, nodding at my phone. "You can start that up."

I tap record.

"Let's go back a little further on the timeline," Gilcrest says. "You got up to go for a run. Who was at the house?"

"Just me," I say. "My mother had a client meeting in Finstock, and my brother left the night before."

Gilcrest waits for me to continue.

"They found out about the podcast," I say. "And I asked too many questions about my father. Reid didn't want to talk about what had happened."

"It got heated?" Gilcrest asks.

I nod.

"Who else was there?"

"My mother, Hadley, Paul Burke."

"Paul must have gone to Burkehaven Farm for the night. And your aunt Hadley?"

"She walked to the bungalow."

And she didn't answer the door when I used the landline to call 9-1-1 the next morning, but my guess is that Seton has already filled the detective in on her suspicions. Unlike Seton, Gilcrest is direct in his questioning. "Your aunt wasn't home when you used the phone," he says, pausing for a confirmation I don't provide. "Fine," he says. "The chief told me your aunt arrived on the scene after you'd pulled Andrea from the fire. Does your aunt get along with Paul Burke?"

"They get along fine," I say. "But Hadley travels a lot. She's not here often."

"What about your mother? Does Hadley get along with her?"

"Mostly," I say. "They're sisters. And my mother always lets Hadley stay at the bungalow when she wants to."

Gilcrest looks up, grasping the implication of what I've said at once. "Your *mother* owns Idlewood. Did she buy Hadley out?" When I don't answer, he adds, "Property records are public, Charlie. You can tell me now, or I can make a quick visit to town hall."

"My grandfather left the property to my mother."

This time, Gilcrest does make a note on his phone. The morning's conversation with Freya has me questioning everything and anything that's happened. And if this were an episode of *Scene of the Crime*, wouldn't Hadley's actions warrant a second look?

"Even if Hadley has a grudge against my mother," I say, "why start a fire? And you told me the arson team would take the lead on this case."

"They take the lead on the fire. I'm trying to find out who assaulted you."

"My aunt Hadley wouldn't hit me with a tree limb," I say. "And a state detective investigating an assault? This is hardly a major crime."

"It is when it's wrapped up with arson." Gilcrest intertwines his fingers. "See, it all connects. How's the cash flow at Reid Construction? Any talk about unpaid debt?"

"My mother runs the business."

"Closing ranks."

"More like, I don't know."

And if Vance Moodey's visit to the site yesterday has business implications for my mother, the detective can find that out on his own.

"Okay," Gilcrest says, "back to the timeline. You and the chief were on the shore with her mother, then Hadley arrived. Who came next?"

"The fireboat."

"After Hadley?"

I work through the events in my mind. "Before," I say. "It went Seton, the fireboat, Hadley, then the EMTs and a fire truck. After that came Reid. He blocked in the ambulance."

"And what about Paul Burke? Or your mother?"

"I told you, my mother had already left for Finstock. Paul must have come later, after Hadley drove me to the hospital."

"Paul's farmhouse is about a mile from here," Gilcrest says. "The smoke was thick. I saw it from my cabin on the other side of the lake in Kingston. I was getting ready to respond when the call came in. I could smell the smoke, too."

Like with Hadley, he's turning Paul, my mother, and Reid into suspects. Where was Paul when his own property was in flames? Could my mother have set the fire before she left? And where had my brother been all night?

A text beeps into Gilcrest's phone. "The arson team's about to arrive," he says.

We retrace our steps along the shore, where two cars pull into the parking lot alongside Gilcrest's SUV. "That's Detective Cornell Stamoran," Gilcrest says as a tall man emerges from one car. "He's helping me out on this case. Give us a minute."

He crosses to where the other detective waits. The two men talk in hushed voices, while another group unloads equipment. A moment later, Gilcrest waves me over. "Charlie's working on a podcast," he says to Stamoran. "True crime."

"Duncan here is your man," Stamoran says. "He'll talk to anyone."

"Thanks a lot," Gilcrest says.

"I call it as I see it, pretty boy," Stamoran says.

◆ ◆ ◆

A few minutes later, Gilcrest stops his car in front of the Landing and turns to where I sit beside him in the passenger's seat. "Send me the recording you just made."

I flick it to his phone.

"Don't think I forgot our conversation earlier about your father," Gilcrest says. "Let's say he's been alive all this time, hiding out. Could he have survived on his own? Or would he have needed help?"

It's a good question, one I should have asked myself. My father wasn't the back-to-the-land type, though who knows what he learned in the years since he disappeared. If someone did help him, I doubt it was my mother, after what he did to her, and Andrea Haviland seems unlikely, too—unless she was having an affair with him. That leaves Paul Burke. Or Hadley. "My father doesn't have a lot of allies," I say.

"Your father grew up here. Maybe someone we haven't thought of helped him out. Someone with resources. Or maybe—" Gilcrest stops himself. "If you're looking to explain who gave you that head wound, your father could be a suspect."

"Maybe," I say.

"Charlie," Gilcrest says, "if there's something you're not telling me, now's the time."

I take a deep breath. "My father was at the Landing last night," I say, and it's such a relief to say it out loud I wonder why I haven't done it earlier.

Gilcrest doesn't attempt to mask his shock this time. "Your father, Mark Kilgore, was at the Landing last night? Who else saw him?"

"The bartender. He served him a beer."

"Blancy's too young to recognize your father, and so are you. He's twenty-five years older."

"Some things don't change," I say.

"You should have told me about this the moment I showed up at Freya's condo," Gilcrest says. "In fact, you should have called me last night. If you see your father, call me, no matter the time of day. I have kids of my own. Three of them. The oldest is fourteen, and I can't imagine putting them through what your father did to you and your brother."

Something Gilcrest said yesterday at the crime scene returns to me. "You watched the Lantern Festival with your kids," I say. "And your wife. You're married."

"I'm married on paper. Her name's Nicole, and Freya doesn't appreciate the paper part. I suspect that's how you wound up tangled in my personal life."

Another text beeps into Gilcrest's phone. He glances at the screen. "That's Stamoran," he says, back in cop mode. "Will you be at Idlewood later?"

"Did he find something?"

"I should get to the crime scene."

I step out of the SUV and around to the sidewalk.

Gilcrest rolls down the driver's-side window. "Don't tell your mother, or your brother, or anyone else about seeing your father. Not yet. Even I don't want the attention a twenty-five-year-old cold case will bring to this investigation."

Chapter Nineteen

During the day, the Landing transforms from a pub into a café, where the air smells of coffee and fresh-baked muffins, and conversation buzzes with local gossip. The cash in the jar for Mrs. Haviland's defense has multiplied, and Blancy works the espresso machine as though he hasn't left since last night. He fills a paper cup with coffee when he sees me and shoves it across the counter. "To go," he says. "Move your boat."

"Any news about Mrs. Haviland?"

He turns to another customer, taking his time steaming milk for a latte, before returning when a lull hits the store. "Was Duncan outside with you? He can't be too happy with you after last night. He and Freya are a thing."

Tell me something I don't know. "You could have clued me in," I say.

"Not my business."

"Everything's your business," I say. "What are people saying about the fire, anyway?"

"If I tell you, will you move your boat?"

"Scout's honor."

"They're saying Andrea's awake, and the DA wants to charge her with arson, but Duncan keeps asking questions on what seems like an open-and-shut case."

"Any theories why?" I ask.

"How would I know?"

"People talk."

Blancy shrugs. "What's the usual motive for arson?"

Money. Gilcrest is following the money.

"Do you remember the guy sitting next to me at the bar last night?" I ask as I AirDrop Blancy my phone number. "Text me if he comes around again."

The door to the café opens. A pack of Spandex-clad cyclists clomps into the store. "Fine," Blancy says. "Now move your boat."

◆ ◆ ◆

I pull the cover from the boat and contemplate the image of my father that continues to take shape. Hadley already told me he may not have been the monster I grew up fearing, and now, thanks to Freya, I've begun to question whether the crimes he committed happened in the way I've believed. Though it will take more than a plotting session in a writers' room to convince me of his innocence.

Still, when I imagine sitting beside him, sharing another beer, the only question I know I'd ask is "Why?"

Behind me, footsteps sound along the planks as I unsnap the final button on the boat cover.

"Charlie?"

I turn to find Seton standing on the pier, wearing that boxy uniform. She kicks off her boots and steps onto the stern. "Do you remember my friend Tammy, the kindergarten teacher?" she asks.

"What about her?"

"She had a few suggestions and lent me some supplies," Seton says, handing me a sheet of pink construction paper with *Certificate of Apology* printed in gigantic font along the top. "I, Seton Haviland," she says, reciting what's printed on the page, "officially apologize for letting the emotion of a difficult day get the better of me. I overreacted and took my feelings out on you, which you didn't deserve. I take full responsibility for my actions and understand this apology is yours to accept or reject, as you see fit. With respect, Seton J. Haviland."

I fold the sheet in half and stow it in the glove box. We could have gone back to being friends without acknowledging yesterday's blip, but I appreciate the effort. Maybe the note represents a new level of maturity in our relationship. "I'll keep the evidence, but apology accepted."

I unfurl the boat cover, and Seton takes the other end to help fold. Ashen skin and dark circles under her eyes tell me she must have been up all night.

"I'd give you money if I could," I say.

"I didn't ask you for money," Seton says. "And thanks, I know you would, but it's better if you don't. Paul loaned my mom money once." She nods toward the Landing. "It was to keep this place going after my father died. She claims their friendship wasn't the same afterward."

More money. Mrs. Haviland owed Paul. Isaac hit Freya up for a loan long ago on a TV set. And based on Vance Moodey's visit to Burkehaven the other day, my mother owes him, too. Who else might be looking to collect on a debt?

We finish folding the cover, and Seton stows it under the rear seat.

"Mom woke early this morning," she says. "She's already demanding to be released from the hospital. She claims she saw the smoke from the boat, and by the time she arrived at Burkehaven, the house was in flames. She says someone else was inside, and she tried to help, which is why she was in the building." Seton touches the stitches on my forehead. "And that same person could have assaulted you. That's why Gilcrest hasn't made an arrest. Too much reasonable doubt."

And why he's asking so many questions.

Seton sprawls across the back of the boat. "I was up most of the night," she says. "But so were you. How's Freya Faith anyway?"

I listen for a tinge of judgment or jealousy in her voice, but all I hear is curiosity. Behind us, some guy in a speedboat pulls in close to the pier. "Hey," he shouts, "make some room."

Seton shifts so the badge on her uniform flashes in the sun. The guy runs his hand through his hair. "Sorry," he says.

"We'll be out of your way in a minute, sir," Seton says as I turn on the blower.

"I don't know how you put up with these Massholes," I mumble.

"These Massholes are *you*," Seton says.

"I grew up here," I say.

"Sort of. On the lake. Off to prep school. And now you live in Boston, which makes you an official Masshole."

"I like to think I'm better than that."

"Keep hoping," Seton says, untying the lines and shoving off.

I back into the marina and drop anchor, while the guy in the speedboat swoops in to take the spot. "Last night," I say, "you could have mentioned Gilcrest had a thing going with Freya before I went home with her."

Seton closes her eyes, her face lifted to the sun. "Do you have any pot in this boat?"

"Aren't you on duty?"

"Don't remind me. And I wasn't talking to you last night, remember? Besides, you wouldn't have listened. You weren't really thinking with your head."

"True," I say. "But now your boss has it in for me. He came to Freya's condo this morning and acted all territorial."

"Gilcrest isn't my boss," Seton says. "We're peers. We manage different parts of the job. And what do you expect? You stepped on his turf."

"I didn't know they were dating. Freya didn't tell me. Besides, Gilcrest is the one who has a wife and kids."

"Take it as a compliment," Seton says. "He's intimidated by your beautiful eyes. You know it's true! Besides, Gilcrest and Nicole have been separated for years. They're still friends, but they're only married for the state health insurance. She probably got sick of him looking at himself in the mirror."

"Speaking of which," I say, showing Seton the photos of Gilcrest at Burkehaven.

She swipes between the two shots. "Be careful what you say to him," she says. "He's not as ridiculous as he presents. His act is how he disarms suspects."

She rolls on her side and props her head on a fist. The stud in her lip glints in the morning light.

"Are you supposed to be wearing that on duty?" I ask.

"I'm too tired to remember regulations," she says, taking the stud out and slipping it into a pocket. "Does Freya really sleep in a safe room?"

"Did Gilcrest tell you that?"

"I won't reveal my sources."

"It's not a safe room," I say, "but it's close. She covers the windows with steel shutters and keeps a gun. And don't forget about Ginger, the dog, who's as sweet as can be . . . until she isn't."

"Cut Freya some slack," Seton says. "She's famous. Or she was. Plus, she had a stalker when she lived in New York. That's why she left *Scene of the Crime* and disappeared off the face of the earth. And it's why she's so paranoid. My department gets about ten thousand calls a week from her security provider, all of which turn out to be false alarms."

Now the steel doors, the perimeter checks, and the gun make sense. "If Freya has a stalker, it's probably Reid," I say, remembering his teenage bedroom covered with images of Freya, and forgetting even a sleep-deprived Seton Haviland is all cop.

She swings her feet around and leans forward. "Why Reid?" she says.

"It was a joke. Forget I said anything."

"Details, or I'll talk to Reid myself."

I groan and tell her about sneaking into Reid's bedroom and finding Freya's signed headshot on the bedside table. I omit the other photos taped to the walls. "It was teenage stuff," I say. "Plus, Paul knew her and talked about working with her."

"I suppose having your photo in the bedroom of random teenage boys comes with the territory when you're on TV," Seton says. "But

Freya came to New Hampshire to escape that. And to see where things went with Gilcrest. Seems as if they may be going nowhere."

"Last night, she sounded ready to go back to New York," I say as a boat passes by, and we rock in the wake. I trail my hand through the water, grateful to be here with Seton, to have someone I trust, someone who won't judge me for succumbing to the charms of a TV star. "It's better when you and I aren't angry at each other."

"Who says I'm not angry?" Seton asks. "But I'm not angry at you. What did Gilcrest ask about anyway?"

"Mostly the podcast. He wants to be part of it. He mentioned getting a book deal, though I'll believe that when I see it."

"Don't do that fucking podcast," Seton says.

I shift and feel the weight of my father's pint glass in my coat pocket. "The podcast isn't about you," I say, though as I say the words, I hear how lame they are.

"Will you mention my name?" Seton asks. "Or my mom's? Or my dad's? Will you talk about what happened to my family as though it's your story to tell?" When I don't answer, she adds, "Your stupid podcast *is* about me."

"What do you remember about your father anyway?"

Seton clenches her fists and lets out a groan. "Nothing, Charlie," she says. "I'm two months younger than you. He's been dead and buried my whole life. And if you're secretly recording me right now, I'll kill you, then turn myself in for murder."

"I'm not recording," I say. "But didn't you ever wish your father had been living another life somewhere else? And that he'd never been murdered?"

"Only all the time."

"If there's no story to tell," I say, "I'll drop the podcast. I promise. And I'll avoid using your name as much as possible. But tell me what you used to imagine about your father. Where did you think he'd gone?"

Seton stands, fists on her hips. "I want my certificate of apology back."

The boat bobs in the water. I should be recording this conversation, but I want the answers for myself, not to share. If Seton and I are honest, we might learn what we actually mean to each other. "Please," I say.

"My name's Seton Haviland. My father was killed when I was ten months old. His murderer's son was one of my favorite people till he told me he was working on this podcast. Now I hate his guts."

Julian would encourage me to forge a personal connection and make Seton feel heard, but what I really want is to push through the imaginary wall between us to see what might be on the other side. And maybe that'll mean having Seton hate my guts for a while, but it could mean something better, and we won't know until we try. "You told me you used to imagine your father was alive. Where did you imagine he went?"

"Anywhere but here."

I touch her hand, but she yanks it away. "Take me to the pier," she says.

"We're friends, you and me," I say. "But there's this thing sitting right there between us, watching what we say, what we do. This thing we don't mention. Wouldn't it be better to talk about it, to see where the conversation leads?"

For a moment, I worry I've said too much of the unspoken, that I've damaged things between us for good, but Seton sinks back onto the seat. "When did you get so deep, Charlie?" she asks.

I smile, relieved, but I won't let her off the hook, either. "I'm not saying anything we both haven't already thought."

She rolls away from me and stares over the gunwale into the water. "I imagined my dad all over the place. It was typical kid stuff. Fantasy. For a while, I decided he'd joined the circus. I'd watch TV shows about spies whose long-lost parents returned, and imagine him as a CIA agent. We live close to Canada, so for the longest time I pictured him up in Quebec, speaking French and running a maple syrup factory with a team of elves."

"Did you tell anyone?"

"Not till right now. My mom, she had to work hard after my dad died. The Landing is a twenty-four-hour-a-day job once summer begins."

"What would you do if your father walked into the Landing one night and ordered a beer?" I ask.

Seton trails her hand through the water. "I'd give him a big hug and ask about the maple syrup factory. How about you?"

"I might get a beer with him."

Push further, I tell myself. Be bold. It's the only way to get to the heart of the story.

"I asked you about DNA testing last night," I say, taking the pint glass from my pocket and handing it to her. "Get the lip tested." I spit in a tissue from the glove box. "Test this, too. See if there's a familial match."

Seton unwraps the glass from the paper napkin. "You stole this from the Landing," she says, and I can see the pieces falling into place for her. "Who could you possibly be related to?"

Gilcrest will report what he and I talked about this morning to Seton, including my claim of seeing my father, and besides, didn't I challenge Seton to be honest? "Glasses. Ponytail," I say. "That was my father sitting next to me. At least I think he was. I've seen him before. Usually I convince myself it was my imagination, but last night he was there. I mean, you saw him. So did Blancy."

Seton takes my hand in hers, weighing her next move and choosing her words with care. "You didn't see your father. And it doesn't matter how much you wish you did."

"I want to be sure."

"If the glass is related to the fire, I'll need to turn the evidence over to Gilcrest."

I wouldn't expect anything else. "Gilcrest knows about most of it anyway," I say.

"If he knows *most* of it, what doesn't he know?"

"He knows I saw my father, but not about the glass or the DNA."

Seton holds out a hand, and I drop the tissue in her palm. She tucks it into her own bag. "We'll see what happens," she says. "But I wouldn't hold your breath."

Chapter Twenty

After dropping Seton at the town pier, I speed across the lake in the boat toward Idlewood Cove and text Julian: I met an old friend last night.

A moment later the phone rings. "I'm driving," Julian says when I pick up.

"Same," I shout. "In the boat."

"Tough life," Julian says.

I cut the engine. "I saw my father last night at a pub in town."

"Now I'm pulling over," Julian says, mumbling something about Daddy being on a work call, and to use inside voices. I picture him out and about in Newton with his two kids in the back seat.

"Details," he says, and I fill him in on what's happened in the last twenty-four hours.

"A house burns to the ground," Julian says. "You're assaulted. Your long-lost dad drinks a beer, and you go home with a TV star who questions the very story you've spent your whole life believing. Please tell me you captured every moment of this in high-quality, easy-to-edit audio footage."

"Not quite," I say, adding in what happened with Freya when she caught me recording her.

"Make nice with her," Julian says. "Convince her to sign a release. You never know what you can recover. Are you positive it was your dad at the bar?"

"My friend's running a DNA test. I'll know soon enough."

"We could know sooner than that, Charlie," Julian says. "This case went cold years ago, but from what you've uploaded so far for me to listen to, you have enough material for a teaser. Let's release something. You never know who's out there, sitting on a secret."

We could harness the true-crime community and follow the leads that come to us. "Give me the day to think about it," I say.

And to warn people about what's coming.

"I'll touch base tonight," Julian says. "In the meantime, talk to your mother. If anyone's lying, it's probably her."

He clicks off the call, leaving me drifting in the boat. Julian's words echo Freya's from earlier: The wife is usually a prime suspect in a homicide. Maybe the answers to my questions do lie with the woman who fought off her knife-wielding husband and then crawled through the woods to safety.

When I pull the boat along the dock at Idlewood, the sun glints off the yellow Volvo's windshield in the parking area. A thought skips across the back of my mind, too fleeting to capture. I try to find the thought, knowing it's important, but it's gone.

Inside the cottage, the rooms on the main floor and the back deck are empty. "Jane, are you here?" I shout, but my mother doesn't answer.

In the kitchen, I stand at the same stove my father cooked at on the day he killed Isaac Haviland, imagining the scene all over again: twelve-year-old Reid at the table doing homework, my mother by the back door, me in my bassinet. I imagine my father's rage simmering alongside the Bolognese as my mother listened to the wall phone and checked her reflection in the mirror. I remove a chef's knife from the butcher block, the steel sliding on wood. This isn't the same knife my father used—that wasn't recovered—but it probably has a similar weight and feel.

I step out onto the wraparound porch. In the quarter century since the murder, the trees have probably grown in, but I have a clear view of the parking area a hundred yards away. I picture my mother out here, Reid beside her, as my father confronted her lover. That thought

I had on the dock flares up. This time I nearly pin it down before it flits off again.

Knife in hand, I march down the steps and onto the path. I charge through the trees, across the footbridge, and emerge where Mr. Haviland would have stood by his truck. Even in playing the role of my father, I forget to hide the knife behind my back. Instead, I grip the handle in a fist, the steel blade glinting in the sun. As Freya said earlier, the knife *should* have alerted Mr. Haviland to danger.

I start a new recording on my phone. "Earlier," I say, "Freya Faith told me audiences were smart, that they can spot holes in a plot. Here in the parking area on the shore beside Idlewood, in the place my father stabbed Isaac Haviland, I can see the porch on the house where my brother observed the crime as it unfolded."

I envision my mother approaching, her hands extended, her voice soft. I wonder if she understood that my father had the capacity to kill. "Even with the knife," I say, "my father would have been outnumbered two to one. Mr. Haviland was tall and strong. My mother runs a construction firm. She's hardly a shrinking violet. They should have been able to put up a fight."

I cross the footbridge again. As I pass the dock, raised voices sound from the other end of the island. I follow the noise through the woods, toward the firepit. When I catch notes of anger, I start to run, recognizing Vance Moodey's voice. "Pay up," he says. "It doesn't get any simpler."

"I need a week," Reid says. "It's not as though I planned on a fire."

"What good will another week do?" Vance asks. "Did you think I wouldn't find out?"

I burst from the trees, my breath ragged. Reid spins to face me, then stumbles back, hands raised. "We're fine," he says. "Just a friendly conversation."

It didn't sound friendly to me.

"Come on, son," Vance says, rising to his full height. "Drop it."

I look at the knife in my hand—forgotten—before letting it fall to the ground.

"That's better," Vance says.

"I didn't see your truck," I say to him. "I heard you arguing."

Vance holds his palms out. "It's business. Nothing more. And I parked at Burkehaven, but there were cops all over the place. I decided to walk over here and see if I could get a straight answer." He holds Reid's gaze. "You have a nice view of the lake. It'd be a shame to lose it, son. You're lucky your mother and I have an understanding, but maybe I should fill her in anyway."

"Don't call me *son*," Reid says. "And leave my mother out of this."

"One week, Reid," Vance says. "Then it's on to plan B."

He brushes by me, leaving along the path. Reid waits until he's out of earshot. "What's with the knife, Charlie? You looked like you were in a slasher film."

"What was Vance talking about?" I ask.

"Nothing for you to worry about," Reid says, adjusting his glasses and making his way along the path toward the cottage. I grab the knife from the ground and follow.

"I deal with assholes like Vance Moodey every day," Reid says. "It's part of the job. You should stay in radio, where everyone's nice. It suits you." He punches my arm. "And I heard about your misadventures with Freya last night."

I feel my face turn red. "Are you jealous?"

"Hardly," Reid says. "My Freya Faith fan club closed shop decades ago. But your tryst is the only thing anyone's talking about, that and the fire. What I haven't heard is when Gilcrest plans to arrest Andrea Haviland."

"He asked me a million questions this morning," I say. "He wanted to know where you were when the fire started. Paul and Mom, too."

"Tell him to ask me himself," Reid says.

"He's looking at the money and trying to find another motive," I say. "Other suspects, too."

Reid clucks his tongue. "Like a disgruntled lumber supplier. That's what has you all worked up. Listen, sometimes projects turn into high-stakes shell games, but it all works out in the end. I have to figure out what to move where."

I haven't stopped recording since I started in the parking area. I hold up my phone and show Reid the screen. "Idlewood," I say. "Reid Kilgore, Sunday morning after the fire."

My brother's expression turns stony. "I'm not doing this," he says.

"Do you remember the time I saw Dad? I was at a soccer game here in town. Mrs. Haviland was there, too. Later that night, you read me a story, and I told you I'd seen him."

"Honestly, Charlie," Reid says. "You claimed to see Dad so many times, it all runs together."

"You told me not to mention seeing him to Mom, that it would upset her."

"It *would* have upset her. Who wants to hear that your six-year-old son is conjuring up images of your dead husband?"

"I saw Dad last night. He came to the Landing."

Reid takes off his glasses. "If Dad started the fire, you could turn that into a podcast, too."

"I'm not making this up," I say.

"I don't care," Reid says. "I need to get to Burkehaven and talk to the foreman, because if you haven't put two and two together, I'm in a mess right now, and it's not one that digging up ancient history will solve. And I don't give you permission to use anything on that phone. Not one word."

Reid leaves me beside the cottage. He crosses the footbridge and disappears into the woods. A moment later, he appears on the opposite shore by the cars. I sit on the wraparound porch, in the same spot where Reid stood twenty-five years ago, and that thought I tried to capture earlier returns, this time fully formed. And it makes my blood run cold.

"I'm on the back porch at Idlewood," I say into my phone. "Sunlight shines off the windshield on my father's Volvo." I may be by myself, but when I say these next words, I won't be able to unsay them. "Reid told the police he heard Mr. Haviland say *my love* to my mother, but Reid was here, where I am now, a hundred yards from the parking area. He wouldn't have heard what Mr. Haviland said, not from this far away."

I pause the recording, my feet rooted to the porch, not sure what my next move should be or who I could possibly trust with what I've realized. Freya poked holes in the story, but this—this is an actual lie, one I can point to and see, one that's been told to me my entire life.

My mother must know the truth. Maybe this was what she planned to tell me the last time we spoke, and maybe Julian and Freya were right to call her the prime suspect.

I pull up her name on my phone and get voicemail, so I send a text. I need to talk to you. As soon as you get this. It's about Dad.

Right then, my phone rings. I pick up without looking at the screen, expecting to hear my mother's voice. Instead, it's Gilcrest. "Would you come by the station in Hero?" he asks.

"I'll be there in ten minutes," I say.

I'm halfway to my car when my phone rings again. This time, Seton's number flashes across the screen. "Where are you?" she asks as soon as I click into the call. "I'll come get you."

"I'm on my way to the station."

"Charlie," Seton says, her voice barely a whisper, "keep your mouth shut. Don't say a word."

Then the call disconnects.

Chapter Twenty-One

A local news truck is parked outside the police station. I hurry up the granite steps and into the small municipal building. Inside, a secretary stops pecking at her computer, her eyes wide, her ponytail swaying back and forth. Behind her, Seton paces in the chief's office. She glances toward me, but it's Gilcrest who approaches. "Charlie Kilgore," he says, taking my arm and steering me into a conference room where he's set up camp.

He waves toward a chair. "Can I get you something to drink?"

"I don't want anything to drink," I say. "I want you to help me sort this out."

Gilcrest rests a hip against the conference table and waits until I find myself sinking into the padded chair.

"Someone's protecting my father," I say.

Gilcrest opens a laptop and clicks a few buttons. "Do you mind if I record? I'll send you the file when we're done if you want to use any of the audio. And you should say that again: *Someone's protecting my father.* It's a great line."

I parse through each of the conversations I've had since the fire, starting with Seton as we left the hospital yesterday, then Freya, Reid, and Gilcrest himself. I come back to the threads of the story Freya unwound, and attempt to explain them now—the soccer game, and that Reid couldn't have heard what Isaac Haviland said, and the tiny inconsistencies in the accounts of the murder—and I hear myself rambling, trying to fit the pieces together in a way Gilcrest will understand, in a way *I'll* understand.

I take a deep breath. I pretend I'm narrating the story for a radio show, that I'm speaking directly to an audience of strangers. "When I saw my father, it wasn't the first time I'd seen him."

"You saw him at a soccer game when you were a kid, am I getting that right?" Gilcrest asks, and when I nod, he adds, "Say it out loud for the tape."

"I saw my father at a soccer game," I say.

"And Andrea Haviland was at the same soccer game?"

"I'm not sure. I can't remember if she was there or if we met up with her later on. But if I recognized my father that day, then Mrs. Haviland would have, too. They've been friends their entire lives."

Gilcrest makes a note. "But only if she was there. And last night, your father came to the Landing, which Andrea Haviland owns."

Gilcrest is easing me into my story in the same way I would if I were interviewing him. But he's listening. And having him listen is helping me work through what I've learned. "My father knew about the fire," I say. "He mentioned it to me when we talked, and he said he was concerned about an old friend. He must have known Mrs. Haviland had been taken to the hospital."

"So maybe he was there to check on her condition," Gilcrest says.

A knock sounds, and Detective Stamoran opens the door. "Podcast," he says, pointing at me with both index fingers.

"Let me get you up to speed," Gilcrest says to the detective. "I'll be back in a sec, Charlie. You sure you don't want anything?"

"I'm good," I say.

Gilcrest closes the door after himself, and I hear the detectives whispering on the other side. When they return, Gilcrest's demeanor has changed. He moves deliberately, crossing the room and pulling up a video on his phone. "You should see this," he says.

The video shows a view of the lake, with the edge of the dock at Burkehaven in the right-hand corner.

"My team found a camera Andrea Haviland missed with the sledgehammer," Stamoran says.

"We don't know Andrea destroyed those cameras," Gilcrest says.

"Good point," Stamoran says. "We don't assume. Regardless, whoever took the cameras out missed one. These things only record when there's movement. See that?"

I squint at the screen. Thick black smoke wafts across the water.

"That's from the fire," Gilcrest says. "And—"

"Wait for it—" Stamoran says.

Five seconds later, a boat speeds into the cove, with Andrea Haviland at the helm. She jumps onto the dock, barely pausing long enough to wrap a line around a piling before dashing out of the frame.

"The fire had already started when she arrived," Stamoran says.

That's why no arrest has been made.

"Maybe my father set the fire," I say.

"Maybe your father set the fire," Gilcrest says, mirroring my words as he leans back in his chair. "You did see him at the Landing, after all."

"I talked to Paul Burke earlier," Stamoran says. "He was at the Landing last night, too. You'd think he'd have recognized an old friend hanging around, especially one who's supposed to have been dead. But he didn't see your dad. You know who else knew Mark Kilgore back in the day?" Stamoran jerks a thumb toward Gilcrest. "This one's girlfriend, Freya Faith, and she was at the Landing, too. Have you asked her about seeing Mark?"

"Not yet," Gilcrest says. "I'm in the doghouse with her, but we'll catch up later."

"That's two people who should be able to corroborate your story, Charlie," Stamoran says. "What do you think they'll say if we ask them?"

I take in the conference room for what seems like the first time: me, squashed into a corner, readily allowing what's been said to be recorded, the two detectives hammering me with questions. I glance from Gilcrest to the laptop to the gray walls. At least there isn't a two-way mirror for someone to observe through. "You're interrogating me," I say.

"We're having a conversation," Gilcrest says. "Nothing more. Take your time. I'm not going anywhere." He pulls up something on his phone and reads for a moment. "The night before the fire, you and your mother were home at Idlewood alone. Just the two of you. She told you she was driving to Finstock."

"For a site visit," I say. "She mentioned a lease."

"When did she tell you that?"

"Right before we went to bed."

"Did anyone else hear her?"

"It was the two of us."

Gilcrest taps a note into his phone.

"You live in Somerville," Stamoran says. "My daughter lives there. You're about the same age. I'll connect the two of you after this is over. It's expensive there."

"It's expensive everywhere," I say, my eyes moving between the two detectives.

"It's nice when you don't have to think about money," Stamoran says.

I start to speak but can't find any words. I've seen enough TV cop shows to know this conversation has taken a turn, and I'm a person of interest, if not a suspect.

"That tightness in your stomach," Stamoran says. "It'll go away when you tell us what happened. You'll feel better. It's like magic."

I haven't had a stomachache, not until this very moment. "I didn't start the fire," I say.

"It's not the fire that concerns us, Charlie," Gilcrest says.

Stamoran smiles. "Listen, Podcast. If you cooperate, we can go easy on you."

"Where's my mother?" I ask, as a feeling of dread descends on me.

Gilcrest stands and leans over the table, his voice low. "You tell us," he says.

"Charlie," Stamoran says, "your brother gave us a list of his current contracts. There's nothing in Finstock. No projects. No leases. Nothing."

"I want a lawyer," I say, right as a commotion begins in the lobby.

"Ma'am, you can't go in there," the secretary says, but the door to the conference room slams open.

Freya Faith appears wearing a fitted gray suit and flats, her auburn hair swirling around her face as if she brought along a portable wind machine. She lifts her sunglasses to the top of her head, and I can almost hear the credits for *Scene of the Crime* begin to roll.

Beside her, Ginger stands at attention.

"Get out of here, Freya," Gilcrest says. "This isn't a TV show."

Ginger trots toward Gilcrest, tail wagging. "Heel," Freya says, and the dog stops. "Is Charlie under arrest?"

Gilcrest glances at Stamoran, who barely shakes his head.

"Not yet," Gilcrest says.

"Get up, Harold," Freya says to me. "And keep your mouth shut."

I do what she tells me, following as she backs out of the room. In the lobby, the secretary stands at her desk, eyes wide. Behind her, Seton stares at her computer monitor. We all freeze in place, as though we don't know our next move.

"I heard you sing last night," the secretary finally says to Freya. "I love those old songs. And *Scene of the Crime* was a really good show. But not after you left. It went downhill fast."

"Thanks," Freya says, taking my arm.

"What do you think I did?" I ask no one in particular, though in my heart, I suppose I already know.

Freya turns on Gilcrest. "You're such a possessive, controlling prick, Duncan."

"Stamoran only confirmed everything now," Gilcrest says. "I didn't have a chance to tell Charlie what happened."

"You had every chance," Freya says.

Gilcrest faces me. "This morning, our team discovered an abandoned car in the woods a mile outside of town. An hour ago, they uncovered a body in the wreckage of the fire. It was buried under a wall we needed a backhoe to move. The ME made the identification while we were talking. I'm sorry to tell you this, Charlie, but it was your mother. She's dead."

Two weeks later

Chapter Twenty-Two

I sit on the end of the dock at Burkehaven with my feet in the water. Behind me, the burned-out shell where my mother's body was found two weeks ago looms on the shoreline. Reid has returned to work as he attempts to rebuild his crew and kick-start the Burkehaven development. Mrs. Haviland was released from the hospital, Seton patrols the streets, my aunt Hadley canceled her trip to the Mideast, and Paul Burke decided to stick around New Hampshire for a few weeks rather than returning to New York.

The world moves on.

But not for me.

I took a leave of absence from the radio station that lasts another week. Each morning, I follow the path through the woods from Idlewood here to Burkehaven, searching for answers in the ruined house, in the placid lake, in the surrounding trees. I search for peace, too, but I don't find that, either.

Meanwhile, Duncan Gilcrest continues to probe my mother's murder. He hasn't brought me in for another interrogation, though I have no doubt I remain a suspect. After all, I'm the one who ran around town claiming to have seen my long-dead father to distract from the investigation.

I close my eyes, wary of sleep. I've had a recurring dream nearly every night since my mother died. In it, she and I lie side by side in the hull of a rickety old rowboat. She's young, the same age as I am now, a woman I never knew. A mass of blond curls splays beneath her head, and her skin is clear of scars. The air smells skunky as we pass a joint back and forth. Above us, paper lanterns float like balloons in a darkened sky while, off in the distance, a coyote howls.

"I saw Dad," I tell her.

My mother props her head on a fist and smiles. "Of course you did. He's right there."

I peer over the side of the boat, expecting to see my father coming for us with a bloody knife.

Instead, he stands on the dock at Idlewood, wearing that pink apron. The paper lanterns light up his dark hair and blue eyes. Like Mom, he's young, the same man pictured in the photo I have pressed between the pages of an old thesaurus. He waves, beckoning us toward shore. "Dinner's ready," he shouts. "Bolognese!"

I slump down into the boat.

"Why Bolognese?" I ask.

"It's a tradition," my mother says.

"Dad didn't look like that when I saw him," I say. "It was recent. Now. When you're old."

My mother squeezes my hand. "We're not old. You only think we are. And cut your father some slack. He watched out for you the best he could. He'll still watch out for you, but don't mention seeing him to anyone, especially not Reid. You'll upset him. He thinks your father's a bad man."

"He is, though," I say.

"More like misunderstood."

The boat bobs on the water. "Where is Reid?" I ask.

"In the kitchen. Working on his math homework. He wants to be an architect."

"He's the only one on the island with Dad."

"Reid can take care of himself," my mother says. "Trust me."

The lanterns drift down toward the lake as, one by one, the candles flicker and go out. Soon we'll need to retrieve them from the water. "Was it you who hid Dad all those years?" I ask.

"That's the type of question you don't want answered," my mother says, a hint of warning in her voice. "It's the kind of question that takes you from the light."

My mother's suddenly older, her hair graying, the scars around her neck red and inflamed. Blood spews from a gash in her forehead. "You did this," she says as she gasps for breath. "Everything that happened is your fault."

Above us, a candle flickers as the final lantern plummets toward the water.

I sit up, awake, sweat pouring down my face.

Chapter Twenty-Three

I try to shake away the images from the dream as I rub the imprint of the dock's wooden slats from my cheek.

Out on Burkehaven Cove, a man paddles a blue kayak along the shore until he faces the wreckage. The site of the fire continues to draw onlookers and will continue to do so until Reid erases the scar by building a new house.

"Was this your place?" the man asks.

He could be a reporter. A few have lurked around town, looking for an angle on my mother's death even as the locals shut them out and the news cycle moves on. Or he could simply be taking a morning paddle. I suspect it's the latter.

"I live in the next cove," I say.

"You own your place?"

I do now. Along with half of Reid Construction. I haven't begun to dig into the business side of things, or learn how many other Vance Moodeys are out there, waiting to be paid. Each time I bring it up with Reid, he deflects the conversation, though I did get access to the books. Maybe I'll find some answers there.

"It's a family cabin," I say.

"I'm renting for the week," the man says. "Got in last night. We come every year—same week, same house, Saturday to Saturday. The first morning, I get out on the lake and see what's changed, and what's the same."

I wish he'd paddle away, but the wreckage seems to draw him closer. "Let's hope no one got hurt here," he says, in a way that makes me wonder if he'd rather hear the gruesome details of a painful death.

Eventually, he tells me to have a nice day and zips across the cove. As much as I wanted him to leave, I want to be alone with my thoughts even less. I linger on the hours and days after my mother died, the events that led up to my visit to the station, to my interrogation.

I think about the night I got out of the hospital and went to the Landing rather than staying at Idlewood. I should have noticed my mother hadn't returned from wherever she'd gone. And the next day, when Gilcrest brought me here to Burkehaven, I should have been wary of his offers to help with the podcast. He has the recording of what I told him that morning. And I can picture him behind the steering wheel of his SUV when he dropped me off outside the Landing, the way his expression changed when he read the text that came through on his phone. That must have been when the arson investigation transformed into a homicide. It was the instant my whole life changed, though I wouldn't know for another few hours.

Later, after Freya burst into the police station, after Gilcrest admitted my mother was dead, I stood in the lobby of the station as the news washed over me. Seton stepped out of her office, and I heard myself saying, "You knew. You knew and didn't say anything."

"This isn't on the chief," Gilcrest said. "She was doing her job."

"I'm sorry, Charlie," Seton said as Freya pulled me toward the door.

Outside, a reporter from the local news station waited with a cameraman. "Keep your head down," Freya said. "Get in your car and leave. Don't let them figure out your name."

Then she transformed into a TV star, flashing a smile and tossing her hair. With her tailored suit, she'd dressed the part of Gina Shock, and she provided enough of a distraction for me to make an escape. As I sped away in the Volvo, I caught Freya in the rearview mirror, pausing long enough to let the cameraman capture her in action. It would be a lengthy enough clip to run on the evening news along with a caption that read Beloved TV star caught up in local tragedy.

◆ ◆ ◆

The following few days went by in a blur as we planned a memorial service, and I learned more about my mother's death. She didn't die in the fire or from smoke inhalation, which, I suppose, came as a relief. The medical examiner's report indicated she died from blunt-force trauma to the head, maybe from the same tree branch used to assault me. Or maybe with one of the many two-by-fours that lie around a construction site. Or maybe from a beam that fell from the ceiling.

A pair of teenagers stumbled on her car, backed into a thick copse of trees. My mother, it turns out, hadn't driven to Finstock.

While I remained in a state of shock, Reid threw himself into planning the memorial service. He made lists and wrote the obituary and served as the family spokesman by reaching out to old friends. When we met with the minister, he answered her questions. And though he asked whether I wanted to speak at the memorial service, he seemed relieved when I declined.

The day before the service, I tried to take my mind off things by sliding under the Volvo to assess the damage to the rusted-out floor and sussing out which holes to patch. A stone popped from beneath a tire as a car pulled up beside mine, and a pair of familiar-looking leather sneakers stepped onto the rutted ground. Duncan Gilcrest leaned over and peered beneath the car.

"Got a minute?" he asked.

"Not without my lawyer," I said.

"These questions aren't hard," Gilcrest said, back to playing good cop. "And they may help me solve the case."

I slid out from beneath the car and ripped off my protective goggles. "I say *lawyer*; you stop talking."

"Do you have a lawyer?"

"Talk to Paul Burke."

"You might get another one," Gilcrest said. "Everyone's a suspect until eliminated, Paul included."

"I still don't want to talk to you."

"One question, then I'll leave. Why did your mother tell you she was going to Finstock when she wasn't working on a project there? Reid Construction hasn't had any work in that area of the state in years."

"I haven't a clue," I said, then wanted to kick myself for answering.

"If you had to guess, what would you say?" Gilcrest asked. "Had she gone there before?"

Not that I could remember. "I have a car to repair and a memorial service to plan," I said.

On TV, that kind of line usually cuts the cops off and provides a transition to the next scene. I turned on the sander, grateful for the noise as Gilcrest paced in his leather sneakers.

"The night before the fire," he said, "your mother called Paul Burke."

"They talk all the time," I say.

"She also called Andrea Haviland."

I turned off the sander. "I don't think so," I said. "My mother and Mrs. Haviland barely speak to each other."

"They talked for over two minutes. According to Andrea, your mother asked to meet at Burkehaven, which explains why Andrea was out on the boat. But why would your mother call in the first place?"

I turned the sander on again and slid under the car.

Gilcrest got on his hands and knees. "There was a third call," he said. "But not from your mother's phone. She used a burner we found hidden in her bedroom to call another burner phone, and here's where you're in luck. We pinpointed that phone to somewhere near Finstock. Who would she have called?"

I thought back to the recurring dream, to asking my mother whether she was the one who'd hidden my father all these years. If Mark Kilgore was alive, he was the only person I could think of mysterious enough to warrant a burner phone.

But I'd let the detective figure that out on his own.

The following morning, a week after my mother died, we gathered in the small Unitarian church in downtown Hero, where I sat in the front pew with Hadley, Paul, and Reid. Reid took to the pulpit. He wore a tailored black suit and talked about my mother through the lens of working with her at the firm. He focused on her commitment to the business and her dedication to family, and inserted a line about overcoming obstacles, the only reference to my father, however oblique.

Behind us, the church's pews were packed. Some of the attendees I recognized—friends from town; Seton and Mrs. Haviland; even Gilcrest, who came with Freya—but the majority of the people I'd never seen, and it made me wonder what vast, complicated life my mother had lived outside of my tiny world. Who had she spent time with, who had she loved, what mysteries lay deep within her heart?

I searched for my father, too, but if he was there, I didn't find him.

At the end of the service, the minister invited attendees to Idlewood for a reception, where Blancy and a few others from the Landing served food and drinks from folding tables, while Hadley, Reid, and I greeted the line of mourners, each face melding with the last. Reid fended off the inevitable questions that came when one of these camps changed hands: What do you plan to do with the property?

"No decisions yet," Reid said, no matter what form the question took.

When Vance Moodey's turn came, he barely met Reid's eyes. "I'm so, so sorry, son," he mumbled to me.

Freya followed, pulling Hadley in for a long hug.

"It's been too long, friend," Hadley said.

"Almost forty years, but who's counting," Freya said, catching my eye. "Your aunt and I, we used to do everything together."

"We'll have to catch up," Hadley said. "I'll be around for another week or so."

The night Freya and I had spent together seemed like another lifetime. Here, especially with Gilcrest hanging at her shoulder, I wondered why she'd shown up at the police station. Had she come to rescue me, or in the hope of generating headlines? Or for some other reason altogether? Whatever the answer, now wasn't the time to ask. "Thanks for coming," I said as she gave me a quick hug.

Gilcrest offered a hand as if neither the interrogation nor our conversation from the day before had ever happened. "I'm sorry for your loss," he said.

Beside me, Reid said, "Made any arrests, Detective?"

Despite the exonerating video evidence, Reid remained convinced Mrs. Haviland had started the fire.

"It's an active investigation," Gilcrest said. "I'll make an arrest when I can guarantee a conviction."

I turned to the next person in line and thanked them for coming. I thanked a lot of people for coming, including Seton and her mom.

"You shouldn't be here," Reid said to Mrs. Haviland.

"We'll be gone soon enough," Seton said, placing a hand over mine and closing her eyes. "You okay?" she asked softly.

There was so much I wanted to say: that I was wrecked, that I hadn't slept in a week, that I wanted her to tell me why she'd let Gilcrest browbeat me at the station, and that I'd give anything to get a beer with her at the Landing and sit quietly in the comfort of being together without saying a word—but if I said any of it, I'd start to bawl, and I wasn't ready for that. "I'm fine," I said.

She put a hand to the back of my head and mussed my hair. "Find me when you're ready."

Julian was the last person through the receiving line. He'd driven up from the city with some friends from the station. He wore a slim black suit and had his hair tied in a man bun.

"Take whatever time you need from work," he said. "We'll be there when you're back, and it might be worth sticking around here. You have some great material already. Now's the time, while the story's hot."

It took a moment to realize he was stuck on the podcast, and it was all I could do not to hurl every bit of pent-up rage from the last week at him. If I had, I suspect Julian would have turned my reaction into material for the podcast, too.

"Thank you for coming," I said, and left the reception, crossing the footbridge and following the path through the woods to Burkehaven, where the burned-out house loomed over the cove.

Here, I pictured the fire raging around my mother's body, threatening to consume her. And I mourned.

Since then, I've come to this dock almost every day to be alone. I used the podcast as an excuse to open old wounds, to start difficult conversations, but what I wanted was to uncover the truth. The one thing I haven't been able to admit, not even to myself, is that I'm terrified my questions got too close to that truth and forced someone's hand. Maybe if I'd left well enough alone, my mother would still be alive.

Chapter Twenty-Four

Footsteps echo along the dock. I sit up, expecting to find Reid or Hadley trying to entice me to Idlewood. Instead, Freya Faith stands at the foot of the dock, heels in one hand, a bottle of Scotch in the other, the sun shining off her auburn hair. She pauses, as though assessing whether to intrude. "I looked for you at Idlewood, Harold," she says. "Your island isn't meant for heels."

I turn and face the water.

"Do you want to be alone?" she asks.

When I don't answer, she crosses the dock and settles beside me, twisting the cap off the Scotch and taking a slug before passing the bottle to me. "Don't worry. It's after noon."

I sniff the liquor and can tell it's peaty and undrinkable, disgusting, but I take a sip anyway, letting the alcohol warm my insides. Somehow, I avoid spitting it out.

Freya takes another glug from the bottle and lights a cigarette.

"I'll have one," I say.

"I don't think so," she says. "And I should quit, anyway."

"Why don't you?"

She turns her face toward the sun. "I'm on the precipice, see. I've been fading away for years. If I stop smoking and get fat, if I stop dyeing my hair and give in to my age, I'll disappear completely."

"You won't disappear."

"We all fade eventually. It's just how long we put up a fight and where we land in the end. It's nice here in this cove, in this little town. It would be a good place to land. A good place to retreat. There are lots of good memories for me here, too."

My memories of Burkehaven are anything but pleasant.

"We can sit here quietly," Freya says, "or if you want to be alone, say the word and I'll take off."

I might be tired of being alone. I take another sip from the bottle. This time, it goes down easier. "I barely recognize you without your companion," I say.

"Ginger got the morning off. She's at the condo."

"I meant Gilcrest."

"Him, I'm not so sure about. He's on probation." Freya dips a bare toe in the water. "Cold," she says.

"Reid swims every afternoon. Memorial Day through October."

"I don't have that resolve," Freya says, stubbing the cigarette out and tucking the butt into the pack. "You know what I like? A big-city gym with bikes that don't go anywhere and hot men who spend their workouts watching each other instead of hassling me."

"Sounds like New York," I say. "You just said that Hero would be a good place to land?"

"I keep going back and forth," Freya says. "Your brother hasn't made much headway on building the house since the fire, though. And my decision depends on a few other things, too."

She means Gilcrest and his marriage and whatever choices he needs to make to make *her* choice worthwhile.

"Talk to me about something besides my mother," I say. "Anything but being sad."

"I can do that," Freya says. "I saw your aunt for a few moments just now. She's the one who told me where to find you. It was nice to catch up, but I want to hear more about where life has taken her. I'd forgotten what good friends we used to be, how much fun we had together, and in a way it was as if no time had passed. Hadley's lived the exact life she talked about living when we were teenagers. She's done good work and seen the world. I hope we'll keep in touch now. At the very least, we can be friends online, unlike before."

Freya swivels around and faces the shore. "You remember the old Burkehaven cabin. Two bedrooms and a bathroom that barely worked. It was about there, close to the path that leads to your cottage. My dad thought Hadley was bad news, so I had to sneak out and meet up with her on the sly."

I can't imagine anyone considering Hadley bad news, and it makes me laugh, and when I laugh, I realize I stopped thinking about my mother, if only for a few seconds, and even though the grief swings around and wallops me in the gut, I welcome the respite. "Hadley's such a do-gooder," I say. "Why would your father think she was a bad influence?"

"He was in the air force," Freya says. "He expected order and wanted a daughter who did what he told her to do, and for the longest time, I went along with it without question. He thought I should earn a teaching certificate, get married, and have kids, and I probably would have—not that there's anything wrong with any of those choices—but Hadley told me I could move to New York and do whatever I wanted. She dared me to have a dream. She told me about Juilliard and encouraged me to apply. I don't know if I'd have come up with that plan on my own. That's a lot to owe someone you haven't talked to in a long time." Freya cups water in her hand and splashes it on her face. "It's as if she opened a door, and I walked through it and found my whole life on the other side."

The night before my mother died, she also mentioned passing through a door, a metaphor I understand better now. Like my mother and Reid, I have a before, one I won't be able to return to, no matter how much I wish I could. I flip onto my stomach. In the shadow of the dock, a school of sunfish darts along the lake bed. "Tell me more about Burkehaven," I say to Freya.

"We stayed here every year for two weeks. The Burkes would come over most nights, or we'd visit friends around the lake. On the last night of our stay, my parents hosted talent night. It's the first place I ever sang in public." Freya pauses. "If I tell you what I sang, it can never be repeated. Ever. You have to swear."

"I swear."

"'Physical,' by Olivia Newton-John. I wore a leotard and a headband. I bet you don't know the song." She sings a few of the lyrics. "You must have heard it in the grocery store."

"And the oldies stations," I say.

"Stop with the ageism. Anyway, I took my performance very seriously. Hadley helped me with my dance moves. I remember rehearsing for most of the week, and that some of the kids around here would come by to watch. They probably spent the whole night laughing at me."

"Like Paul Burke," I say. "And my father."

"Yep. Paul. Isaac Haviland, too. Your father was there, but he was too nice to make fun of a kid like me. Speaking of your father, any new sightings?"

"Do you think I imagined seeing him?"

"Do you?"

"Sometimes."

Freya hands me the Scotch, and this time I take a long swig.

"Are you doing okay, Harold?" she asks.

"I'm fine," I say, as I've said to anyone who's asked so far. "Actually, not really."

"It's okay to be sad," Freya says. "You might be sad for a long time. I think about my parents when I come to this cove. My dad was an amazing person, even if he was a disciplinarian. So was my mom. She was a computer programmer when a lot of women didn't have jobs. They both died about five years ago. My mom first, and then my dad a few months later. It takes a while to fill the hole from losing a parent, and part of you may never heal—I know I haven't—but eventually the grief fades into the background."

"I don't feel anything," I say.

"That numbness protects you until you're ready to face what's behind it."

I rest my chin on my fist and watch the sunfish poking their mouths at the lake floor. If Freya keeps pressing, I may have to face what's behind the numbness, and I can guarantee I'm not ready for whatever I might find. To change the subject, I ask, "Are you pissed off at me for recording you?"

"All's forgiven," Freya says.

"I'm sorry anyway. It was a dick move."

"Apology accepted."

Behind her, a pickup truck rolls into the parking area by the construction equipment, and a man gets out. I squint across the water. "That's Vance Moodey," I say to Freya. "He runs the lumberyard."

We're far enough away that I'm not sure if Vance notices us at the end of the dock as he moves along the shore and snaps photos of the cove and the construction site as if he's collecting evidence. A few moments later, he retreats to the truck and pulls away.

"That was weird," Freya says. "What do you think he wanted?"

I sit up. "Where did you park?" I ask.

"Over at Idlewood," Freya says. "Why?"

I could stay here on the dock all day and be sad and angry. Or I could find a way to distract myself, and I could do it with Freya.

"Because when we follow Vance, my yellow Volvo will be too easy to spot."

Chapter Twenty-Five

By the time Freya and I reach her truck and hit the main road, Vance Moodey is long gone. Freya speeds away from the lake. "Start with the obvious," she says. "Moodey Lumber is out on Route 44."

She drives quickly, and soon the thick forest alongside the road transitions into a two-lane highway lined with strip malls and restaurants. "Has Vance Moodey come up in Gilcrest's investigation?" I ask.

"Let's get one thing straight, Harold: Duncan doesn't confer with me on his open homicide investigations, and that's too bad for him, because I'd make an excellent consultant. Even if he did, I wouldn't tell you what he said. It would be a breach of trust. Let's stick to finding Vance Moodey for now. What do *you* know about the guy?"

"I met him at Burkehaven the day I arrived for Memorial Day weekend," I say. "He confronted my mother. And two days later, he came by Idlewood and got into it with my brother. Vance attended my mother's memorial service. Now he showed up at Burkehaven again."

"If he owns the lumberyard," Freya says, "he's probably worked with your mother for years. There can't be that many suppliers in the region."

"Reid owes Vance money," I say. "Vance said as much when they were arguing."

"And the Burkehaven project is stalled," Freya says. "Cash flow may be a problem at the construction firm. Vance could be taking photos for a lawsuit."

Something from the earlier conversation between Vance and my mother returns to me now. After Vance left that day, I'd asked my mother what she owed him, and she'd replied that everything wasn't about money. If Vance hadn't come to talk to her about the Burkehaven project, what could he have come for?

We drive in silence for a moment, until Freya says, "That night we met at the Landing, you weren't straight with me, and you should have been. But I wasn't up front with you, either. Duncan and I were supposed to go out on his boat the night of the Lantern Festival, but he canceled and spent the evening at his cabin with his wife and kids. I wanted to get back at him. And I used you. So we're more even than I want to admit."

"Is that an apology?" I ask.

"I don't know if it's an apology, but it's my explanation for what happened, and it's part of the reason why I came to find you this morning."

"You were Gilcrest's date to my mother's memorial service."

"I don't know if *date* is the right word. *Chaperone*, maybe. I had to be sure he didn't act like an asshole. Besides, he's working an open homicide, and plenty of suspects were there."

Including me.

"Did he learn anything?" I ask.

"I told him he could observe, but no questioning," Freya says. "And I told *you* I wouldn't talk about what I learned from Duncan. So stop asking."

"I can't make any promises," I say, swiveling around to face her as she drives. "And I didn't mind being used."

Freya's eyes glint in the sun. "Lascivious," she says.

"I thought we were being honest," I say.

Freya pulls up beside a lumberyard. A chain closes off the entrance. "Well, I didn't mind using you, either," she says, cutting the engine and turning to face me. "You made me feel young."

Sunlight streams across her face. She's beautiful, and in another life, we might have given things a go. We came together when we both needed each other for different reasons, but that night won't be something I forget anytime soon. "What's the game plan here?" I ask. "We could ask Vance why he came to Burkehaven this morning."

Freya's eyes search my face, as though she might have something else to add about our night together. If she does, she lets it go and returns to the business at hand. "We need more of a strategy, especially if the guy's keeping secrets. We'll start by asking about your brother. I'll take the lead. I have plenty of experience talking to persons of interest."

"You don't, though," I say.

"I have more experience than you."

We get out of the truck and step over the chain and into the empty yard, where the air smells of split pine and mulch. "It's Sunday," Freya says. "They must be closed."

We take a few steps across an empty parking lot toward a beat-up trailer. The truck that came to Burkehaven is parked beside it. "I wish Ginger were here," I whisper.

"If it comes down to it, I'm packing," Freya says.

"You brought a gun?"

She opens her bag, and I flinch. "Pepper spray," she says, showing me the canister. "Don't leave home without it. But I have a gun too. It's locked in the truck."

The door to the trailer slams open and Vance Moodey emerges, a bottle of Wild Turkey in hand, his eyes red and swollen. He wears a blue flannel coat and a backward baseball cap over his close-cropped hair. "We're closed," he says, squinting into the sun.

"We wanted to ask you some questions," Freya says. "About your relationship with Reid Kilgore."

"He's a shithead," Vance says. "And a liar. What about it?"

I feel myself rising to my brother's defense and take a step forward, but Freya puts a hand of warning to my arm. "You and Reid," she says to Vance. "You got into an argument a few weeks back."

Under my breath, I whisper, "Start with some softballs."

Vance reaches into the trailer, leaving the bottle of Wild Turkey on the step and retrieving a two-by-four. "I told you I was closed. Come tomorrow when the staff is here, and we can help you then. And I'm not answering any nosy questions."

Freya stands her ground, hand in her bag, while I step back, ready to run. A shadow passes over Vance's face as the sun disappears behind a cloud. He slips on a pair of glasses from where they hang from his collar, then focuses in on Freya. "I know you," he says, his shoulders softening. "You're the lady from that TV show. Sorry. I had a robbery a few years back on a Sunday. I've been jittery ever since."

"We saw you over at Burkehaven," Freya says. "You were taking photos."

"What about it?" Vance says.

"You came to my mother's funeral," I say.

Vance turns, as though seeing me for the first time. He smacks the two-by-four against his palm. "Damn," he says.

He comes at me as Freya fumbles with the pepper spray in her bag. I raise my hands, but the two-by-four clatters to the asphalt, and Vance has his arms out, and he pulls me into a bear hug, and I struggle to free myself until I realize he's sobbing. "Son," he says as he swipes at his eyes with a meaty fist, "I didn't want to intrude. It didn't seem like the time or the place."

I stop fighting, as I try to make sense of his words.

"I can't believe it happened," Vance says. "I can't believe she's gone."

Suddenly, the pieces fall into place as I hear my mother's voice in my ear: *Everything isn't always about money.*

"You and my mother," I say.

"I miss her," Vance says. "All the time."

I've been fighting feeling anything since the moment Gilcrest told me my mother died. When Seton came to the reception at Idlewood, I was too withdrawn to lean on her, and even when Freya found me at the dock earlier this afternoon, I wanted to talk about anything but being sad. Now, here, with Vance Moodey, this man I've barely ever met, I sob, huge ugly tears that won't stop no matter how much I try.

Vance swipes at his eyes too. "Your mother and I, we used to meet at Burkehaven to watch the sun set. Things are changing there so quickly, with all the building. I wanted to capture what the cove looked like in my memory before those houses go up. That's why I went over there to take photos."

"How long were you together?" I ask.

"A few months, though we've known each other for years. We've worked on dozens of projects, saw each other socially, but my wife, Evelyn, got sick last winter. Jane was kind to her. She'd come to the hospital almost every week to play cribbage, bring cookies, try to get Evelyn to eat. Evelyn kept telling me, right up until the day she died, that there'd be someone for me after she was gone. It was the last thing in the world I ever could have contemplated, but then later . . ." Vance blows his nose. "I shouldn't have come to Burkehaven that day, when you and I met the first time. I tried to force your mother's hand. I wanted her to tell you about us and to make it official, but Jane wasn't sure if you were ready."

I think back on the night I spoke to my mother in her room. She said there was something she wanted to tell me, and I'd assumed it was a secret about my father. Maybe all she wanted was to share that she was ready to move on with her life. I wish she'd had the chance so I could have been happy with her.

"You look stunned," Vance says. "It's a lot to take in."

"This isn't what I expected," I say.

He offers a hand. "I'm glad to know you, though I wish it was better circumstances."

I take his hand in mine, and in a way it feels as though I'm reaching through time and touching a part of my mother's life I never knew existed. We talk for a few more moments and promise to get together sometime soon, a promise I'm not sure we'll keep. Though now that I own half of Reid Construction, we'll probably work together in some way or another. "We owe you money," I say. "We'll get that settled sooner rather than later."

"It's a few thousand dollars," Vance says. "Leave it to Reid, okay? Your mother wouldn't want you involved, and neither do I."

◆ ◆ ◆

In the truck, Freya hands me a box of tissues. "I feel like an idiot," I say.

"For crying about your mother?" Freya asks. "That's nothing to be embarrassed about."

"For not seeing what was right in front of me."

"Sometimes things don't make sense until they do," Freya says. "One mystery's solved, and now other pieces will fall into place. Clear the clutter to see what's really happening—or that's how it worked on most of my cases."

"You didn't work any cases," I say.

"So you keep telling me," Freya says. "But I'm working one now. With you."

Chapter Twenty-Six

"Let's make a pit stop at my place," Freya says as she pulls away from Moodey Lumber. "We'll pick up Ginger and head to a spot where we can think."

Back in downtown Hero, Freya rolls her truck by the police station, where two news reporters linger. I swear she slows to give them enough time to recognize her. One of the reporters actually gives chase. Freya guns the engine, skirts the harbor, and skids into the garage beneath the condo complex. "The trick with reporters is to escape without killing anyone," she says, her eyes sparkling. "We're lucky they aren't paparazzi. Those guys never give up."

I wonder if she welcomes the renewed attention. "You can spin a reboot of *Scene of the Crime* out of this mess," I say as we get out of the truck. "They can base the script on what's happening right now. And if you play Gina Shock, who will play Freya Faith?"

"How meta. But I think I'll pass."

"You love it," I say as she enters the code into the security system and the steel door unlocks.

"Not as much as you might believe," Freya says.

A moment later, the elevator door opens on the condo, where Ginger waits for us, her head cocked, her ears alert. I like to think the dog remembers me, and when Freya gives permission, she comes right to my side, tail wagging. I crouch beside her and stroke her thick coat.

"Take your time with her," Freya says as she runs upstairs.

I fall on my back and let Ginger walk across my chest and lap at my salty cheeks.

"Need anything?" Freya asks a moment later.

"Bathroom," I say, dashing up the stairs.

Back in the truck, Ginger rests her snout on my seat and sighs as Freya heads away from town.

"What made you come to the station that day Gilcrest was interrogating me?" I ask. "I'm surprised he didn't arrest me."

"He doesn't have anything on you," Freya says.

"I was at the scene of the crime," I say. "And I'd been running around town claiming my long-missing-and-presumed-dead father appeared out of nowhere on the night of the fire like someone trying to establish an alternative theory for a crime."

"But what's your motive?" Freya asks.

That one's not hard to come up with. "Money," I say. "I inherited an expensive piece of property. And half a construction firm."

"As motives go, it's not terrible," Freya says. "But if Duncan had any evidence, you'd be in jail. He was trying to scare you, and I think it had more to do with me and Duncan's jealousy than you. I was saving you from yourselves."

"Unlike Seton," I say. "She sat in her office and let Gilcrest grill me."

Freya careens along Lake Avenue and turns up the rutted road, past Burkehaven Farm, to the trailhead at the end of Paul's property. "You should have more faith in your girlfriend," she says.

She cuts the engine, steps out of the truck, and opens the back. Ginger leaps after her and sits at attention before Freya releases her to run into the trees.

"Seton?" I say, struggling with my seat belt, then tripping as I alight from the truck. "She chose her job over friendship."

"Be more than a pretty face, Harold," Freya says. "Put two and two together. I showed up at the police station because I heard you were on the verge of making a mess for yourself, and Duncan was being a competitive prick."

I remember the phone call with Seton on my way to the police station, how she told me to keep my mouth shut. "Seton called you," I say.

"I'm not confirming a thing," Freya says. "In my day, a cop would get fired for that. Also, you need a lawyer. A criminal lawyer. Until we find one, I'll play the role. I was a defense attorney in a Lifetime movie about twenty years ago, and if I know one thing, it's that a good lawyer can make the difference between life in prison and a sweet plea deal."

That pit in my stomach returns. I'm not sure what Freya can do if Duncan Gilcrest sets his sights on me.

She opens the truck's covered bed, where a pair of rifles sits in a gun rack.

"You told me you had *a* gun in the truck," I say. "I didn't take you for the home-arsenal type."

"Two is hardly an arsenal, and our relationship isn't that old. Let's hope we can surprise each other. Please don't tell me you've never shot a rifle. It's a good skill to have, especially if you need to protect yourself."

I've never seen a gun except on a cop. Or on TV. And when Freya pulled a handgun from her safe the morning I woke next to her. She unlocks the rack, lifts one of the rifles to her shoulder, and looks through the lens. "I learned to shoot on the show. Unlike those guns, these have live ammo."

She tosses the second rifle to me, as if we're in an action movie. I jump away, and it clatters across the gravel road.

"It's not loaded," Freya says. "Yet. And here, take these." This time, she tosses me a bag of dog treats. "You can bribe Ginger into being friends."

Freya perches on the back of the truck and swaps her heels for a pair of hiking boots. She hefts a backpack over her shoulders. At the trailhead, she pauses and asks, "Are you coming, Harold?" then disappears into the trees, with Ginger dashing after her.

Despite my reservations, I slip the dog treats into my coat pocket and grab the second rifle from where it lies on the ground. I hold it out in front of me, cautiously balanced between my thumbs and index fingers, and follow Freya along the brook and up the familiar trail. At the summit, we reach the clearing studded with wooden posts and surrounded by an overgrown stone wall. "We shot BB guns here when I was a kid," Freya says. "Target practice should help you reset."

She jogs into the clearing with the backpack and places aluminum cans on top of five posts across the field. When she returns, she lights a cigarette and hands me a pair of noise-canceling headphones. "I'll walk you through the steps," she says. "Don't worry. I won't let you kill anyone."

For the next few moments, she demonstrates holding the rifle against her shoulder and finding the target through the lens, while the cigarette dangles from the side of her mouth.

"Are you ready for ammo?" Freya asks.

"No."

"Too bad," she says, stubbing the cigarette out.

She spills open a paper box of long copper-colored ammunition, each of the bullets seeming large enough to take out a battleship. She also attaches a cord to Ginger's collar and fastens it to a hook on a gate. "Even the best-trained dog in the world can get spooked." She breaks open the rifle and loads the chamber. "These are single-shot. You load one bullet at a time, pull back the hammer to release the safety, and it's ready to fire."

She puts an eye to the sight, and the rifle kicks back as she squeezes the trigger. Even with the headphones, the blast reverberates through the trees. Down the field, one of the aluminum cans no longer sits atop its post.

"Nice shot," I say.

"With this equipment, you have to be pretty shaky to miss."

She loads my rifle and holds it toward me. I contemplate the firearm before carefully taking it. It feels heavy and dangerous now, as if it might explode at any moment. "Don't be so nervous," Freya says, leading me to the stone wall and guiding my hands to the hammer.

"Find the target in the lens." Her breath feels warm against my neck, and even though I don't expect anything to happen between us, being this close to her gives me goose bumps. "And when you're ready, squeeze the trigger. No more."

She moves away. I find the closest aluminum can through the lens and squeeze the trigger. But I don't squeeze. I pull, and the kick knocks me over into the grass, and Ginger starts to bark, and Freya has her hands over her face, and I panic that I somehow shot her until I realize she's laughing, and the aluminum can is exactly where it was before. I rip the headphones from my ears. "That was awesome!"

Freya removes the spent casing, loads the rifle, and stands behind me again.

This time, I'm gentler with the trigger and more prepared for the kick. I miss the target, but at least I don't sprawl across the ground.

"We'll make a rifleman out of you before the end of the day," Freya says.

Ever since Gilcrest told me my mother had died, I've felt numb, helpless, unable to process the death or any of its aftermath. Maybe I've felt that way my entire life, as I've tried to understand events from my childhood I can't remember and yet shape my whole existence. Now I don't know if it's that Freya cared enough to come find me, or that I found out about my mother's secret love, or that Seton risked her career to keep me from incriminating myself, or simply that I'm getting off on firing a rifle, but something in me has awoken. I want the truth, the entire truth, about my father, about my mother's death—all of it.

And I want to tell my story.

I lay my phone on the stone wall. "Do you mind if I record our conversation?" I ask.

Freya takes a moment to answer. "You're back," she says.

"I'm back," I say.

"Thanks for asking this time. Go ahead."

I hit record and mark the time and location. "Your boyfriend accused me of killing my mother," I say.

"Duncan's not my boyfriend."

"Do you spend most nights together?"

"Except when I'm pissed off at him."

"Then I know two things for sure: Duncan Gilcrest is your boyfriend, and I didn't kill my mother, no matter what he believes."

Freya loads the chamber and fires off a round. Another aluminum can flies off its post. "Let's figure out who did," she says.

"How?" I ask.

"Examine the evidence: motive, means, and opportunity. That's where Gina Shock would start. We'll divide and conquer. Tomorrow, I'll swing by Hadley's place to see what she can tell me. It'll be good to catch up with an old friend."

"And I'll start with Andrea Haviland," I say. "I've barely seen her since she got out of the hospital."

Mrs. Haviland took her boat to Burkehaven for a reason that morning, and it's time to find out why.

◆ ◆ ◆

We leave the shooting range and return to Freya's truck, where I say goodbye before walking the rest of the way to Idlewood. There, Reid swims across the cove, while Hadley and Paul sit on the Adirondack chairs drinking gin and tonics.

"Where have you been?" Paul asks.

"Out and about," I say.

"It's good to have you here," Hadley says.

When Reid finishes his swim, we make our way up to the house and turn on music while we cook dinner as if nothing's changed, even if everything has. Tonight Hadley's in charge, and she's concocted a complicated Afghani dish of pumpkin and homemade pasta that keeps us busy as the sun sets and darkness descends. After dinner, we play Hearts on the back porch. Later, Hadley and Paul head into the night toward their respective homes. As I lay in bed, I wonder what secrets they reveal on their walk. Soon Reid slips out of the house and drives away, like he did the night before the fire.

Everyone's a suspect until eliminated.

That's what Gilcrest said to me while I lay under my car the day before my mother's memorial service. Paul. Reid. Hadley. Any of them could have murdered my mother. I'll find out who committed the crime. I'll ask the questions that need to be asked. I'll find the truth and tell my mother's story. No matter the consequences.

When I wake in the morning, I change into my running gear and head into the hills. It's not until I've passed the shooting range and reached the summit overlooking the lake that I realize I slept without dreaming.

Chapter Twenty-Seven

The bells over the door at the Landing ring as I walk into the café. "Is Mrs. Haviland around?" I ask Blancy, who works the espresso machine.

He jerks a thumb toward the kitchen, where Andrea Haviland and the chef are getting ready for lunch. She wears a black apron, her gray ponytail peeking out from the back of a baseball cap.

"Hey, Blancy," I say. "Did that guy who sat with me at the bar ever come back?"

"Not when I've been working, but I have your number. I'll let you know if I see him. And Charlie, your brother owes me. Tell him if he doesn't return my calls, I may show up at the house."

Great. Reid probably hasn't paid the catering bill from the memorial service. "Will do," I say as Mrs. Haviland takes off her apron and greets me with a long hug, then piles chocolate chip cookies from the bakery case onto a plate. She leads us through the café to the back porch, where we sit at a high-top. "You're looking better," I say. "How're the lungs?"

"Functioning," she says, "though it was touch and go there for a few days."

She pushes the cookies toward me, as though she doesn't know what to say next. I break one in half. It's salty and sweet, the chocolate warm.

"I baked them this morning," Mrs. Haviland says. "But don't tell Seton. That girl eats my profits, especially now that she lives upstairs. Are you two talking to each other yet?"

That's part of the reason I stopped by here this morning. "I owe her an apology," I say.

Mrs. Haviland reties her ponytail. She can't be much older than Freya, but she carries a life lived in the lines around her eyes. "Don't wait too long," she says. "The summer's short. So is life." She glances down at the table. "I'm sorry about Jane, about your mother, Charlie. I wanted to talk more at the memorial service, but—"

"But Reid was showing his charming side," I say.

"Making myself scarce seemed like the respectful option. These last few weeks must have been impossible."

There's that grief again, rearing its ugly head right when I thought I might have tamed it for good. And *impossible* is an understatement. "I'm distracting myself by playing cop," I say.

"Is that why you're here? Do you think I started the fire? Your brother does."

"Reid needs someone to blame. You have to admit the whole situation is suspicious, though. The cameras at Burkehaven are destroyed, and then the house burns."

"*Suspicious* is a good word for it," Mrs. Haviland says. "I heard I'd destroyed those cameras before I'd heard the cameras had been destroyed. Seems to me someone wanted to cast blame, and I was the easiest target."

"Tell me what happened," I say, laying my phone between us.

"The infamous podcast," Mrs. Haviland says. "There are consequences for telling other people's stories, Charlie."

"You owe me for saving you from the fire."

Mrs. Haviland leans back on her stool, skepticism etched into her expression. "How do you decide what you'll use on a podcast? How do you know which parts of the story you'll tell?"

"I don't know until I hear it," I say. "And sometimes I don't know then. Connections show up when you least expect them."

"Which story are you telling?" Mrs. Haviland asks. "Past or present?"

I'm not sure anymore, or how the strands intertwine, but I do know understanding what *was* is essential to understanding who we've become. "Right now," I say, "you're telling me your story. Later on, I'll see how it weaves into the whole."

Mrs. Haviland considers the phone for a moment and gives me a curt nod. "Go ahead," she says.

I start recording.

"Tell me about my father," I say.

"You first," Mrs. Haviland says. "I heard Mark bought you a beer."

There really aren't many secrets in Hero, though I'd hoped Seton would keep this one to herself. "Seton tells you everything," I say.

"Except what she doesn't."

"Well, yeah. My dad sat with me at the bar and told me he was worried about an old friend. And since you're getting right into it, you're an old friend he could have been worried about."

The corners of Mrs. Haviland's mouth turn up. "Now I get it," she says. "You're wondering whether Mark heard I was in the hospital and had almost died. I could buy into that story if it were true, but I haven't seen your father since he disappeared. If he was here, it wasn't for me."

I try reading her expression to determine whether she's holding back, but her face doesn't reveal much. "Not once," I say, "in the years he's been gone?"

"I wish I had, but no, Mark hasn't been sneaking in and out of my life for a quarter century."

"What would you do if he showed up right now?"

"I'd call my daughter and let her do her job." Mrs. Haviland breaks the edge off one of the cookies and eats it slowly. "Let's pretend you actually saw Mark that night. What could have brought a man who's been in hiding to the very town he fled all those years ago? Maybe he was worried about his son, Charlie. You were in the hospital that day, too. And maybe when he saw you at the bar, once he got to talk to you, he felt okay leaving."

"How would he have known about the fire?" I ask.

"He could have heard about it on the local news. Both of our names were made public."

I'm slightly annoyed that Mrs. Haviland came up with this idea so easily, one I should have thought of on my own. But the concept of my father seeking me out—worrying about me—isn't something I could have contemplated until recently. For years, my only impressions of Mark Kilgore have been of rage and anger. Now a person has begun to emerge and replace those emotions, and enough doubt has been raised about what happened that I could almost buy into Mrs. Haviland's theory. "As he was leaving that night," I say, "he told me I was all he could think about."

"Sounds like I may be right, then," Mrs. Haviland says. "What else have you got? Ask, and I'll tell you what I can."

"My mother called you the night before the fire. You talked for more than two minutes."

"It was after midnight, and she wanted to meet at Burkehaven in the morning."

"Did she mention a project in Finstock?"

"We didn't talk business. She said she had something important to tell me but wouldn't say what."

"You and Jane—"

"We hated each other?"

"You said it, not me."

"Time mellows grudges. Jane and I knew each other long before she had the affair with my husband. We've managed to coexist in this tiny community. We could have been friends again if the circumstances were right."

I like Mrs. Haviland. She's been kind to me when she hasn't had to be, but she also had a long-standing grudge against my mother, one I doubt had mellowed as much as she wants me to believe, so I remind myself to remain impartial, to take in the facts without allowing my feelings to influence my judgment.

"What happened that spring before Mr. Haviland was killed?" I ask. "How did you find out about the affair?"

Mrs. Haviland takes a moment to collect her thoughts. "That's the part I try not to think about," she says. "Mark, your father, found out about the affair first. One of the foremen on a project had seen Jane and Isaac at a hotel bar in Concord, and they hadn't left much to the imagination. Mark confronted your mother and then came to see me, and . . ." She pauses and shrugs. "I didn't believe him. Or maybe I didn't want to hear what he had to say because it would have forced me to make too many choices. I had a new baby and no job and no idea what I'd do if what Mark had said was true. I'd gotten myself into a spot where I was completely dependent on Isaac financially, so I told your father I never wanted to see him again. When Isaac came home that night, I let him into the house, and we acted as if none of it had happened, even though Jane had to have told him that Mark had confronted her." Mrs. Haviland sighs. "Talk about compartmentalization. The day Isaac was murdered, he tried to convince me to go to Idlewood for the Lantern Festival. I almost said yes."

She rests her forehead on her palm as she sits with the memories, working through her own scenarios for what could have happened had she made different decisions, I imagine. Eventually, she says, "I don't blame myself for what happened. Or, I mostly don't. But what if I'd swallowed my pride and gone to the party? Maybe we wouldn't be where we are now."

"Paul said almost the same thing to me," I say.

Mrs. Haviland sits up. "What does Paul know? He thinks he's better than the rest of us, and has for as long as I've known him. I don't owe him a thing."

Something Seton mentioned in the boat two weeks ago flashes into my mind. "But you did owe Paul at one point," I say. "He got you out of a bind. He lent you money for the Landing."

"Paul lent *Isaac* money, not me. Isaac convinced Paul to invest the fifty grand he needed to finish the rehab on the Landing. The two of them tried to keep it secret from me."

"Isaac showed up in New York, too," I say. "He asked Freya to invest in the restaurant."

"Isaac probably asked anyone who gave him the time of day for money. Once my husband got an idea in his head, good or bad, he went with it. But imagine this: What if Paul *hadn't* given Isaac the money? Isaac and Jane wouldn't have had a reason to work together all spring, or to do anything together, for that matter, and none of us would be in this mess. But I paid Paul back as soon as I figured out what had happened. He was the last person in the world I wanted holding a favor over my head."

"Fifty thousand dollars is a lot," I say. "Why would Paul loan that much money in the first place?"

Mrs. Haviland taps the table beside my phone. "I'll help you spin a tale for the podcast. Maybe Paul had a secret and he's the one who killed Isaac. If you could prove that, you'd make my day."

I scowl at her. "If Paul killed your husband, then my mother and Reid covered for him for decades. Why would they do that?"

"They wouldn't. That's my point." Mrs. Haviland rests a hand over mine. "You lost your father. And now you've lost your mother, too, and you're trying to make sense of things that don't make sense, and it's terrible in every possible way. I get it, more than you realize. For decades, I've been trying to understand why my whole life zigged when I wish it had zagged. On the night Isaac was killed, Seton was ten months old, and I was home, stewing because she was screaming her head off, and I didn't have two nickels to rub together and felt trapped in a marriage I wanted to end. The only way I could get her to sleep was to put her in the car, so I drove to Sunapee on the other side of the state, bought a soft-serve cone at the Anchorage, and parked by the lake there. In the space of a week, I'd lost two of my best friends and been betrayed by my husband. I'd never felt so tired or lonely or hopeless in my life. I fell asleep, and it must have been midnight when I woke. It took me an hour to drive home to Hero, and when I got to the house, the police were already there." She pauses, collecting herself. "And nothing's been the same since. I'd give anything to see Isaac again. Mark, too. For your sake, I hope your father *was* here the other night."

I almost pause the recording for what I have to say next, but somehow I suspect Mrs. Haviland wants this conversation on the record, that she's been waiting to tell this story for longer than I've been wanting to hear it. "You loved my father," I say.

"I did love him. I still do, despite what he did."

"When my mother first met you and my father, she assumed you were high school sweethearts. Were you dating?"

"You mean in high school?"

"Or later?"

"Did Jane tell you we had an affair?"

"She implied he had one with someone."

Mrs. Haviland puts a hand to my cheek. "I wish Mark and I were sweethearts. But we weren't. Not in high school. Not ever. If your father had an affair with someone, it wasn't with me." She stands. "I've talked enough for one day, and I have to get to work, anyway. Good seeing you, Charlie. Remember, we promised to go water-skiing this summer. Come find me when you're ready."

As she heads up the ramp toward the restaurant, I call after her. "How did you know about the loan Paul gave to Isaac? You said they tried to keep it from you."

"Your father and I studied accounting together in college, and I'm good when it comes to finances. Every bit of information I needed was in the books for the restaurant, buried in a spreadsheet. I should have been a forensic accountant. I'd be a lot richer now."

That gives me an idea. "I could use your help."

Chapter Twenty-Eight

The landing field in Kingston sits behind a chain-link fence right outside town, with a single hangar rising from the center of an expanse of asphalt. I park the Volvo in a dusty lot and head toward the only aircraft present, a helicopter with a slowly spinning rotor blade, where Seton preps for a flight, exactly where Mrs. Haviland told me I would find her.

Seton works through a checklist, talking to someone in the cockpit. She laughs, sweeping a hand over her spiky hair as she jots something on the clipboard, showing a placid ease I don't see often enough.

I call her name and wave.

"Charlie Kilgore," she says, stepping away from the helicopter blades' rhythmic pulsing. "My mother called to tell me you might show up."

I hand her a sheet of yellow construction paper. "Turnabout is fair play."

Seton unfolds the note and reads through the large font. "The unicorn stickers are a nice touch," she says.

"I, Charles R. Kilgore," I say, "officially apologize for making assumptions about my friend Seton Haviland's actions. I thought she didn't have my back, but I was wrong."

Seton folds the paper and slides it into her pocket. "The less said about the day Gilcrest brought you to the station, the better."

"Your secret's safe with me," I say, turning to leave.

Seton calls after me, "Where do you think you're going?"

The next thing I know, I'm strapped into the back of the helicopter while Seton and her instructor, some guy named Lee with an Australian accent, chiseled features, and a sleeve of tattoos that makes Seton's seem restrained, get ready to take off. "I don't know about this," I yell over the noise.

"You don't have to shout," Seton says, her voice coming over the headset. "And tough. Lee knows what he's doing, and I'm getting there. Don't you want to see the lake from the sky?"

"It's not on my to-do list," I say.

Seton hits one of the controls. The rotor blades speed up. Beside her, Lee mumbles about antitorque pedals, and suddenly we're rising into the sky.

"Mind the altimeter," Lee says.

I grip the edge of my seat and double-check that the straps are buckled as Seton arcs across the airfield. Out the window, the foothills stretch to the horizon, and soon we're flying over the surface of the lake to where tiny Hero sits nestled on the shore. It would be thrilling if I weren't so terrified.

"I can't believe the town approved a helicopter," I say into the headset.

"You sound like Paul Burke, complaining about taxes," Seton says. "And it's not as if Hero *bought* the helicopter. We share it with Kingston and a whole slew of other towns. You'd be surprised how many day hikers get lost. Dogs, too. My whole team was out for two days this spring looking for a missing goat."

"Manage your torque," Lee says.

Seton touches another pedal. The helicopter lurches, and I grip the edge of my seat.

"Calm down, you wuss," Seton says as we level out. "Where do you want to go?"

Down to solid ground, though I manage to say, "I've never seen Idlewood from the sky."

A few moments later, we swoop over the island, the main cabin's metal roof glimmering in the sun. The boat's gone from the dock. "No one's home," Seton says, hovering over the cove.

A patchwork of water, forests, and lawns extends to the horizon.

"Give us the 360 view," Lee says. "Use the cyclic stick."

The helicopter starts to turn in a smooth clockwise motion until we're facing the foothills to the west. "How much of this land does your family own?" Seton asks me.

"The island," I say. "And everything around the cove. And the property out to the bunga . . . to the house on the street."

"Good catch there." Seton jerks a thumb toward the back of the helicopter. "Charlie here lives in an eight-bedroom bungalow. That's when he's not staying in the lake house."

"Shut up," I say, though it feels good to be teased.

"Invite me over anytime," Lee says.

Seton checks a gauge on the console. "Watch out for my mother, Charlie," she says. "She'll be after you soon enough to put this property in conservation. She tried to convince Jane to do the same thing."

"Reid won't agree to that," I say.

We leave Idlewood and pass over the cove to Burkehaven. From up here, the burned-out house looks small, insignificant, a darkened scar nestled among the trees. "Charlie and I hung out here when we were teenagers," Seton says to Lee. "We must have tossed back hundreds of cases of beer. Now I'm the one who has to break up the parties."

"Screwing the mood," Lee says.

Seton punches his arm, and I swear her eyes spark with attraction as she banks to the right and swoops over the water. "There," she says, a moment later, moving in over a Bryant 219 anchored in a cove. Two faces look up into the sky, and I recognize Freya and Hadley from under their sun hats, a bottle of wine between them.

Freya's catching up with an old friend, like she told me she would yesterday. I wonder if Hadley's told her anything new.

Seton heads inland over Burkehaven Farm, then rises to the summit of the Ridge Trail. She turns the nose of the helicopter to face the lake, hovering above the spot where I witnessed the fire begin.

"I could take us in for a landing right there by the old cabin," she says.

"That stone shelf is narrow," Lee says. "Practice landing on flat ground a few more times."

"Yes, please," I say. "Practice on flat ground."

"Now who's screwing the mood?" Seton says to Lee.

I lean over the seat as, in my mind, I suddenly hear Reid's voice as he confronted Mrs. Haviland on the dock at Burkehaven. *You won't screw me.*

"Take me to Rocky Nook," I say.

We soar past the shooting range where Freya and I went yesterday, then across the lake to an undeveloped point jutting into the water. Below us, boats have begun to drop anchor for the day, and a single house sits up on a hill, as though standing guard. "Reid mentioned Rocky Nook and a connection to your mother," I say. "What happened here?"

"It's still happening," Seton says. "Some guy from Los Angeles inherited Rocky Nook from his uncle and aunt last year. He'd never been to the lake. He saw dollar signs and went to sell, but there's no access." She points to the land rising from the lakeshore. "That's all conservation land. Thanks to my mother. Reid wanted to bid on the project and was pissed off when it fell through. So was the owner, who's been filing lawsuits trying to find a way to develop, but nothing's worked so far."

"And Reid's been helping him," I say.

"I wouldn't be surprised," Seton says.

◆ ◆ ◆

When we set down at the landing field, I'm grateful to be back on solid ground and ready to head up into the sky all over again.

"See you next week," Seton says to Lee as they finish closing down the helicopter.

"Or sooner," he says, adding, "Cheers, mate," to me.

He has to be six five, all muscle, with that sexy Australian accent. Seton doesn't even pretend not to watch as he makes his way toward his car.

"What's up with the two of you?" I ask.

"He's new to the area and doesn't know anyone. I told him to come to the Landing some night and I'd introduce him around."

That's not what that seemed like to me. "He's really good-looking," I say.

"Believe me, he's well aware. And he's old enough to be my father . . . or my much older brother. I'll pass, thank you."

"The two of you could get matching tattoos—"

"Cut it out," Seton says. "Those Certificates of Apology only last so long. Besides, I hear you spent yesterday with a certain TV star. Are you two a thing again?"

"We never were a thing," I say as we move toward our cars.

"Probably for the best," Seton says. "Gilcrest is *obsessed* with her. He calls her his second chance, but he's convinced Freya's about to hightail it back to New York and is in Panicsville." She tosses her bag into her cruiser. "Watch yourself, Charlie. Freya can be intoxicating. Don't get a broken heart on top of what else is going on."

I let the advice settle in, knowing that it comes from a place of kindness. "You're a good pilot," I say. "Let's get drinks tonight . . . or dinner."

Seton opens the driver's-side door on her cruiser. "Are you asking me on a date?"

"Should I be?"

"Not till you figure out what's going on with Freya."

"Freya and I are friends, nothing more," I say. "You might mention that to Gilcrest next time you see him."

Seton sweeps hair out of my eyes, letting her hand linger on my cheek. "I told you already, I don't want to make a mistake."

I press my hand over hers and inch closer. "How about a friendly drink, then?"

"I'll have to take a rain check, unless you want to get together later."

"Are you meeting Lee?"

Seton steps away from me, her hand dropping to her side, relegating us right back to the friend zone. "I'm not dating Lee! Stop being weird. I'm on duty till ten o'clock. If you're at the Landing when I get there, we can have a drink. Otherwise, you're on your own."

She slides into the driver's seat and starts the car. I lean on the open window. "The night before the fire, Jane called your mom—"

"I know," Seton says, cutting me off. "I know everything about the case, except what Gilcrest doesn't tell me, which I hope isn't very much. You, on the other hand, don't need to know anything. In fact, the less you know, the better. It'll keep you out of Gilcrest's line of fire."

"Did you get that pint glass tested for DNA?"

"I told you I would. I should have results in a few days."

"Would you tell me if someone reported seeing my father?" I ask.

Seton closes her eyes. "Probably not," she says. "If I help you think through why your mother called mine, will you leave the rest of the investigation alone?"

"Maybe," I say.

"That's the best I can hope for," Seton says. "Occam's razor: Start with the simplest explanation possible, not a crazy one, and go from there. In this case, the simplest explanation is Jane called my mom about catering, because the Landing caters most events on the lake, and that's what most people call my mom about. Also, Jane's hired my mom to cater events before, even if they don't like each other. It helps being the only game in town."

"Why would my mother want to meet at Burkehaven? Wouldn't she place the order over the phone?"

"Okay, think through some other ideas. Try it. *What if*—"

"What if," I begin, my voice trailing off. At first my mind's blank, but then a fully realized idea snaps into place. "What if my mother was planning to meet my father at Burkehaven, and somehow she wanted your mother to be there, too. What if your mother was the one who helped my father escape. She told me she drove to Sunapee the night your father was killed because you couldn't sleep, but your mother could have been anywhere. There was no GPS tracking then. She could have had my father hidden in the trunk of the car, and no one would have bothered to look because she was the victim's widow—"

"Stop!" Seton says. "Remember what I said about going with the obvious? That sounds like a plot for *Haviland and Kilgore*, not real life."

"It's convoluted," I say.

"More like ludicrous," Seton says. "But here's another one for you: What if Jane wanted to tell my mom to stop getting in the way of the Burkehaven project? My mom's annoying. That's what I'd have done in Jane's place."

It's a simpler explanation. And it actually makes sense.

Seton glances at her phone. "I have to get to work," she says. "But keep going. What if . . . ? And keep it real. Think of the things my mom does, and how they overlap with Burkehaven. She's a selectperson, she owns the Landing, she's on the conservation commission. My mom has a foot in almost anything that happens in this town. Where did those things overlap with your mother? If you come up with something useful, let me know."

After she drives off, I sit in my car. Why did my mother go to Burkehaven that morning, and why did she ask Mrs. Haviland to meet her there? And who else was lurking in the trees, waiting?

I don't have the answers, but I know in my heart that the solution must be more complex than a catering order.

What if . . . what if . . . what if . . .

Then I remember something Seton said as we hovered in the helicopter. What if Mrs. Haviland and her crusade to save the lake had more to do with the fire at Burkehaven than anyone has realized?

Chapter Twenty-Nine

Paul stands by the sugarhouse in Burkehaven Farm's front yard as I speed up his driveway and skid to a stop beneath an ancient maple tree. He wears work boots and a red overshirt that swallows his thin frame. His normally coiffed salt-and-pepper hair stands on end, and dirt smears his face as though he's been working the fields. "You look like there's something on your mind," he says as I approach.

I have questions about the call between him and my mother the night before the fire, though I'm not sure where to begin. I worked out a whole scenario at the landing field after I talked to Seton, but what seemed clear then now seems muddled. "It's nothing," I say.

Paul lifts the door to the sugarhouse, where a large evaporator sits at the back of an open space and tools line the walls. "It was a good year for sugaring," he says. "We got over ten gallons of maple syrup. Remind me to give you some before you go back to Somerville." He takes a shovel and hatchet from the wall and hands me a long iron crowbar and a pair of work gloves. "I could use help in the south pasture. Whatever's going on, a little hard work will help you think it through."

Paul has a way of calming the loudest of internal voices, and I can feel my resolve seeping away. *Keep pushing for answers,* I tell myself, as he steers me across a field where tufts of new green grass have begun to poke through the winter gray. We follow a fieldstone wall, up and over a hill, where we pass the bloody remains of an unfortunate creature.

"Coyotes," Paul says. "They're all over the place. You can hear them howling at night."

A moment later, we come to a spot along the wall where lichen-covered stones lay scattered across the ground, along with the remnants of a fallen tree.

"One of the beech trees gave up the ghost during a storm last winter," Paul says. "I lost count of the rings on the stump when I got to 150. Some of the guys from Reid's crew cleared most of the debris a few weeks ago, but we can cut these last limbs for firewood, and the wall needs repair. See if you can move that stone."

I wedge the crowbar beneath a round stone, inching forward until Paul rolls the stone toward the gap in the wall. "You and Freya hung out yesterday?" he says.

I ease the stone into place. "She taught me how to shoot."

"Freya's used to being in control. She'll hold a grudge, too. You don't want to find yourself at the end of a lawsuit, especially when the other party has money to burn."

"There's no lawsuit," I say.

"You recorded her without consent."

"And I deleted the recording."

"*That* recording," Paul says.

I work another stone into place. I've made the mistake of assuming my conversation with Freya was confidential. Now I wonder how much of what I said she reported to Paul. "She gave consent," I say. "I have it on record, and I'll get it in writing, too. Are you talking to me as a family friend or as Freya Faith's lawyer?"

"Maybe a little bit of both," Paul says. "But mostly, I don't want to see you hurt. You're a kid, Charlie."

I start to protest, but Paul holds up a hand to stop me.

"I know. You're not a kid," he says. "I have to remind myself of that. But Freya's definitely not a kid, and now that . . . now that your mother's gone, I have to look out for you. Freya doesn't know what she wants, but I can guarantee you she won't be moving to Somerville or sticking around New Hampshire much longer. This town isn't her style, even if she's convinced herself it is for the time being. Freya prefers the city, and she craves the spotlight. She won't settle for singing in a run-down bar for the rest of her life."

"Freya's not a kid," I say. "You said it yourself. She's a grown woman who makes her own choices."

"And those choices put one person on center stage. Not Duncan Gilcrest. And definitely not you."

"I can handle myself," I say.

Paul crouches beside a wide, flat rock. "Get on the other side of this," he says.

We lift the rock together and use it to form the top edge of the wall.

"Freya's using you because Gilcrest won't let her control his every move," Paul says. "That's what she does. That's what she's always done. And Gilcrest is probably keenly aware that the moment he gives in to her, she'll get bored with him. But he's getting desperate, too."

Paul's worked with Freya for decades. He probably knows her better than nearly anyone else, but the person he describes now doesn't mesh with the woman I spent the day with yesterday. Still, she admitted she'd used me to make Gilcrest jealous. She also posed for the cameras outside the police station and slowed her truck to be sure that reporter gave chase. Maybe she's using me in other ways, too.

And maybe she's a better actor than I realized.

Half an hour later, we set the final stone in place along the top of the wall.

"These projects never end," Paul says, admiring the work. "I prefer New York, where I call the super when something needs attention."

I sit on the wall to test its stability. "Solid," I say. "Satisfying, too."

"Keep telling yourself that," Paul says. "I noticed a crack in the firepit at Idlewood. Guess who needs to fix it now. You." He leans on the crowbar. "That cut on your head healed. Send me the hospital bill, and I'll take care of it while we settle the estate. Any thoughts on who whacked you? Or why?"

"I had a suspect," I say, "but he didn't pan out."

Paul takes in the information without comment, waiting for me to fill the silence.

"Vance Moodey and my mother were dating," I continue.

Paul raises his eyebrows. "Your mother was good with a secret," he says.

"Secrets like why Reid owes Vance money."

Paul swings the crowbar over his shoulder and begins to retrace the path to the farmhouse. "Once your mother's will is out of probate, you, Reid, and I should sit down and go over the estate so you can get a sense of what you're dealing with. If you have questions about creditors, we can cover them then. Reid Construction is a complicated business. The condos by the marina, the ones where Freya's staying, haven't sold. Reid's the owner, so it's been a strain on the firm. Now that spring's fully underway, they should move."

I don't know a lot about real estate, but I do know brand-new lakeside construction sells quickly. Or it should. "That project finished over a year ago," I say.

"They need to repour the foundation. It's not a big deal."

"That sounds like a huge deal."

We reach the crest of the hill. Below us, Burkehaven Farm sits nestled among the trees. In the distance, an SUV glides into the driveway. Duncan Gilcrest gets out and peers up the hill toward where we stand, then begins hiking our way.

"I wondered when he'd show up," Paul says.

"Did my mother know Reid had money tied up in those condos? Or about other creditors like Vance?"

"Jane was the president of the company."

And my mother would hardly be the first company president who lost track of the accounting at her organization, but like any good lawyer, Paul's made a career of evading answers.

"My mother called you the night before the fire," I say.

"Your mother and I talked a lot," Paul says.

Down below, Gilcrest has begun to cross the pasture toward us, his black anorak blowing in the breeze. I need to ask Paul my questions before the detective reaches us. "You were my mother's lawyer," I say. "The night we played cards, Jane said what was happening at Burkehaven would never happen to Idlewood, even when Reid mentioned property taxes. Mrs. Haviland is the chair of the conservation commission. And when I was out in the helicopter with Seton just now, she told me Mrs. Haviland had been after Jane to put Idlewood in conservation."

Paul turns to face me, and I can see him calculating how much to reveal. "Andrea can be persuasive," he says. "I'll give her that."

"You're not answering the question," I say.

"I didn't hear a question."

"Did my mother talk to you about changing her will?"

Paul glances to where Gilcrest has begun the final ascent toward us. He lowers his voice. "Your mother wanted Idlewood protected against anything that might happen in the future, but stop asking about this, Charlie. If we're lucky, Gilcrest and his team will make an arrest soon. Andrea Haviland should have been in jail weeks ago. There's a good case against her, and she had plenty of opportunity to kill your mother and start the fire. I should have made a bigger deal of what happened with those security cameras, but I let false loyalty sway me. If I had, maybe your mother would be alive."

"Mrs. Haviland rode into Burkehaven *after* the fire began. It's on tape."

"And she knew that camera was in place because she made sure it was there when she destroyed the other ones. Then she killed your mother, moved her car into the woods, set the fire, got in her boat, and drove into the cove at the one angle she knew the camera would capture. It's pretty simple."

It's not simple, and it's hardly the *simplest* explanation. "What happened between you and Andrea Haviland, anyway?" I ask. "Why do you hate her so much? You loaned her money, but there has to be more to the story."

"Charlie Kilgore," Gilcrest calls out, his breath ragged from the hike, "you're always one step ahead of me."

"I fronted her a few thousand dollars, nothing more," Paul says, his voice low, his tone a warning.

He wants me to leave this alone.

Chapter Thirty

"What's that about a loan, Charlie?" Gilcrest says to me as he completes the climb up the hill, the lake extending to the horizon behind him. "Is Seton hitting you up for money again?"

Paul catches my eye. "It's nothing, Duncan," he says. "Charlie's taking a loan against his mother's estate to pay his hospital bills while I get things settled. Perfectly standard."

"Must be nice to have a well to draw from," Gilcrest says.

I brush past the detective without answering. "I'll see you around, Paul," I say.

"By the way, thanks for the lead," Gilcrest calls after me. "I was over at Moodey Lumber this morning. Vance told me what he could about your mother."

I turn, taking a few steps backward over the uneven ground. Gilcrest looms a few feet above me, hair tousled, hips thrust forward with practiced ease, testosterone exuding from his very essence. He's letting me know Freya reported on our day together and anything I tell her will get back to him one way or another. "You're playing good cop," I say.

"I am a good cop," Gilcrest says. "How's the aim? Have you managed to hit the target yet?"

"I'll let you know," I say.

Gilcrest is also making sure I understand he's in control.

I leave the detective with Paul and descend through the field. At my car, I send a text to Freya: Meet me in our spot.

An hour later, Freya emerges from the hiking trail onto the shooting range. She carries the two rifles slung over her shoulder. Ginger trots along beside her. The dog growls and wags her tail when she sees me, as though she doesn't know whether to attack. "Release," Freya says, making the decision for her.

I roll onto the ground and wrestle with the dog while Freya heads into the field to set up aluminum cans as targets. When she returns, I take the bag of treats from my coat pocket.

"Make her earn it," Freya says.

I palm one of the treats. Ginger's haunches hit the ground, and then she swallows the biscuit in one bite.

"Good girl," I say, scratching her behind the ears. "I'll get you to trust me. Maybe we can be friends."

"More like frenemies," Freya says, loading one of the rifles, then attaching the line to Ginger's collar before firing into the range.

"No cigarette?" I ask.

"I think I quit," Freya says, leaning the rifle against the stone wall. "I've earned it."

I get up from the ground. I'm not sure how I'm supposed to greet Freya—a peck on the cheek or a quick hug or something more—so I offer a hand.

She almost laughs. "Nice to meet you, sir," she says, adding a nod to a firm handshake, then releasing Ginger from the line. "Go play," she says to the dog, who dashes into the woods after a squirrel.

"I saw your boyfriend," I say. "He came to the farm to talk to Paul."

I tell her about my conversation with Andrea Haviland earlier this morning and that I made up with Seton while out in the helicopter.

"That was you flying over Hadley and me when we were on the lake," Freya says.

"Did you learn anything from her?"

"Not really. We had forty years of catching up to do."

I lift one of the guns and find an aluminum can in the sight. The weapon still feels dangerous pressed into my shoulder, even with an empty chamber. "It's as though I'm watching myself move through my own story while I gather pieces and try to fit them together. And I'm not sure what the pieces are right now, because nothing seems to make sense."

"Stay here," Freya says, disappearing into the trees and returning with a long stick she uses to scratch a grid in the muddy ground. "On *Scene of the Crime*, Gina Shock would gather the CBI team at a whiteboard after the mid-episode break, especially if the story was complex. We'd bat around ideas, but it was also a way to refresh the audience on who the suspects were. So, who are our suspects?"

Only everyone I know. And it feels coldhearted to reduce my mother's murder to a grid, but I also want to learn what happened. "Start with me," I say. "Gilcrest did."

Freya scratches *Harold* into the grid. "Motive?" she asks.

I walk her through my theory that my mother planned to put Idlewood into conservation.

"Getting cut out of a big inheritance, not bad." Freya adds an X to the Motive column. "Means: a tree limb; opportunity: you were at the scene."

"But I didn't do it," I say.

Freya x-es out my name.

"You'll take my word for it?" I ask.

"Gina wouldn't, but I will. And eliminating suspects is as helpful as identifying them. Your brother has the exact same motive as you: money. But not necessarily the same means or opportunity."

She adds Reid's name to the grid, but seeing my brother as part of a list of suspects makes me uncomfortable, especially when the list—so far—only consists of one other person.

"It was probably a stranger," I say.

"Maybe," Freya says, placing a question mark at the bottom of the grid. "But not very satisfying, story wise. A random act of violence would never make it out of the writers' room. What about our friend Vance Moodey at the lumberyard, with his handy two-by-fours? Motive could be greed, jealousy, envy, rage. He could be a serial killer. We only have his word he was dating your mother, and even if they were dating, maybe she met him at Burkehaven to break things off and he lost his temper."

"Gilcrest told me he went to see Vance this morning," I say.

Freya pauses. "Yeah, Duncan's a real cop, so if I have a theory about a crime, I have to tell him, whether he's earned it or not."

Duly noted.

I take the stick from her and scratch Vance's name beneath mine. "And my father," I say, adding his name, too.

Freya clucks her tongue. "Viewers love stories where the past comes around and connects to the present. This could be as easy as discovery. Maybe your mother found out your father was alive and threatened to expose him. Your father could have killed your mother, started the fire, and retreated into the trees when he saw Andrea Haviland approaching in the boat. Then, when you arrived, he could have attacked you with the tree limb." Freya adds three check marks next to my father's initials. "Motive, means, and opportunity equals a viable suspect."

She's getting a little too into this. "We're not in the writers' room," I say.

"Sorry," Freya says, touching my arm as she seems to search for something to say. "How are you feeling, anyway?"

Tired of talking about how I feel. "Let's keep going," I say. "But honestly, focusing on the crime helps me forget about the rest of it. I know it doesn't make sense, but at least I'm doing something."

"Back to your father, then," Freya says. "On the show, we'd work your father into the plot early in the episode, but we'd put him aside as a long-shot theory. One of the junior agents would pursue it, while Gina Shock followed other leads. Your father would come back in the last act, when he'd become the main focus of the investigation."

"Since this isn't a TV show," I say, "maybe we should keep him in our sights."

"Or," Freya says, "maybe there's another storyline we're forgetting, one your dad's distracting us from, and *that* storyline will come around and connect. What did Andrea Haviland have to say about your father?"

"She insists she hasn't seen him since he disappeared."

"Plus, there's the recording showing her arriving at the scene *after* the fire started. No opportunity."

I tell Freya Paul's theory that Mrs. Haviland left the single camera in place on purpose so she could start the fire and be recorded arriving on scene.

"That's a lot of detail to keep track of," Freya says, adding Mrs. Haviland's name to the grid. "For it to work, we'd have to shoot a flashback, maybe in black and white. The explanation's too convoluted otherwise."

"God forbid we shoot a flashback," I mumble, though it gives me an idea. I pull up the audio files on my phone. "I have my own flashback right here. My mother and I talked the night before . . . the night before everything happened."

I hit play as my mother's voice washes over me: *Good marriages don't end. And bad marriages don't have a good guy and a bad guy. We all play our parts. I played mine, and so did your father.*

I hit pause.

"Doesn't that sound as if my father had an affair, too?" I ask. "Mrs. Haviland denied it was her. I don't know who to believe anymore, and Seton—"

I add Seton's initials to the grid, and this time it really does feel like a betrayal. "She's been against the podcast since the moment I told her about it."

"She doesn't want to dig up the past," Freya says.

"Or she's protecting someone," I say. "Seton and Mrs. Haviland tell each other everything. Could Seton know something the rest of us don't?" I shiver. "What if Seton is my half sister?"

"That's a little too soap opera, even for me," Freya says. "And if it were true, my guess is your mothers would have kept you very, *very* far away from each other. Let me hear that recording again."

I hit play.

"Your mother's saying that both your parents did things they shouldn't have, but she doesn't say your father had an *affair*. He could have been a drug addict or a drunk or worse."

I draw a line connecting Mrs. Haviland's name to my father's. "Or maybe the simplest explanation is he slept with an old friend."

Freya's eyes crease in thought as she calls to Ginger. The dog barrels from the trees and sits at attention. Freya attaches the line to her collar, loads the rifle, and shoots. "When Hadley and I were out on the boat this morning, I got to thinking about firsts and lasts. Sometimes you know they're happening, and sometimes you don't see them until they're far off in the rearview mirror. Like that night we met at the Landing. That was a first for us. When we talked on the sidewalk in the rain, I never would have guessed we'd be here together in the woods two weeks later."

Freya breaks open the rifle again, loads the chamber, and fires. This time, she misses the target.

"You're shaking," I say.

She pops out the spent casing. "I had a memory come back to me right this very moment, fully formed, something I haven't thought about in decades. The last time my family stayed at Burkehaven was the year before I started college. I don't think any of us knew we wouldn't return, or that we'd lose touch with so many of the people we'd spent summers with. Hadley and I were good friends. And even though we only saw each other for two weeks each summer, I knew she'd be part of my time here. We couldn't have known the last time we spoke to each other would be *the* last time, that I'd blink and decades would melt away."

Freya lays the rifle on the stone wall.

"I took the path to Idlewood on our last day," she continues. "Hadley and I went swimming. It was hot, and the sun was beating down on us, and the water felt silky against my skin, and it was one of those days that should never have ended. Hadley's a year older than I am, so she'd been out to California already for her first year of college. For as long as I'd known her, she'd talked about leaving New Hampshire. She wanted to travel the world, and by then I knew I wanted to live in New York, to be an artist. She'd instilled a desire for independence in me."

"You both got what you wanted," I say.

"That's just it," Freya says. "I'm glad she got what she wanted. It was a relief to learn that, actually, because that last time I spoke to your aunt, her whole outlook had changed. As we floated in the lake, she was smiling and laughing in a way I hadn't seen before. She told me she was considering staying in Hero and transferring to Kingston State." Freya's eyes suddenly focus. "It's a snapshot in time, a single moment Hadley probably doesn't remember."

"Hadley didn't transfer to Kingston State," I say. "She went to Berkeley and finished med school at UCSF. I can't imagine her staying in Hero. She makes fun of it the whole time she's here."

"But she had a boyfriend that summer," Freya says. "Or a boy she was obsessed with talking about." She crosses over to the grid and adds Hadley's name beneath Andrea Haviland's. Then she draws a line connecting Hadley to my father. "Her boyfriend was Mark Kilgore. Your father."

Chapter Thirty-One

I scuff Hadley's name from the grid of suspects with the toe of my shoe. While I'm at it, I erase Seton's name, too. "Hadley couldn't have dated my father," I say. "He was too old. He'd never have dated a kid like her."

"Stay objective, Harold," Freya says. "And stick to the facts. You don't know your father or what he'd do, but if I remember correctly, your father was a junior at Kingston State that year, two years older than Hadley, who'd just finished her freshman year at Berkeley. If I was eighteen, she was nineteen, and he'd have been twenty-one. Seems okay to me."

She's right, of course. My mother was four years older than her sister, and my father was right between them.

"If you talked to your father at the Landing," Freya says, "he's either managed to live on the lam on his own, or someone's been helping him. Maybe it's Hadley: the sad sister with the long, unrequited crush on her brother-in-law. He gets himself in trouble and needs help. Maybe he knew she had feelings for him and exploited them to manipulate her."

"Men don't manipulate Hadley," I say. "And, reminder, she was in Kosovo the night Isaac Haviland was killed, so she wasn't here to hide my father, no matter what she felt about him."

"She could have flown home without telling anyone."

"Hadley flies halfway around the world, rents a car, drives to New Hampshire to . . . what? Seduce my father? *And* she manages to fake a photo showing her surrounded by eyewitnesses who can attest to her being in Kosovo. I mean, did Photoshop exist in 2001?"

"Believe me, Photoshop existed long before 2001. The producers used it on my publicity stills all the time."

"Well, that's a pretty far-fetched scenario, even for *Scene of the Crime*."

"My show was *not* far-fetched. And you're pretty protective of Hadley."

"What can I say? She's my cool aunt. And she makes me feel special."

"And she's my cool friend, so I'd be glad to clear her name, but didn't you tell me Hadley came home from Kosovo as soon as she heard what happened here, and stayed all summer? Even if she'd been out of the country on the night of the murder, Mark could have found her after she returned. Maybe she helped him get set up in a new life." Freya returns Hadley's name to the grid. "Who's left?"

"Paul Burke," I say.

"How well do you know him?"

"How well do *you* know him?" I ask.

"Are you asking if we dated?"

"It could be an interesting plot twist."

"Paul and I have a professional relationship, and I suppose we're friends, too," Freya says. "But that's all. I mean, I've known him most of my life. He handles my relatives, making sure they stay happy and out of my hair with about a thousand trusts he manages. *Scene of the Crime* was good to me. The residuals roll in, and my money rolls out. You wouldn't believe how much it costs to be rich. He's helped me with some thorny issues over the years, too, especially my divorce. It was rough when those photos of my ex-husband hit the tabloids—they were pretty racy—and I had to be on set with him until we killed off the character. Paul was there, watching out for me. We used to spend a lot of time together before I met Duncan, especially after I left *Scene of the Crime*. So that's my relationship with him. What's yours?"

"He stepped in with my father being gone," I say, adding his name to the grid.

"Motive?" Freya asks.

I add a question mark as I review the conversation I had with Paul earlier. I have a loyalty to him like I do with Hadley, but he was also keeping something from me when we talked. That thing—the loan to Mrs. Haviland—had more to do with the past than the present. "We keep asking if there could be a connection between Isaac Haviland's murder and what happened to my mother," I say.

"Two violent deaths in one tight-knit group," Freya says.

I add Isaac Haviland's name to the grid. "Paul lent Isaac fifty grand."

"That's not chump change," Freya says.

"Paul wasn't at Idlewood when my father stabbed Isaac Haviland. It's in the police reports. He'd gone to a party his parents were throwing at Burkehaven, and there were witnesses who confirmed he was there the whole time. But the two properties are connected through the woods, and it only takes two or three minutes to run the path from Idlewood to Burkehaven. I do it most mornings."

"So, questionable opportunity," Freya says. "But if Paul killed Isaac Haviland and framed your father, why would your mother have covered for him?"

And why would Reid have told the police my father killed Isaac? It's the same argument I made to Mrs. Haviland earlier.

"We could add Duncan to the mix, too," Freya says. "He was the responding officer at the Haviland murder, and now he's working this case years later."

"I don't see a motive," I say.

"That's big of you."

Score one for Charlie Kilgore.

I smile at Freya, forgetting for an instant that these aren't storylines, and this isn't a TV episode. But that grief comes out of hiding all over again, nearly knocking me off my feet. I rest my palms on the stone wall and gasp for breath. "Wow," I say, the smile gone.

"Let's take a break," Freya says. "Duncan has a whole team working on solving this case. We don't have to do this."

We do, though. Or I have to.

I thought I wanted to know what happened next, who my father was, how he could have ruined his whole life in a single instant of rage, but what I need is to understand where I belong, how I've fit into this story for all these years, and what's kept me on the outside, looking in. "What if I asked the wrong question?" I say. "If I'd kept my mouth shut and not run around trying to tell this story, would my mother be alive?"

"You can't own someone else's terrible decision," Freya says. "Whether the choice was made twenty-five years ago, or twenty-five minutes ago, the choice was theirs to make."

We gather the rifles and retrieve the aluminum cans from the shooting range. Freya releases Ginger from the line, and we make our way down the trail. When we reach the stream, a text beeps into my phone. Then another. And another. I glance at the screen. A text from Julian sits over all the others. This thing is gaining traction! he writes.

I click his name. He picks up on the first ring. "We're at two thousand downloads," he says.

"Of what?" I ask.

"I edited together some of your narration," Julian says. "There's a story here! I posted a teaser for the podcast."

Right then, a growl begins at the back of Ginger's throat.

"What's wrong?" Freya says to her.

The dog takes off toward the trailhead. Freya swears and chases after her.

I imagine the other texts on my phone, from Reid and Paul—from Seton—each expressing some version of betrayal. "Take the teaser down," I say to Julian. "Now. Right now!"

Then I disconnect the call, sling the rifle over my shoulder, and run down the path toward the road, my boots pounding through mud. A few moments later, I emerge from the trees. Freya stands beside Ginger, her hand on the dog's collar.

"I'm going to strangle my producer," I say, between gasps.

Freya doesn't speak. I follow her gaze. Sun glints off her truck's windshield, where WELCOME HOME has been smeared in what looks like blue paint. "He's back," Freya says.

I search the forest for whoever she means. Something moves in the trees. I lift the rifle and find the scope as someone tackles me from behind.

Chapter Thirty-Two

As I crash toward the ground, the rifle slips from my grasp and clatters across the forest floor. I struggle to escape the weight on my back, trying to catch a glimpse of who took me down. I scramble after the rifle, but my arm twists, and I'm back on the ground, my face shoved into a pile of wet leaves. An elbow presses into my back. And auburn-colored hair cascades across my face. "Do you have any idea how many perps I've taken down in my day, Harold?" Freya hisses into my ear.

I try to turn. Ginger lunges, and Freya shouts "Off!" before the dog's jaw can clamp onto my leg.

"Don't point a gun at anything besides a target," Freya says, tightening her grip on my arm. "Ever. You're not trained, and I don't need a protector."

"The rifle wasn't loaded," I say.

"It doesn't matter," Freya says.

I breathe in the loamy scent of wet leaves and mud and will my heart rate to slow. Usually, I do my best not to act the part of an alpha male, but getting taken down by a woman crushes the ego. I stop struggling, and Freya relaxes her grip, if only a bit. "Can I trust you?" she asks.

I nod.

She releases my arm and rolls off me. "Are you hurt?"

I spin away from her, keeping my hands visible, until I'm sitting cross-legged. Dampness seeps through the back of my jeans.

Ginger crouches at Freya's side, transformed into a snarling, drooling killing machine.

"She'll rip you to pieces if she thinks I'm in trouble," Freya says, catching Ginger's eye. "Down."

Ginger drops to an active down, but the snarls don't stop. Freya crawls to the rifle, breaks it open, and checks the empty chamber. Then she sits by the truck, her legs splayed out. I join her, but when I put my hand on the rifle, she yanks it away. "You lost your privileges."

Another text beeps into my phone. I silence it without looking at the screen, and nod toward the graffiti on the truck. "What's that?"

"Nothing for you to worry about," Freya says.

"What if whoever did that is still here?"

"Ginger will let us know. And I can load a rifle in two seconds flat."

Despite Freya's tough demeanor, she's shivering. I go to wrap my arm around her waist. "Do you mind?" I ask.

"Don't make a move on me," she says. "You won't be likable."

"I don't care if people like me."

"I don't believe that for a second."

Freya rests her head on my shoulder, and Ginger's growls are replaced by a whine.

"Come," Freya says, and the dog shimmies right in between us. "Paul warned me not to play those shows at the Landing." She adds, "Too much publicity. I didn't think it would be a big deal, but anything can be a big deal these days with social media." She inhales. "I have a stalker. I've had one for years. He comes and goes, disappearing for months and years, then reappearing out of nowhere like we're planning storylines for May Sweeps."

I scratch Ginger's belly. A canine tooth peeks out from under her lip. "What can I do?" I ask.

"I don't want you involved," Freya says.

"I'm involved already. I'm so involved, I nearly set myself up for a murder charge with that rifle."

Freya manages a tired smile. "Manslaughter, actually. There was no intent. And being famous isn't what it's cracked up to be. When you're beamed into millions of living rooms every week, the line between what's real and what isn't gets blurred."

"How long has this been going on?" I ask.

"Since I was on *Eternal Flame* in the nineties. The first time it happened was at a mall event in Albany. There was a problem with the car service, so I rented and drove myself. Hundreds of people were there—soap fans were so devoted then—and when we finished, I found a handwritten note under my wiper that said, *Nice to see you in person. You look great in green.* I didn't think anything of it. I'd been sitting by a fountain at the mall meeting strangers for hours at that point, and any one of them could have left the note, but on my way to the city, I started feeling like someone was following me. I pulled over when I saw a state cop, and he listened and sat with me for a bit, but I couldn't show him anything tangible. After the cop took off, I realized whoever had left the note had seen me *arrive* at the mall, like they were waiting for me."

"Otherwise," I say, "how else would they have known which car was yours?"

"Exactly. So, they were either there when I pulled into the parking lot—"

"Or they followed you."

"A few days later, I found a second note in my dressing room on the set—same handwriting. This time he wrote, *I wish we could have spent the weekend upstate.* The cops took a statement and collected the note as evidence, but didn't do much about it. I was a public figure at a public event. There were no stalker laws on the books then in New York, so the cops couldn't do anything unless he physically harmed me. The producers on the show wrote it off, too. As far as they were concerned, stalkers came with fame, but the notes kept coming, and they got more aggressive, more threatening. In the last one, he told me not to leave my apartment after dark. It said, *You should be terrified.* That's the real reason Brenda Jackson disappeared at that costume party.

Paul arranged for me to get out of New York and stay with a friend in the Hamptons. He told the producers I wouldn't return to set without additional security."

My voice tightens. "What happened next?"

Freya puts a hand to my chest and pushes me away. "Don't go all testosterone on me. I have Duncan for that. You're my gentle soul."

I don't want to play that part this time. "Didn't you see how I wielded a rifle?"

"And I don't want to see it again," Freya says. "But I walked away from the soap for good a few months later. I couldn't take being afraid anymore, and once I left, the stalking stopped for a while. I had a fallow period between Brenda and Gina Shock where I took guest spots or had roles in off-off-Broadway or waited tables. I hoped he'd moved on to someone else, or—"

"Or he believed he'd won and had you to himself."

Freya nods. "*Scene of the Crime* debuted in 2000, and it was as if I turned on a faucet. The threats started at once, and we suddenly had the web and internet cafés to protect his anonymity. He'd send emails and attach photos of me on the set or leaving my apartment. In the second season, there was a continuing storyline about a serial killer who targeted gay men. This guy hated that storyline. He thought we were writing about him and implying something about his masculinity, and he went from annoying to threatening." She nods down the road toward Burkehaven Farm. "One night, I got home from meeting Paul for dinner and there were photos in my inbox of the two of us at the restaurant. That time, the stalker threatened to kill me. He threatened to kill both of us."

"You told me you and Paul hadn't dated," I say.

"We haven't, but the stalker couldn't have known. He imagined whatever he wanted. By then, the laws had changed in New York, and the cops took stalking more seriously. They traced the source of the email to a public computer but couldn't identify who'd used the machine. I almost left *Scene of the Crime* like I had with the soap.

Instead, I learned what I could about self-defense. Journalists used to come to set and focus on how much of my own stunt work I did, how I was in such great shape. The stories were supposed to be empowering, but I did all that work because I didn't feel safe."

She stops for a moment, her brow furrowed.

"What are you thinking?" I ask.

"It's nothing."

"Tell me."

"That time Isaac Haviland showed up on the set," Freya says. "When he asked me to invest in the Landing, part of me suspected he might be the stalker. He'd always given me the creeps, as though he was watching me no matter what I did. One summer, this necklace I'd gotten for my birthday went missing, and I'm certain Isaac took it. I asked him to go to the diner because I wanted to see if I could get him to confess."

"I'm not the only reckless one," I say. "Sounds dangerous."

Freya waves a hand. "We were in a public place in the middle of the West Village. Nothing would have happened to me, and besides, it was clear Isaac had no idea what I was talking about. I felt bad enough that I gave him the hundred bucks in my wallet."

"Maybe he was playing you," I say.

Freya jerks her thumb toward the truck. "From the grave?" she asks. "Isaac Haviland's dead and buried. My stalker's very much alive. I hadn't heard from him much since I left *Scene of the Crime*, but last year, when I shot the true-crime pilot with Duncan, the threats started again. I was almost relieved when the show didn't get picked up. That's part of the reason why I came to New Hampshire. I thought I could escape."

She stands and looks at the letters written on the windshield. She taps the blue *W* in *Welcome* with her fingertip. "Nail polish," she says, holding her own painted nails against the glass. "It's the same color I've been using. I have a bottle of it at the condo." A shadow crosses her face. "You were in my bathroom."

I back away, holding my hands out where she can see them.

Freya snaps her fingers. Ginger leaps to her feet, the fur at her neck standing on end.

"Ginger's fickle," I say.

"She sees who people really are."

"I'm taking my phone from my pocket, that's it," I say, retrieving the phone and entering the code. "I've been with you at the firing range since you left your truck down here, so I couldn't have done this without help from someone else. Go through my texts. See if I plotted with anyone."

I hand her the phone.

Freya scrolls through the first few texts and whistles. "Wow, you pissed off nearly everyone you know."

The podcast.

"Tell me about it," I say.

Freya keeps scrolling. "There's nothing connecting you to this crap," she says, returning the phone to me. "You're off the hook, for now."

"Who else has been to your condo lately?"

"You, Paul," Freya says. "And Duncan."

Maybe Duncan Gilcrest is a suspect, after all. "Gilcrest went to Columbia," I say, remembering my conversation with the detective at Burkehaven.

"What about it?" Freya asks.

Columbia is in New York. And Gilcrest is forty-eight years old, which means he'd have gone to college in the nineties, right when Freya's stalker first appeared. "What was the name of the security company the producers used on *Eternal Flame*?" I ask.

"I don't want to play detective anymore," Freya says.

"Humor me."

"You're testing my memory. That was a long time ago." She thinks for a moment. "It was a pun, Safety Pin, or something similar."

I pull up Gilcrest's résumé on LinkedIn. There, in the first entry, is a part-time job working for Pin Safety in Manhattan.

"Do you have security footage at the condo?" I ask.

"What do you think?"

"You probably have all the evidence you need sitting somewhere in the cloud," I say. "We should call Seton. She can meet us here."

Ginger suddenly growls. I turn to the thick forest surrounding us. Beside me, Freya slides a bullet into the rifle's chamber. I tap Seton's name on my phone. A twig snaps, and Ginger charges into the trees. Freya takes off after the dog, rifle in hand.

"Charlie," Seton says on the other end of the line, "what's with this teaser? You couldn't give me a heads-up?"

I cut her off. "We're at the trailhead by Burkehaven Farm," I whisper. "Come. Now."

I sprint into the woods after Freya. In the distance, a snarl follows a splash.

"Off," Freya shouts.

I emerge from the trees. Freya stands on the banks of the brook, the rifle pointed at someone sprawled in the water wearing a pair of black capri pants. As I approach, Reid rolls onto his back, his hands raised, his thick-rimmed glasses slipping down his nose.

"Get your dog away from me," he shouts.

Chapter Thirty-Three

Between Freya's rifle and Ginger's teeth, I don't dare move or ask Reid what he's doing here, sprawled in the brook by the trailhead, or if he had anything to do with the message smeared on Freya's truck. I certainly don't ask if that message is somehow connected to the photos of Freya he had taped on his bedroom walls as a teenager. Instead, I focus on sounds: water flowing over rocks and birds chirping in the trees. It could almost be peaceful here.

Except then Reid shifts, and Ginger lunges, and Freya shouts, "Heel," and the dog backs off, her body quivering, every part of her ready to attack.

"If he bites me," Reid says, "I'll have him put down."

"If *she* bites you," Freya says, "you'll have earned it."

I manage to find my voice. "This is Reid, my brother."

Reid probably wants to lay into me about the podcast, like Seton. That could be why he came to the trailhead in the first place.

"Reid and I have met plenty of times," Freya says. "Paul used to bring him to the set when he was at NYU, and he's been trying to talk me into buying the house at Burkehaven for months. What the hell are you doing here?"

For a moment, Reid seems as though he might not answer, but he relents. "I came looking for Charlie. Paul told me you were up at the summit, but the two of you were having a moment, and I didn't want to interrupt whatever was about to happen. Then *Teeth* here came charging."

"Put the gun down," I say to Freya. "What will he do, anyway? He's wearing capri pants."

Freya lowers the barrel and hands me the rifle.

"I thought I lost my gun privileges," I say.

"You got a reprieve."

"This water is freezing," Reid says.

"Release," Freya says.

Ginger relaxes. I pull a treat from my pocket, and the dog comes to me. Reid has the good sense to stand slowly. His sodden clothing clings to his body, outlining the wallet and phone beneath the fabric, but no bottle of nail polish, which Freya seems to realize, too, as she says, "The police will need to set up a perimeter and find out what he did with it."

"With what?" Reid asks.

Freya catches my eye and barely shakes her head.

"Someone used blue nail polish to write on Freya's windshield," I say. "She has a stalker, and now he's in New Hampshire."

"Thanks for the discretion," Freya says.

Reid steps out of the river, the soles of his espadrilles slipping on the slick stone. My brother came dressed for a garden party, not to terrorize.

"Walk in front where I can see you," Freya says. "And Charlie, tell Seton what's happening."

It's only then I hear Seton's voice shouting from the other end of the call I never disconnected.

"What the hell is going on there?" she says. "I'm two minutes out."

"How much did you hear?" I ask.

"Enough to call for backup. Maggie's on her way, too."

"Meet by the trailhead," I say.

A moment later, Seton speeds up the road in her cruiser, lights flashing. She gets out of the car deliberately and approaches with her hand poised over her holster. "Lock those firearms away," she says to Freya.

Freya checks the chambers on both rifles and stores them in the gun rack at the back of her truck.

"And the dog," Seton says. "Let's put her in my cruiser."

"Is she under arrest?" Freya asks.

"She should be," Reid says.

"Zip it," Seton says. "Both of you."

Ginger follows Freya to the cruiser and leaps into the back seat. As soon as the car door closes, Reid says, "That thing tried to kill me."

"You have all your fingers and toes," Seton says. "Don't make something out of nothing. Can everyone get along, or do I have to wait for my deputy?"

Reid kicks a stone into the trees. "We're fine."

Seton glances at Freya, who nods.

"These two seem to have something between them," Seton says to me. "Charlie, why don't you tell me what happened?"

"Freya came at me with a rifle and an attack dog—" Reid begins, but Seton interrupts him.

"Walk it off," she says.

Reid charges up the road. Seton watches him for a moment. "Is he hurt?"

"Only his pride," I say. "He got taken down by two women . . . or two females. Freya and Ginger. Now you're here to berate him, too."

Freya suppresses a smile, one that feels good to see after these past twenty minutes.

"Keep talking," Seton says to me, "and don't believe for a second you're off the hook for what you did with the podcast. How could you have posted that file without telling me?"

I don't bother with excuses. "My producer's taking it down," I say.

"It's too late," Seton says. "The story's out there and spreading like lice. Ollie from the *Kingston Gazette*'s been hounding us at the station for the last hour. There'll be others soon. But we can deal with your mess later. Let's focus on what happened here."

I cover the events of the last half hour, beginning with emerging from the trail, and ending with pursuing Reid through the forest. "What did I miss?" I ask Freya.

"Only the part where you went commando with the rifle," she says.

"I wasn't the only one," I say.

Seton ignores the bickering as she examines the windshield. "And you didn't see anyone else in the area besides Reid?"

"Gilcrest was at Burkehaven Farm earlier," I say.

Seton's eyes narrow. She's in full cop mode now. "Meaning?" she says.

I wave a hand toward Freya's truck. "Shouldn't the boyfriend be a suspect?"

"That would make *you* a suspect, too," Seton says. "So quit playing detective." She turns her attention to Reid as he joins us again. "Have you cooled off?"

"For now," he says.

A second cruiser speeds up the rutted road, and Maggie, the deputy, gets out. So does Paul, who storms toward us, his face red. He glares at Reid and then me, before pulling Freya in for a protective hug. She crumples against him.

"This road goes right past your place," Seton says to Paul. "Tell me what you saw."

"Nothing out of the ordinary," Paul says. "Charlie was there earlier helping me fix a wall. Duncan Gilcrest came by, too. Then Reid stopped in and asked if I knew where Charlie had gone. I sent him to the trailhead."

Seton barely touches my forearm, a warning to keep my mouth shut. "When did Gilcrest leave the farm?" she asks.

"About an hour ago," Paul says. "Jesus, Freya. I told you not to play those shows at the Landing. We were trying to lie low here."

"I can't hide," Freya says. "I should have learned that by now."

"Thank God nothing worse happened," Paul says.

Seton punches a text into her phone and confers with the deputy, who begins to cordon off the area with yellow crime-scene tape.

"Normally I'd have to do backbends to get the state cops to focus on an incident like this one," Seton says, "but Gilcrest is sending a couple of techs this way. And before anyone asks, Gilcrest was driving his daughter to a softball game. Now he's on his way here."

From the trees, the deputy shouts. Seton joins her and takes more photos, before emerging from the woods with a wad of paper towels smeared with blue. She drops the wad into a plastic bag. "Let me see your hands," she says to Reid.

Paul gives Reid a quick nod, and Seton snaps a photo of both sides of Reid's outstretched hands. "You, too," she says to Paul.

Before she can ask, I hold out my hands, too.

"I need to talk to Freya," Seton says. "The rest of you head to the farm and wait. I'll have questions for you, too."

"I'll stay," I say.

"You won't, though," Seton says.

"I can handle myself, Harold," Freya says. "I'll be at the house soon."

Paul, Reid, and I make our way down the unpaved road toward Burkehaven Farm, the two of them walking together and talking softly, while I trail behind and replay the afternoon's events: the conversations with Seton, Mrs. Haviland, and Paul; the grid we scratched in the dirt; the theories Freya and I put forth; Julian's stupid move with the podcast. And that's not even taking into account the mysteries that keep converging: the fire, my father's reappearance, my mother's murder, now Freya's stalker. Four separate, unrelated incidents. Or maybe not so unrelated.

What if . . . what if . . . what if . . .

Start with the simplest explanation.

Gilcrest was at Burkehaven Farm earlier. And he worked for the security firm in New York when Freya was on *Eternal Flame*. And he lured her here to New Hampshire, far away from her life in Manhattan. He's touched every part of that plotline.

We arrive at the farm and enter Paul's converted barn, an enormous kitchen built from reclaimed materials, with ceilings that soar to the rafters, and a wine cellar in the old hayloft. "Gilcrest and his team should be laser focused on Andrea Haviland," Paul says. "We don't need him distracted with protecting his girlfriend."

Reid raises an eyebrow. "Or maybe Gilcrest will learn something about his girlfriend he doesn't want to know. It's pretty convenient having a stalker return in the middle of a murder investigation, especially when the woman being stalked has been trying to revive her flagging career for decades."

I've had similar thoughts, but they don't jibe with what I observed in the moment. "Freya was terrified," I say.

"Freya's an actress," Reid says. "She'll play any role she needs to, including damsel in distress. What do you bet she's on the phone with her agent right now trying to book a gig?"

"Freya's been *avoiding* the reporters," I say.

Or she mostly has.

"That makes them want to talk to her more," Reid says. "We'll see what the cops dig up. They might find connections they never imagined."

"Watch it, Reid," Paul says, resting his hands on the marble counter. "We need to stick together and keep the story tight and to the point. That's the way you get through these things. I know both of you are upset about . . . about everything. I am, too." He catches Reid's eye. "Let's not go creating links where none exist. The FBI hasn't managed to find Freya's stalker. Why would it be different for the New Hampshire state police?"

"There are a lot fewer suspects than there were in Manhattan," Reid says. "Plus, we have Seton Haviland on the case, and Charlie here, too. He gets off on digging into things that should be left alone. Any new sightings of Dad?"

I ignore the jab. I also haven't forgotten Reid's teenage bedroom, the walls covered with images of Freya he'd torn from magazines, images my mother thought made him feel safe. "What were you doing at the trailhead?" I ask.

"I was looking for you," Reid says. "What were you thinking, releasing that podcast? You've done enough damage. And stay away from Vance Moodey, or anyone else I work with. Your questions are making trouble I don't need. People are talking and calling in debts."

Off in the distance, a police siren sounds as a thought suddenly takes shape: The simplest explanation for what happened to Freya's truck has nothing to do with Duncan Gilcrest or a long-ago connection to a soap opera set. Instead, it's standing right here trying to convince me Freya did this to herself. Reid owns the building where Freya lives and showed more than a passing interest in her years ago; he has access to her condo and its security system, which means he could have easily slipped into the apartment and taken that bottle of nail polish; and we found him hiding in the woods by the truck.

But the question is why. Could the answer lie in the money he owes? Reid and I do need to talk. But not here, not in front of Freya's lawyer, and not with the police on the way. "We'll finish this later," I say to him.

When we're alone.

Chapter Thirty-Four

Outside Paul's farmhouse, the sky has turned gray as storm clouds sweep in over the foothills. Duncan Gilcrest careens up the driveway, sirens blaring. As I step from the converted barn, the cruiser skids to a stop.

"Where the hell is Freya?" Gilcrest asks.

"At the trailhead," Paul says as he emerges from the farmhouse behind me.

Gilcrest comes close enough that I can feel his ragged breath against my face. "Listen close, Charlie," he says. "Maybe you didn't understand you were stepping on my turf before, but you do now." He shoves his finger into my chest. "First we find you at the scene of an arson and you run around town spreading rumors about your long-lost father. Then you decide to post a podcast about an active investigation. Now you're right here in the middle of things when Freya is threatened. Too many coincidences. And if anything happens to Freya, you'll regret the day you were born."

Somehow, I manage to keep my voice steady even as my heart threatens to beat out of my chest. "Save your anger," I say. "Freya doesn't need you to prove how masculine you are right now."

"I don't take advice on my personal life from a man-child."

Thankfully, Reid emerges from the house and heads toward his Audi.

"I have questions for you, Reid," Gilcrest says. "We have you on video filling a gas can at the station in Kingston two days before the fire."

"Backhoes don't run on solar power," Reid says. "And sometimes gas isn't delivered when you need it. If you have other questions, you know where to find me."

He slides into the car and speeds off as Seton's cruiser pulls out of the trees and down the hill toward us. Freya emerges from the passenger's seat and releases Ginger, who's on high alert.

"You okay?" Gilcrest asks, keeping his distance.

Freya puts a hand to the dog's head and doesn't answer. Gilcrest approaches slowly and gently sweeps a stray lock of auburn hair from Freya's eyes. Freya steps into his embrace and lets her head fall to his chest.

Score one for the detective.

I approach them. Ginger growls, and Freya lifts her head, her eyes swollen and bloodshot. "Harold," she says, "thanks for watching out for me. This would have been so much worse if I'd been alone."

"And you can move on now," Gilcrest says to me. "I have this covered."

"Charlie and I are having a tender moment, Duncan," Freya says. "Don't be a jerk."

"I don't know if he can help it," I say.

Freya's eyes flare. "Same goes for you, Charlie," she says, her voice icy. "In fact, the two of you can have at it, but keep me out of whatever's going on between you."

She leaves us in the driveway as Ginger trots after her into the farmhouse.

Gilcrest goes to follow, but Paul stands in the doorway and shakes his head. "Don't make the situation worse," he says, before heading inside.

"Good job there," Gilcrest says to me.

"You're the one who was a territorial asshole," I say. "Freya and I . . . we're friends. Nothing else."

Gilcrest's phone rings. "I need to take this. It's the fucking FBI. When I'm done talking to them, don't be here. If I have questions, I'll find you."

He moves out of earshot as he clicks into the call. I cross to where Seton's watched us from her cruiser. "He's protective," she says.

"You think?"

"But he's not the only one. Stop acting jealous. It makes you look guilty."

"I'm not jealous," I say. "If someone had bothered to tell me Freya had a boyfriend, I wouldn't have gone home with her in the first place. I'm not that kind of person. Besides, I was *with* Freya when she saw what had happened to her truck." I hear the defensiveness in my voice. I close my eyes and will myself to calm down. "If you want to treat me as a suspect, I suppose I could have had a partner," I say.

Such as my brother.

"Freya told me you were at her apartment yesterday, in her bathroom," Seton says.

"Where I could have stolen the nail polish," I say.

"She also said you were the one who proposed meeting up this afternoon."

"I texted her," I say.

"If you had a partner, you could have asked him to lurk in the woods and wait for Freya to head up the trail."

"I could have," I say.

Seton shakes her head. "Except Freya already told me she checked your phone to see if you'd texted anyone, and you hadn't."

"Texts can be deleted," I say.

"I suppose, and we'd be able to recover them, so there's that. But if you want to be a suspect, you're not doing a very good job of it."

"Tell Gilcrest," I say.

Seton rests a hip against her cruiser and watches the detective talking on the phone. "You're an easy target. Gilcrest needs to choose between his ex-wife and Freya, and he keeps messing up the situation so badly he wants someone else to blame."

"You told me Freya was being stalked when we were on the boat a few weeks ago. Maybe Gilcrest believes I convinced myself that if the stalker returned and I was there to offer comfort, Freya would choose me over a rival."

"Or maybe Gilcrest told himself the same thing," Seton says. "As crazy motives go, I don't hate it. Gilcrest did come barreling in to the rescue." She lowers her voice. "I don't know who to trust, so I guess I'm stuck with you."

"You're asking for help?"

"*Haviland and Kilgore*, right?"

"You told me to go with the simplest explanation."

"Indulge me. Go complex. And I'm asking as a cop, not a friend."

"All I know is the threats against Freya mostly stopped after she left *Scene of the Crime*, but they started again when she met Gilcrest on the set of that true-crime pilot. Ask Freya who had the idea for her to leave New York, to leave her life behind, and move to a place where she'd be dependent on one of the few people she knows. Maybe it's love, or maybe Freya really did need a change, or maybe—"

"A controlling prick has been manipulating her."

"You said it, not me."

Seton keeps her eyes on Gilcrest. "Leave the rest to me," she says. "I don't need things to be worse than they already are between you and Gilcrest. Lie low for the next day or so. When this is over, you can play detective all you want. And don't think I've forgotten about that podcast you unleashed on the world."

I rub the bridge of my nose. "My producer posted it without telling me."

"There wouldn't have been a trailer to post if you hadn't come up with the idea in the first place."

"I'm sorry," I say.

"Try starting with the apology next time around," Seton says. "And I guess you're forgiven, though I don't have much of a choice. This town's too small to have enemies."

Freya and Paul emerge from the farmhouse with Ginger in tow. Gilcrest finishes his call. "We can grab some things from the condo before we head to my place," he says to Freya.

"Is your wife there?" she asks.

"Nicole has her own house," Gilcrest says. "You know that. How many times do I need to tell you we're only married on paper. And you can't stay by yourself tonight, safe room or not. Either come to my house or I'll stay with you."

"Paul," Freya says, "you're getting a houseguest for the night. And when can I have my truck?"

"We'll process it for evidence as quickly as we can," Seton says. "Give us till the morning."

"Call me if you finish earlier. As soon as I have the truck, I'm taking off for New York and my beloved co-op. Paul was right—at least in the city there are people wherever you go." Freya looks at Gilcrest. Off in the distance, thunder rumbles. "And plenty of assholes to date."

"Don't do this," Gilcrest says.

"I'll see you around, Duncan. You, too, Harold."

Freya retreats to the farmhouse. Fat raindrops begin to fall from the sky, and the fog that swept in with the storm hems us in. Gilcrest stares after Freya, his expression cold. I imagine he's seeing two versions of his future laid out in front of him—the one he wanted with Freya, and the one he has now. "I just got off the phone with the FBI," he says. "They're sending an agent, and I'll be taking lead on the stalking case. You're free to go, Chief. Take Mr. Kilgore with you so I don't have to look at him anymore."

"*I'll* be taking the lead," Seton says. "Tell your contact at the FBI we'll coordinate from the station."

"Back off, Chief," Gilcrest says.

"You're the one who needs to back off, *Detective*," Seton says. "Get in your car and drive away."

Gilcrest makes a move toward the farmhouse, but Seton blocks his path. "Freya puts up a good front," she says, "but she's scared out of her mind. If you care about her, that's what you should remember."

"I love her," Gilcrest says, the words catching in his throat.

"Then stay as far from the investigation as you can. You aren't objective."

The detective takes another step toward the house. "Duncan," Seton says. "Stop. Be smart."

For a moment, it seems as though Gilcrest might try to force his way past her. He gives one last look toward the front door, then gets in his car and leaves. Seton waits until he's driven out of sight before sending a text. "That was to Paul," she says. "I told him to call me if Gilcrest shows up again. Jealousy makes people batshit crazy."

"This whole situation makes me feel helpless," I say.

"You feel helpless?" Seton says. "Imagine how Freya's felt all these years, and multiply that helpless feeling by infinity. Get out of here, Charlie, and don't come back."

She watches, arms folded, standing guard, as I drive away in the Volvo and rain splatters the windshield.

Nothing will happen to Freya. Not tonight.

◆ ◆ ◆

When I arrive at the turnoff by the bungalow, I pull to the side of the road while the rain pounds at the roof of the Volvo. I delete text messages from Reid, Seton, Paul, and Gilcrest, all expressing some variation of *What did you do?* about the podcast trailer. I delete the messages from Julian, too, where he rationalizes posting the trailer without telling me first. When I come to a message from Mrs. Haviland that reads Call me when you get this, I nearly delete it. Something stops me, though, and I click on her name.

"Charlie," she says, "you made it onto the Hero Board. Vote's split on whether or not to run you out of town."

"Which side are you on?" I ask.

"You can stick around, for now," Mrs. Haviland says. "You asked me to look at the books for Reid Construction. Wait till I tell you what I found. I really should have been a forensic accountant."

After we hang up, I make another call. Thirty minutes later, I park beside a construction site in Finstock, where rain falls in sheets across mounds of earth. Idle equipment dots a recently cleared landscape, and a sign advertises a new outdoor mall and residence. Placards advertise a rival construction firm.

Rain soaks through my clothing as I make my way to where a cement foundation and cinder blocks mark the perimeter of what will eventually be a big-box store.

As I emerge on the other side, footsteps squelch through mud. I swipe wet hair from my eyes and spin to face Vance Moodey.

Chapter Thirty-Five

When I return to the lake, the rain has passed, and the sun casts a golden glow across Idlewood Cove. On the dock, Reid stretches before his evening swim. I leave the Volvo and cross the footbridge, through the blueberry bushes, over the exposed roots and granite, as though I'm in a dream. At the house, I go through the motions of mixing a pitcher of martinis and setting snacks on a tray, before heading toward the dock to join my brother.

It's happy hour.

And we might as well drink.

Reid turns at the sound of my footsteps. He sits on the dock, one leg twisted over the other. "We're celebrating?" he asks. "After today?"

I pour myself a cocktail and balance on the arm of an Adirondack chair, letting the icy gin linger on my tongue. Beside me, the boat tugs at its lines, thumping in rhythm as the wake sloshes at the dock. This is the time before: before words that can't be unsaid are spoken, and theories become reality; before I step through another door.

I strain a second martini and rest it on the edge of the dock. "You shouldn't swim alone."

"So I've heard, though I haven't listened yet." Reid takes a tiny sip of the cocktail. "I'll have the rest when I'm done."

"Did you know about Vance Moodey?" I ask. "About him and Jane?"

"Mom didn't tell me," Reid says, moving from his stretch into a set of push-ups. "She thought it was her secret, though they weren't that great at hiding. All the guys on the crew knew."

The sun has begun to dip toward the foothills, its light filtering through the trees. In my mind, I go over the earlier phone call with Mrs. Haviland, trying to make sense of what she told me. "I found a ledger," she said, "with four payments from Vance Moodey to Reid Construction. The payments aren't small."

"Vance is a supplier," I responded. "Wouldn't money usually go the other way?"

"That's what caught my attention," Mrs. Haviland said. "The payments are on a lease in Finstock. Vance may have invested in the project."

Now, before I lose my nerve, I say, "The first time I met Vance, I was with Jane. He told her she'd have to deal with him eventually. I assumed she owed him money, so that day I overheard you and Vance out by the firepit, I thought you were talking about an overdue invoice, nothing more."

Reid's movement catches mid-push-up, if only for a second. "Mom hated when you called her Jane."

"Okay, Mom, then. But it turns out," I continue, "that if you run the only lumber supplier in the region and live in a trailer, you can save some bank. Vance thought he'd impress Mom by helping you out with a lucrative new project. I bet he thought he'd get a good return, too. Is that what the lease in Finstock was supposed to be? A good investment?"

"Investments are always risky," Reid says.

"As long as the investments actually exist," I say. "You were supposed to secure a lease for that outdoor mall. Vance wrote you a check to get in on the deal, but you lost the bid, and you never returned Vance's money."

Reid stands. "Is this for your podcast? Where's the mic? Let me be sure you capture this: You're full of shit. You're trying to stir up drama where none exists. Vance was the one who came to me. He thought he could impress Mom by throwing money around. I told him to go to hell."

"But where's Vance's money?" I ask. "He gave you over two hundred grand. Did you think he wouldn't find out? When I finish going through the firm's accounts, what else will I find? How leveraged is the company?" A thought forms at the back of my mind, one that connects two strands of this story. The more I try to push the thought away, the more it takes shape. "Did Mom know what you'd done?"

"What if she did?"

"I met Vance at the mall construction site this afternoon," I say. "He confirmed that Jane . . . that *Mom* planned to put Idlewood into conservation, that she was having Paul draw up papers. Did you know *Mom* was meeting Andrea Haviland that morning?"

"Mom was meeting Andrea to tell her to fuck the hell off, and Andrea hit her in the head and burned down the house. That's what happened. And if Andrea had minded her own business, that spec house would have been finished a month ago, and I wouldn't be in the mess I'm in now."

I keep my voice steady. "I don't think so," I say. "I think Mom saw how you were managing the firm. She knew you owed Vance, and that's why she was so standoffish with him when she saw him at Burkehaven."

"There's nothing wrong with the way I manage the firm," Reid says.

"Except you owe money to Vance Moodey and God knows who else, and those condos on the harbor have to be rebuilt."

"There are some issues with the foundation and the septic system. I can manage it."

I count off on my fingers. "You owe money you don't have. Mom didn't trust you anymore, and she said as much that night we played cards." I pause. "*It's my thirty grand.* She told me she'd never let Idlewood be developed, but you were trying to convince her to sell."

Reid closes his eyes. "Move on with your life, Charlie," he says, his voice softer this time. "The rest of us have."

We haven't, though. We've spent twenty-five years pretending our whole lives didn't change in an instant, and I've spent the last few weeks using a podcast as an excuse to make people talk to me. "Mom's dead," I say, "and Dad's in hiding."

"Dad isn't in hiding," Reid says. "He died after trying to kill both of us, and he got exactly what he deserved. Imagine what it was like for me that night. Imagine having the man who cared for you for your entire life come at you with a knife stained with your own mother's blood. Imagine lying in a boat on a cold night watching paper lanterns floating in the sky while trying to protect your baby brother and hoping to be rescued from a nightmare. I thought Mom was in the woods dying in a pool of her own blood and that we'd be joining her soon. And now, imagine twenty-five years later, having your brother question what happened to you as though it was his to discover. I saved you that night, Charlie. I was a fucking hero."

Reid is the only one left who can tell the story of what happened on the island the night Isaac Haviland died.

"What did Mr. Haviland say?" I ask. "Right before Dad stabbed him?"

"How would I know?"

"It was in the papers. The police reports, too. You told the detectives he called Mom *my love*."

"Then that's what he said. She was having an affair with him."

"But how could you have heard him? You were on the porch. Mom, Dad, and Mr. Haviland were by the cars."

"Maybe I didn't hear him," Reid says. "Or I made it up. Or Mom told me later on, and I reported it to the police as though I'd heard it myself. I was twelve years old, and didn't understand how important it was to stick to the facts."

"Mom hated what Paul was doing to Burkehaven," I say. "And today, you were lurking by Freya's truck. You used to have photos of her posted all over your bedroom walls."

"When I was a teenager trying to convince my mother I was straight," Reid says.

Reid seems to have an answer ready for whatever I throw at him. "Fine, maybe that's true," I say. "But today, by the trailhead, were you trying to distract Gilcrest from the homicide investigation? Is that why you did that to Freya's truck?"

"What, exactly, was I distracting him from?" Reid asks. When I don't answer, he says, "Okay, tell me if I'm getting this right: I lied about what happened to Isaac Haviland and I *also* killed my own mother, to . . . what? Cover up a two-hundred-thousand-dollar debt? In my world, two hundred grand is pocket change."

Pocket change that selling a lake house would provide.

Reid comes at me. I brace myself, but he grips me by the shoulders and looks me in the eyes. "I didn't kill Mom," he says, "and no matter how mad you are, you don't get to say I'm a murderer so you can get a little attention with some podcast no one will listen to. Unlike you, I live in a world where bills come in, and people need things from me, and there are expectations."

Reid strips off his T-shirt and shorts, then swings his arms back and forth as he moves to the edge of the dock. "This house costs tens of thousands of dollars a year in taxes and maintenance," he says. "Way more than you can afford, Charlie. If you want to buy me out, come up with the cash, because I have plenty of others lining up with offers." He fits a red swimming cap over his blond hair and adjusts his goggles. "Tonight, when you're lying in bed feeling awful about yourself, know that I love you and forgive you for every terrible thing you said to me, but I don't want to see you right now. Also, I have an airtight alibi for the time Mom was killed. Do you?"

He dives into the water and takes off across the cove. I could accept what's been told to me: My father killed Isaac Haviland; my mother dragged herself through the woods to save her children; my brother fled with me in a rickety old rowboat and floated offshore until a handsome, young police officer arrived to rescue us. And years later, a widow exacted revenge. That's a story to remember.

But I don't believe it.

Chapter Thirty-Six

As Reid swims across the cove, I pull Seton's name up on my phone. I could text her. I could tell her what happened tonight, what Reid and I said to each other. She's a friend. Someone I trust. But she's also a cop, and not one who'd ignore accusations hurled from one brother to another, no matter how wild.

I'll keep what was said to myself.

For now.

I nearly put the phone away. Instead, I find Freya's text from earlier. I wish she were here right now, that I could test this latest plot twist in the hope that she'd poke enough holes in it to prove me wrong. I could use a friend, I type.

The tip of my finger hovers over send, but I delete the message. As Seton said earlier, Freya's scared out of her mind, and she needs time to be on her own.

In the cove, Reid reaches the opposite shore. He turns and makes his way back, and when he touches in, he pushes away from the dock. "I told you I didn't want to see you," he says, lifting his goggles onto his forehead.

"And I told you not to swim alone."

"Well, I'm finished," he says.

I top off his martini glass. "Have a drink."

"I'm not doing this, Charlie," he says. "Not tonight. I'm too angry. Give me some space and we can talk tomorrow."

I start to argue but stop myself. Reid won't say more, not tonight. The best strategy is to let him stew in his anger until later. I leave him in the water and cross the footbridge, following the path along the shore until I emerge on Burkehaven Cove, where it takes a moment to realize I'm not alone. My aunt Hadley sits at the end of the dock, her feet dangling in the water. "Returning to the scene of the crime?" she asks as I approach.

"I could say the same of you."

She pats the boards. "Join me. The bass are out. They're giving me a pedicure."

I kick off my shoes and settle in beside her, letting my bare feet dangle in the cool water. It seems like weeks ago that Freya found me in this same spot, but it was only yesterday.

"I expected to see you for happy hour tonight," I say.

"Oh, I was there," Hadley says. "I heard you and Reid talking on the dock."

"More like fighting. How much of it did you catch?"

"Enough. Sounds like he wants to sell Idlewood."

"And I sort of implied he killed Jane."

Hadley puts a hand to her mouth to suppress a laugh. "Oof! Just a friendly little conversation between loving brothers, right? Is that what you want to tell the world?"

"I don't know that I want to tell it to the *world*," I say. "It feels as though I'm betraying everyone I know. But Reid's in trouble. He owes money, and my guess is I've only found a small part of it."

"Talk it through with me," Hadley says. "Maybe you'll find the story you do want to tell for the podcast. Or for yourself."

I'm not sure what I want to do with the podcast anymore, but Hadley's been the most willing participant so far. I lay my phone between us. The mic will capture the water lapping at the pilings, and our feet dangling in the water. If Julian ever hears this, he'll appreciate the ambience.

"You and me," Hadley says. "We make our own way when others dismiss us."

"No one's ever dismissed you," I say. "You do whatever you want."

"Not always," Hadley says. "My father—your grandfather—doted on Jane, on your mother, watching what she did, shaping her into a little version of himself. It made me feel invisible. That's why I left for California. It's how I got to become my own person, and not someone my father wanted me to be."

I suppose we do have more in common than I realized. My mother kept Reid close while packing me off, first to boarding school, then into the world. "I wish I felt as fully formed as you," I say.

"You're a lump of clay, waiting to be shaped," Hadley says. "But *you* get to choose the shape. My father, he wanted to ignore me and control me at the same time. He couldn't stand that I'd left, that I didn't hang on his every word."

"Is that why he cut you out of the will?" I ask.

Hadley rolls her eyes. "He and I got into the stupidest fight. I was visiting Idlewood for a few weeks the summer before I started my residency and found out my father had paid Jane's student loans, but not mine. He claimed it was because she went to a state school, and I decided to move away, but it was really because I kept leaving and she didn't. And I wasn't angry about the loans—I was mad because my father favored Jane over me. But I told him I never wanted to speak to him again. He went to a lawyer about the will as soon as I left town. Honestly, once he cooled off, I bet he'd have changed everything back to the way it had been. But he died before he could."

"You haven't seemed to mind," I say.

"I cared more than I let on, and I took it out on Jane in ways I never should have. Hurtful, selfish ways." Hadley lifts her feet out of the water and flexes her toes. "But," she says, her expression brightening, "in retrospect, it was a gift. My father cast me off and made me fend for myself. Jane could only be who he wanted her to be, a good girl who spent her life watching over the homestead and running the family business. I've been all over and made friends everywhere. And I've loved every minute of it."

"How long did it take you to get there?" I ask. "To forgive?"

Hadley laughs. "I talk a good game. I never fully got to a place of forgiveness. Idlewood was this thing sitting between Jane and me, and it would have been kind of me to release her from any guilt. I owed her that."

My phone beeps from where it lies on the dock between us. A text from Freya lights up the screen. Sorry for how things went down today, she writes. The cops finished with my truck sooner than expected. I'm headed to New York. Tonight. I'll see you around, Harold.

"Freya's leaving," I say.

"Where's she off to?"

"New York. For good."

"That's a surprise. When I took her out on the boat earlier, she seemed done with New York, with TV, with having to look a certain way all the time. I thought she wanted to give it a go up here."

I tap, I'll see you around, into the phone, then stare at the screen. I'm more disappointed than is warranted from a one-night stand with someone twice my age. "Reid used to have photos of Freya in his bedroom," I say.

"I remember that," Hadley says.

"I heard you talking to my mother once. She said the photos made Reid feel safe."

"I hope they worked," Hadley says, swinging around and taking in the burned-out shell on the shore. "So much for Paul's castle. Reid will need to find someone else willing to dole out the cash. As for you, Charlie, no matter how exciting Freya may seem, she wasn't right."

I turn on my side, my head propped on a fist. "Freya and I hooked up, nothing more. But don't I get to decide what's right for me?"

"You do," Hadley says. "And that's something I need to remember, even though I am most certainly right."

The last rays of evening sun shine on her face, and for a moment I can picture Hadley here, at Burkehaven, decades ago. "Freya's father thought you were a bad influence," I say.

"I bet he did. I showed Freya how the world worked."

"Do you remember the last time the two of you talked? When you were teenagers? It was the summer after your first year in college. You were dating my father."

Hadley glances toward my phone as though she wants to jump through the lines and strangle Freya. "Mark and I didn't date," she says. "We were friends. But I did have a mad crush on him. He was all I could think about that summer. We'd go out in the boat, and bike around town, and hike the foothills. I returned to California for my sophomore year at Berkeley intending to transfer to Kingston State, but distance and the California sun worked their magic, and I forgot the plan. The next thing I heard was that Jane and Mark had started dating. They got married the year I graduated from undergrad. I had an internship in Nairobi and couldn't make the wedding. Reid arrived seven months later." Hadley stands and steps into her shoes. "And before you ask," she says, "losing your father was another disappointment that transformed into a gift. Imagine my life living in Hero. It's a beautiful town, but this wasn't the place for me."

"I shouldn't have asked about him," I say.

"You should have, though. It's part of your story. Keep asking. Keep pushing until you find that story you want to tell." Hadley nods at the phone. "It's good to have a passion. Don't let anyone stop you. Ever."

Her footsteps retreat down the dock and along the shore as the light fades from gray to black and the first of the evening's bats flits across the sky. In the distance, a coyote howls into the night, as though going in for the kill.

Chapter Thirty-Seven

A full moon rises over the lake as I save the conversation with Hadley to my phone. I'm not sure which parts of this story I'll share with the world, but I've invested too much at this point to walk away. And Hadley's right: It's good to have a passion.

I start a new recording. "Tonight, my aunt talked about turning disappointment into opportunity, though she admitted she had the benefit of hindsight in her favor. I wish I had that hindsight right now. I don't know what to do about my brother. Whether he's guilty of what I accused him of tonight, he's definitely guilty of mismanagement, probably fraud. Maybe we can work those things out between us. Maybe we'll have to sell Idlewood, after all." I pause, surprised when the next words catch in my throat. "Freya Faith left for New York. I'll miss her. Maybe I cared about her more than I wanted to admit. I appreciated having someone to bounce ideas off of, someone who had nothing invested in what's happened to my family. I enjoyed listening to her sing and watching her smoke. I got off on learning how to shoot a rifle."

Something in the water brushes along my foot. I've been coming to the lake long enough to know it's a sunfish or a bass, but I pull my feet out, let them dangle over the surface, and imagine Hadley in her dorm room in California all those years ago, possibly still weighing a transfer to Kingston State. I wonder if it was my mother who called to tell Hadley the happy news about the pending marriage, or what my mother knew or suspected about Hadley's relationship with my father, and whether she cared.

"Being left behind leaves a hole," I say into the phone, "and I barely knew Freya. How did my aunt Hadley feel when she heard my father had started dating my mother, that they were getting married and having a child? How long did the disappointment—the resentment—linger?"

I remember Freya drawing a line in the dirt connecting Hadley's name to my father's. Two and a half decades ago, my father and Isaac Haviland were friends, and then they weren't, and then one of them lay in a pool of his own blood, and the other fled. Now, a house burns. And my mother's dead. Paul and Reid and Andrea Haviland straddle both stories. Duncan Gilcrest, too. Hadley was in Kosovo, dancing with the Swiss ambassador. But she was here, too, on the lake, even in her absence. That can't be the story she wants me to tell.

"Has Hadley ever truly let those feelings of resentment go?"

I stop the recording, slip my shoes on, and make the return journey through the woods. As I emerge into Idlewood Cove, the full moon reflects off the inky water. By now, my eyes have adjusted to the darkness, and I swear I catch movement on the dock even though Reid finished his swim a while ago. I dread returning to the cabin. As with Hadley and my mother, Idlewood now sits between Reid and me, a burden we'll have to face together.

A single light from the cabin shines through the dark. In the water, something floats on the surface, but before I can take it in, a noise begins from the dock, low at first, reverberating across the cove as it rises to an anguished wail.

My feet begin to move on their own, picking up pace as I shout Reid's name. I sprint through the parking area and across the footbridge. Overhead, the trees close in, blocking any moonlight. I slam into something solid and fall back, landing hard. I scramble onto all fours, my heart pounding.

Heavy breathing fills the darkness.

"Who's there?" I say.

I touch the screen of my phone. In the sudden light, a bearded face leans over me. It's my father. His face is scratched, his glasses askew, his clothing sopping wet. This is no figment of my imagination. "I tried," he says. "I should have seen this. I should have known."

Off in the distance, a police siren sounds as the screen goes dark.

"What did you do?" I ask, tapping the screen again.

This time, my father's gone, his footsteps retreating through the trees.

The phone rings and Seton's name flashes across the screen. "Are you coming for him?" I say.

"Where are you?" Seton asks.

"At Idlewood. By the dock. My father was here. He's hiding in the woods."

"Stay exactly where you are," Seton says. "Don't let Reid know I'm coming, Charlie. I need to talk to him before he makes things worse for himself."

The call disconnects. I shove the phone into my pocket and face the cottage. My father was here. He's alive, and my guess is that Reid has known all along.

"Seton's coming," I shout toward the house. "I need the truth, Reid."

And I need it before the police arrive, before the questioning begins, before Paul steps in to play lawyer and Reid stops talking to protect himself.

But I can buy time.

"Come to the dock," I shout, running to the boat and tearing at the cover.

We'll retreat onto the lake. Seton will need to bring in the police boat or circle the lake in the helicopter until she narrows in on us with the floodlight. By then, I'll have asked my questions, and I hope Reid will have answered.

I release the lines and jump into the hull. The boat drifts from the dock as Seton's cruiser skids to a stop on the shore, her lights flashing. She runs across the footbridge and edges onto the dock, her hand poised over her Taser. "Where's Reid?" she asks. "He needs to tell me where he was this afternoon."

"My father was here," I say.

"Come to the dock, Charlie. Get out of the boat and tell me what you saw."

"Give me ten minutes," I say. "That's all. Leave and come back, and Reid and I will be here."

"I can't do that. Gilcrest is on his way. Bring the boat to the dock before he arrives. Please. He can't see you out there."

I search the darkened shoreline for any sign of my brother or father. I feel shaky as I see myself through Seton's eyes, the panic, the desperation. "I don't know what to do," I say.

Seton comes to the very edge of the dock and reaches across the water toward me. "Yes, you do," she says. "This is easy. Toss me a line. That's the *only* decision you need to make. I'll tie off the boat, and we'll go up to the house, where you can tell us what you know."

I turn away from her, facing the lake.

"It's only us," Seton says, "but it won't be for much longer. Right now, as far as I'm concerned, none of this happened. When Gilcrest gets here, that won't be an option anymore."

Out in the channel, a boat passes, its red and green combination lights illuminated against the dark. Seconds later, its wake moves across the still water. Something ripples on the darkened surface, something that shouldn't be there, something that chills me to the bone.

I pull at the laces on my boots.

"Don't move, Charlie," Seton says. "I mean it."

I kick the boots into the boat, tear at my fleece, and struggle to pull off my jeans before giving up and flinging myself over the bow. As Seton shouts into her radio for backup, my head submerges beneath the surface, and the cold of the water expels oxygen from my lungs. I come up for air and pull forward, toward the center of the cove.

Maybe I'm not too late.

My hand brushes something cold and slick. I flail, as Reid's lifeless eyes stare up at the moonlit sky.

Chapter Thirty-Eight

I shiver on Idlewood's back porch, wrapped in a blanket, somehow having managed to change out of my wet clothing. I stare into the night, feeling nothing but remorse for the final, angry words Reid and I hurled at each other the last time we spoke. The last time we'll ever speak.

An hour has passed, maybe two, since I found my brother's body, since Seton threw herself into the lake and surfaced beside me while a second cruiser skidded to a stop in the parking area.

"Oh God," Seton cried out when she saw Reid. "In the water!" she shouted toward shore. "Call an ambulance. Now!"

I struggled to stay afloat as I cradled Reid in my arms. "We fought," I said, the words forming on their own. "I was so angry."

Seton grabbed my face and forced me to look her in the eyes. "Shut up," she said. "I'm a cop. Not another word."

Now I can't get images out of my mind, of Reid's lifeless eyes, of struggling with Seton to drag his body through the water to the shore. There, Seton and the deputy, Maggie, began administering CPR, though I knew it was futile. Hadley arrived soon after, drawn by the police cruisers speeding past the bungalow. She took over compressions while I watched, my body drained of emotion. When Gilcrest arrived on the scene, he stood over Reid, his face ashen.

Eventually, Hadley asked for the time.

"9:52," Seton said.

Hadley stopped compressions. "Take note," she said. "Time of death."

"No, no, no," I heard myself say. "Keep going."

"It's over, Charlie," Hadley said to me, slumping onto her heels. "He's gone. His body's already cooling. He's been dead for a while, but the ME will need to determine when."

"And how," Gilcrest said. "The why, that's up to me to determine."

"I told him not to swim alone," I said, as Seton put both hands on the side of my face and barely shook her head.

"Chief," Gilcrest said, "you threw me off the stalking case earlier. Let me return the favor. Leave the crime scene. Maggie and I can manage till the rest of the team get here. This is an unattended death, so it's the state's jurisdiction anyway."

"I'll help set up the perimeter," Seton said.

"The less you involve yourself, Haviland," Gilcrest said, "the better it will be for all of us, including Charlie. The last thing he needs is rumors about a compromised investigation following him for the rest of his life. Go home, get out of those wet clothes, and be grateful you won't be up all night with the rest of us."

"I wish," Seton said. "If you need Maggie, I'll have to cover her shift. I'll be on all night."

After Seton left, Maggie took my sodden clothes. My phone, too, though I doubted it would work after sitting in the pocket of my jeans while I treaded water. The state police will recover the audio recordings stored safely in the cloud. Maybe something I recorded will lead them to solving this case, the only thing I care about.

Down by the dock, Hadley confers with the medical examiner while a team of state cops sets up flood lamps and fans out across the island to begin a grid search.

In the dark, someone taps on the screen door, and the hinges creak. "Mind some company?" Gilcrest asks, stepping onto the porch before

I can respond. His boots thump across the wooden planks until he looms over me. "I'm sorry for your loss," he adds. "Truly. But I need to ask some questions. Do you want anything before we get started? Coffee? Water?"

"I know where things are," I say.

Gilcrest pulls up a ladder-back chair and sits beside me. "Hit the high points and we can fill in the rest tomorrow, after you've gotten some sleep."

"High points? Does finding my brother's dead body in the lake count?"

"Start with the last time you saw him alive. What time was it?"

I picture Reid tucking his hair into his swim cap and hear him telling me he loved me, despite what I'd said. "It was before dark," I say.

"How much before dark?"

"The sun was on the horizon."

"Okay, that'll give us a range," Gilcrest says. "Did you send a text? Make a call? Anything we can use to mark the time?"

"My phone got ruined in the water. And your team has it anyway."

"We'll see what we can recover." Gilcrest shows me a photo on his own phone of the pitcher of martinis I brought to the dock sitting next to an evidence marker. "Was Reid drinking before he went in the water?"

"I mixed the drinks," I say. "Reid swam every evening. Sometimes the rest of us got started with happy hour. When he finished, he'd join us."

"Who's 'us'?"

"It used to be my mother," I say, "and Hadley, when she's in town. Paul Burke, too. But I was the only one there tonight. I was trying to get things back to normal. Reid had a sip, no more. I left and walked over to Burkehaven, where I found my aunt. There's a recording on my phone of our conversation that should have a time stamp. The last time I saw Reid alive was five or ten minutes before that recording begins."

"Anything on those recordings you should tell me about?"

I glance up. "Hadley and I talked about Freya, who texted to tell me she'd left for New York. I assume you already knew."

Gilcrest's expression falters, if only for a split second. He stands and strides toward the door as if to leave, and then turns, spinning the wooden chair around, the ladder-back creating a barrier between us. "You made a whole pitcher of martinis and brought two glasses, and then left the pitcher behind. Do you usually let your brother swim by himself?"

Behind me, someone steps onto the porch from inside the house. Hadley says, "We've been telling Reid not to swim alone for thirty-seven years, practically since the day he was born. He didn't listen."

"I shouldn't have left," I say.

"Do you mind if I talk to Charlie in private?" Gilcrest says to Hadley, but my aunt comes to my side and slides onto the arm of the chair.

"I'll stay," she says. "And Charlie, you should know Reid had a contusion on the back of his skull. The ME will do the autopsy, but my guess is he may not have drowned, and even if he did, the wound was a contributing factor."

Blunt-force trauma, like my mother.

"Charlie," Gilcrest says, "you were on the phone with Chief Haviland before you found the body. Does she often call you when she's on duty? She was responding to a call to your house. And your brother was dead in the lake."

Hadley puts a hand of warning to my arm, but I speak anyway. "Seton called *me*. She asked where Reid was."

"And what happened next?" Gilcrest asks.

"My father killed Reid," I say as Hadley's fingernails dig into my skin. "He was here."

"Your father," Gilcrest says. "How convenient."

"Charlie," Hadley says, "you need a lawyer."

"First your father shows up when your mother dies," Gilcrest says, "then again, when your brother dies."

Hadley stands. "Lawyer," she says. "Lawyer, lawyer, lawyer."

But Gilcrest continues. "Paul told me you and Reid got into an argument about your mother's estate at his house. Did you fight a lot with your brother? Did you fight tonight? Is that why you left without finishing your drinks?"

"Reid and I fight all the time," I say. "And we make up until it happens again."

"Except there won't be a next time, will there? Your mother's dead, and your brother's dead, and you, Charlie Kilgore, have the most compelling and clear-cut motive. Greed. You own this island now, free and clear. How much is your family's construction firm worth? From living in a shared Somerville apartment to becoming a millionaire in two easy murders—that's the story you should tell for your podcast." Gilcrest shoves the wooden chair aside. He comes at me, the corner of his eye twitching. "You haven't asked why the chief came to your house in the first place."

I haven't asked because I'm pretty certain I already know. Seton came to arrest Reid.

"We have Reid on video," Gilcrest says. "He was in Freya's condo. He had access to the building's security system and turned it off. But here's the thing, Charlie. Freya had a hidden camera set up, and it caught Reid breaking into the apartment, and my bet is you're the one who asked him to do it."

"Why would I do that?" I ask.

"Because you wanted Freya to turn to you."

"Listen," I say, "you're the one who couldn't break things off with your wife, so if you need someone to blame for screwing up your personal life, look in the mirror. Freya's a good friend. Nothing more."

"Lawyer," Hadley says, her voice soft but firm.

"You're lucky your aunt's here," Gilcrest says. "Between her, the chief, Andrea Haviland, and even Freya, you seem to have an entire army of women ready to go into battle for you."

Detective Stamoran appears at the screen door. "What the hell are you doing, Gilcrest?" he says, placing himself between Gilcrest and me, then moving the detective against the wall. Gilcrest shoves him, but Stamoran stands his ground.

"You'll be surprised, Charlie," Gilcrest says, "how many allies you lose once the murder charges hit."

"Leave," Stamoran says to him. "Now."

Gilcrest closes his eyes, and I can almost hear him counting to ten. He steps into the night, slamming the screen door behind him.

"We're done here," Hadley says. "If you need us, we'll be at the bungalow."

Stamoran holds his hands out, palms open. "Let's take the temperature down," he says. "Did you see anyone by the lake, Charlie? Or hear something out of the ordinary? Whatever you tell us could be helpful."

Hadley smiles. "Lawyer," she says.

"Got it," Stamoran says. "I'll get someone to follow you home."

"We know the way," Hadley says. "We've done it thousands of times."

"Not when there's a murderer on the loose," Stamoran says. "And lock the doors tonight. I'll feel better when I find you safe and sound in the morning, because I have questions for both of you. And your lawyer."

Chapter Thirty-Nine

"I didn't kill Reid," I say to Hadley, as soon as the deputy leaves us at the bungalow. "No matter what Gilcrest believes. And I didn't have anything to do with what happened to Freya's truck, either. And I did see my father by the dock."

Hadley slips an arm through mine and leads me into the kitchen. "You were with me at Burkehaven. Don't forget that. Where's the opportunity?"

Only that I was alone with my brother on the dock, and Hadley herself heard us fighting, which, if I'm not mistaken, I admitted to in the audio recording that's sitting on my phone waiting for the police to dissect. I could easily have gulped down a martini, bashed my brother in the head, and calmly retreated from the scene of the crime. "I was only with you for part of the evening," I say.

Hadley puts on the kettle. "Well, the cops'll get there on their own. No need to lead them there by the nose. Besides, we don't know what happened to Reid. That's for the coroner to determine. Yes, there was a contusion, but maybe he dove off one of the rocks in the cove and hit his head. Maybe a boat ran him over. If your father has something to do with what happened to Reid or Jane, let the police find him."

"They haven't found him for twenty-five years."

"Something tells me your father's tired of hiding."

"That makes it sound like you've talked to him."

"I haven't, though you only have my word for it." Hadley roots around in a cupboard until she comes up with a box of tea bags. "Are you sad about Reid?"

I should have deep and profound feelings right now, but I've been pushing something down for so long, something I haven't named, and without finding that name, I'm not sure I can reach what's on the other side or be whole. "None of this makes sense," I say. "I'm panicked because I don't trust Gilcrest, and I'm confused. I should be sad, too."

The kettle whistles. Hadley turns off the gas and pours water over the tea bags. "Peel all that away. What's there?"

Images flood my mind: my father in a crowd; Reid beside my bed reading a picture book; Paul at a Yankees game; Mrs. Haviland buying ice cream; Hadley regaling me with stories of seeing the world; my mother paddling beside Reid, their heads bent together as though no one else in the world mattered. Brief flashes of happiness where I'm on the outside, looking in. Beneath it all, I find a deep, profound sadness. "I'm lonely," I say.

Hadley starts to speak and looks down. She takes a long sip of her tea and swallows loudly. "I should have been around more," she says. "I should have watched out for you."

"I don't know what you could have done."

"More than I did," Hadley says.

I rub the bridge of my nose. "I keep searching for answers, but all I get are more questions."

"And more tragedy," Hadley says. "One question shatters into a thousand new ones, and each time, you scramble to find answers. But keep asking, and don't hold back to protect anyone. Certainly not the dead. Reid did what he did."

I picture Freya's windshield covered in angry letters and Reid cowering by the brook while Freya stood over him with the rifle. I see his bedroom walls covered with images of her. "The police have video of Reid in Freya's apartment," I say. "If he threatened Freya, what else did he do?"

"I don't know what Reid was capable of," Hadley says.

I set my mug down and put a hand on her arm. "What aren't you telling me?"

Hadley won't meet my eyes. Eventually she says, "All I know is that after Isaac Haviland died, I told your mother Reid should go to a therapist. Jane shut the conversation down before it began." My aunt glances up. "She told me Reid saw Isaac as a threat to your family. She also said she worried what Reid might say to a therapist, that Reid would want to own his choices."

A child kills to protect a parent; a parent lies to protect the child. That story was told at least once a season on *Scene of the Crime*. It's the kind of secret a parent would go to the grave to protect, the kind that could make a second child spend his entire life feeling as though he's come in halfway through a conversation, as though he's not quite part of a family.

I stop and try to imagine the world that existed a few seconds ago, the one where none of this was true, but I can't. It's as though a part of me has known what happened all along. "You think Reid killed Isaac Haviland," I say, my voice sounding as if it's coming from somewhere else, from *someone* else.

"I'm telling you what Jane told me," Hadley says, "and now you have a thousand new questions."

Actually, something that hasn't made sense to me now does. Instead of walking through a door to find something new, it's as though I've returned to the night when everything changed and can see it again for the first time. "For my whole life," I say, "I've felt as if what happened on the lake bonded Mom and Reid in a way that kept me on the outside. I thought it was why she sent me to boarding school and kept Reid so close. But maybe—"

"Maybe," Hadley says, "Jane was keeping you from your brother and protecting you all along."

◆ ◆ ◆

I lie in bed, unable to sleep, rehashing the conversation with Hadley, until I get up and cross to a bookshelf. I haven't slept in the bungalow since the holidays, when I came for a weekend visit. Now I scan the spines of the books on the shelf until I come to the old thesaurus and retrieve the photo of my father I hid there years ago.

It's a clipping from a newspaper, the color faded, the edges yellowed, a moment in time. When I've looked at the image before, I've mostly noticed myself in my father's eyes, in his floppy hair, in his angular face. The image is dated from the October before Isaac's death. My father stands against the lake, smiling, a riot of autumn leaves erupting along the shore behind him. The photo must have been cropped from something larger, because this time I note the disembodied limbs and shoulders of others around him and wonder who else might have been with him that day. Could it have been the entire gang of six, Hadley and my mother, Paul and Isaac, Andrea and my father, doing everything together?

In the next few months, my mother would begin an affair with Isaac, and soon after that, Isaac would be dead. Years later, my father would slam into me in the dark while his son's cold body floated in the lake, but on this day, none of that could have seemed possible. They were friends, together, maybe for the last time.

I slip the photo into the thesaurus and place it on the shelf. In bed, I punch at the pillow and force myself to return to earlier this evening, to the sound of Reid stroking through the water, to the burn of gin at the back of my throat, to the warmth of the sun on my face. *I love you and forgive you for every terrible thing you said to me,* Reid said. *But I don't want to see you right now.*

I imagine staying on the dock, waiting until he lifted himself out of the water and tucked his goggles into the side of his suit. "Can we start over?" I ask.

"Give it a try," Reid says, still breathing heavily from his swim.

I could have asked about his life away from Idlewood, his friends in Boston, those trips all over the world he documents online. I could have told him about Seton, that we were both too scared to make the next move because we didn't want to make a mistake. I could have confessed that I didn't want to lose Idlewood because it would eliminate the one link between us. Without it, I feared we'd drift apart. I could have asked why we began each summer with a pot of Bolognese.

"Tell me where you were the morning Jane died," I say. "Tell me why there's no way you could have killed her."

"That would be too easy," Reid says. "And you already know the answer."

I jolt awake, grasping at Reid's words from the dream, afraid I might lose them for good.

I swing out of bed and instinctively reach for my phone before remembering that it's with the police. I slip on my shoes, reviewing the conversation with Reid on the dock, and then careening to my visits to the Landing these last few weeks. More pieces snap into place, and if they mean what I think they mean, I got part of the story wrong—the most important part. And with it, the other threads unravel, too.

◆ ◆ ◆

Downtown Hero is dark except for that single streetlamp Freya and I kissed beneath two weeks ago. I park the yellow Volvo on the street outside the Landing and run up a set of stairs to the apartments above. I pound at a door until a light comes on and footsteps patter my way.

"I'd given up hope," Blancy says as he opens the door, shirtless and toned in a pair of boxer briefs, his white hair standing on end. "Oh," he says. "Charlie. Did Reid send you?"

Every time I've seen Blancy this summer, he's asked after Reid. Even this morning, when I visited Mrs. Haviland, Blancy told me to ask Reid to give him a call, that he owed him.

"Reid was with you the other night," I say.

"You'll have to be more specific," Blancy says. "Reid's here a lot of nights. Or he was. But if he's not into it anymore, he can tell me himself."

"He was in your apartment when the fire started at Burkehaven."

"What about it?" Blancy says.

"The two of you," I say. "You're dating."

"*Dating* might be pushing it, but if you want the details, you should ask your brother. What was going on at your place tonight, anyway? Why all the cops?"

By morning, Blancy will know Reid's dead. Right now, I need his focus. "It was nothing," I say.

"If it was nothing, I'll say good night. I'm freezing."

Blancy moves to shut the door, but I block it with my knee. "The night of the fire, did Reid leave? Even for a little bit?"

"Not till we heard the fire engines heading toward Burkehaven. Then he took off, and I've barely seen him since."

"Did you tell anyone else he was here?" I ask.

"No one's asked," Blancy says, folding his arms over his slim chest. "Reid and I have had a thing since high school. Only when he's here in the summer and not off with his fancy friends. It isn't serious. He knows to come by, and that my door's usually open. Remind him when you see him. It gets lonely in this apartment. Besides, your brother's sexy as hell. You can tell him I said that, too."

I'm halfway down the stairs before Blancy calls after me. "I thought you'd come about my text. I sent you one earlier tonight."

"I lost my phone."

"Ponytail and glasses was here earlier, lurking by the dumpster when I took out the trash. Scared the shit out of me. I told him you've been looking for him."

"He didn't come into the bar?" I ask.

Blancy shakes his head.

"Where was Mrs. Haviland?"

"Andrea?" Blancy asks. "Where do you think? She was in the kitchen, like she is every night. Ponytail told me to tell you he was visiting an old friend."

◆ ◆ ◆

I kill the lights on my father's Volvo and park on the side of the road, then make my way through the dark, along the tree-lined driveway toward Burkehaven Farm. The house is pitch black. In the distance, a coyote howls.

I'm worried. Paul should have been at Idlewood earlier tonight as soon as we found Reid's body, as soon as the cops descended on the island. He should have run interference and made himself known. He'd have heard the sirens, seen the lights, and followed them. Unless something—or someone—kept him from coming.

Someone such as my father.

I test the door to the converted barn. It slides open without a sound. Inside, as my eyes adjust to the dark, the contours of the kitchen come into shape, revealing signs of a struggle: barstools toppled over, dishes smashed. I whisper Paul's name and root in the kitchen drawers until I find a flashlight. I aim the beam around the room and find a chef's knife. The blade is smeared in blood.

What happened here? I take a poker from beside the fireplace and edge up the ancient staircase to the second floor, the treads creaking beneath my weight. Paul's bedroom is empty, the bed made. I check the guest rooms, all of which appear as if no one's been in them in months. Back downstairs, I ease open the bathroom door, flip on the lights, and splash water on my face. Reid rehabbed this part of Burkehaven Farm five years ago. As part of the rehab, he added this bathroom and decorated it in stainless steel and pure white.

I wipe my face dry.

Whether I trust Gilcrest or not, this investigation is for the police now. As I flip off the light, my eye catches something on the floor. I turn the light back on and get down on my hands and knees, where a tiny circle of blue stands out against the white tile. It's the blue of Freya's nail polish. The polish used on her windshield this afternoon. The polish smeared on the paper towels Maggie found in the woods.

I kill the lights. In the kitchen, I use the landline to call Seton. "Something's going on at Burkehaven Farm," I say, running through what I've found. "There's a bloody knife. And I can't find Paul anywhere."

"Get in your car, lock the doors, and drive away," Seton says. "I'm on the other side of town. It'll take me twenty minutes to get there, and I'm calling for backup."

I jog into the cool, damp night, gripping the fireplace poker. Up in the foothills, the coyote continues to howl. Before I've gone ten paces, I stop, drawn by a muffled sound emanating from somewhere in the dark. I turn the flashlight beam toward the trees, following the sound until I come to the side of the sugarhouse, where I lift open the door.

Inside, alongside the boiler, Freya's truck takes up the open space—the same truck that should be on its way to New York right now—and the sounds of someone struggling to escape the covered bed fill the night.

"Freya," I whisper, "I'm here."

I test the locked doors and then use the poker to smash the driver's-side window. I release the locks and tear open the door to the covered bed. But it's my father—not Freya—who lies in a pool of blood, his blue eyes clouding over. Behind him, Freya's gun rack is empty. "Charlie," he says, his voice barely audible.

"Where is she?" I ask. "Where's Freya?"

"Paul," my father mumbles, his head falling to the side.

Blood seeps from a gash in his abdomen. I tear off my fleece and wad it into a ball, pressing the cloth to the wound and laying his hand over it to hold it in place. "Don't move," I say. "Help is on the way."

I drop the poker and run to the driveway. My father's lying in the bed of Freya's truck, bleeding; Paul's nowhere to be found; Gilcrest left the scene of Reid's murder in a rage; and Freya should be on her way to New York. But she's not.

Howls sound in the foothills, this time drawing me away from the farmhouse, up the road toward the trailhead. Because that's not a coyote celebrating a kill. It's a dog.

It's Ginger.

Chapter Forty

I sprint onto the trail, the beam of the flashlight bouncing in front of me as my feet find their way over rough ground, along the brook, and into the hills. I grip a sapling, hauling myself up the incline as I picture the grid Freya drew in the ground earlier today, the names laid out: Reid, Duncan Gilcrest, my father, Paul Burke. Hadley, too. And Andrea Haviland. What part does each of them play in what's happened recently and what happened before? How could Freya be tied to it all? And who could have made her send a text telling me she'd left for New York when her truck is here?

I start with the things I know to be true: My mother told Hadley she worried Reid would own his choices, and my brother broke into Freya's apartment. The police have him on video. Later, Reid hid in the woods by Freya's truck, and he ran when he was discovered. Now he's dead.

But my brother wasn't Freya's stalker, at least not in the beginning, which I should have realized earlier. Even if his bedroom walls were covered with her photos, he couldn't have followed her to that mall in Upstate New York when she was on *Eternal Flame*, because Reid was a teenager. He lived with my mother in the bungalow and attended Hero High School. He also couldn't have killed my mother, because he was with Blancy the night of the murder, right through the morning of the fire. So why break into Freya's apartment and steal a bottle of nail polish? His only connection to Freya was the condo she lived in and the house she toyed with buying. Earlier, Hadley told me she'd thought Freya was leaning toward making the move to Hero. If Reid needed the money from the sale, he wouldn't have wanted to frighten her into leaving for New York.

There's Gilcrest, too. He worked security on the set of *Eternal Flame*, and he was the responding officer at Isaac Haviland's murder, the one who enticed my brother, a terrified young boy, to row a boat to shore, or so he and Reid have claimed. Twenty-five years later, Gilcrest oversaw an arson investigation that transitioned to homicide. He and Freya met on the set of a TV show. He convinced her to move to New Hampshire but refused to leave his wife and commit to the new relationship. Then he tried to pin my mother's murder on me when he believed he had a rival for Freya's affections and started to lose control. And Gilcrest has shown all along how much he demands control.

The trail levels out, and the sound of Ginger's panicked yelps grows closer. I reach the edge of the pasture and stop at the tree line. Moonlight filters over the clearing, the wooden posts we used for target practice rising eerily across the rocky shooting range. By the fieldstone wall, Ginger strains at the line Freya used earlier to keep her from bolting. She stands at alert, her ears perked and eyes locked on an unseen target farther up the trail, toward the summit. The dog seems unhurt, even as she howls.

I edge out of the trees and across the grass. In a low voice, I say Freya's name. Ginger turns on me, eyes narrowed, teeth bared, lunging until the line on her collar pulls taut, her every bark carrying a warning. I offer a hand. "Nice girl," I say, my voice quavering. "Don't you remember me? We slept together a few weeks ago. I gave you a treat earlier today."

Muscles tense beneath Ginger's rough tan-and-black coat. She snarls again.

I pray the line attached to her collar will hold.

One of Freya's single-shot rifles lies on top of the fieldstone wall, broken open. Ammunition spills from a paper box beside it. Out in the field, aluminum cans sit atop their posts, ready to be taken out. I picture the scene. Freya was here, in this field. She must have returned earlier, while the police processed her truck for evidence. She attached the line to Ginger's collar, then loaded the rifle and covered her ears with headphones to start target practice.

"What happened?" I ask Ginger as I try reaching around the dog to retrieve the rifle. She lunges, teeth snapping.

"I could use some support right now," I say.

Ginger's having none of it.

"Fine," I whisper. "Stay there. I'll be back."

I dash around the field, conducting a perimeter check. As I move through the posts, Ginger's barking slows, then stops. By the time I return to the stone wall, she whimpers, and I'm almost convinced she might accept my commands. That is, until I meet her eyes, and a low rumbling begins at the back of her throat. She crouches, her tail firm.

"We'll keep our distance for now," I say.

I glance farther up the trail, to where Ginger was focused when I arrived. I imagine the summit where I watched the fire begin two weeks ago. That old hunting cabin sits near the edge of the cliff, slowly giving itself back to the forest. I shine the flashlight along the base of the wall. The beam lands on a black knapsack, hidden in the shadows of the stones, the same knapsack where Freya stored her phone. I could use that phone now to call 9-1-1, even if I can't unlock it to do anything else.

I retreat into the woods and return with a tree branch long enough to reach past Ginger's snapping jaws. I crouch inches from her teeth, maneuver the branch, and manage to snare one of the bag's straps. Ginger clamps her jaw on the branch and turns the exercise into a vicious game of tug-of-war. "Leave it!" I hiss.

She releases her end of the stick. I land flat on my ass but drag the bag toward me.

"You don't make things easy," I say as I root inside the knapsack for the phone and instead come up with a bag of dog treats. Ginger's growls stop instantly.

"You're hungry," I say.

She whines.

I toss her a biscuit. She looks at where it lands, waiting for permission.

"Okay," I say.

The biscuit disappears in a single chomp.

"Maybe we're friends now," I say, but as I take a step toward her, her haunches come off the ground and the snarls return.

So much for that.

I toss a second biscuit. This time, her tail nearly quivers into a wag, and her ears tilt forward. Again, she sits until I give her permission to gobble down the treat, then returns right away to another sit, her mouth watering. I eye the rifle. It would come in handy, especially if I find myself confronting a killer/stalker/kidnapper.

I throw a fistful of biscuits as far from the wall as possible, on the very edge of Ginger's range, and make her wait until she froths at the mouth with anticipation. "Okay," I say, and when she gallops toward the treats, I make my move.

But Ginger's no fool. She lunges, jaws snapping as I scramble backward and barely avoid losing a chunk of my thigh.

"I get it," I say. "You don't appreciate being underestimated. Neither do I. I won't try that again."

The barking stops as suddenly as it started. Ginger whines, one of her ears flopping over. "What is it?" I ask. "I can't take the mixed signals."

She stares behind me with the same intensity I observed earlier. And in the sudden quiet, a twig snaps.

I spin around. "Who's there?" I say, into the dark.

"Hold your hands where I can see them."

Duncan Gilcrest emerges from the trees and into the moonlight, gun in hand. It's pointed right at me.

Chapter Forty-One

I stand slowly, my hands raised, as Gilcrest edges into the field. "What are you doing here, Charlie?" he asks.

"I should ask you the same thing," I say, though I can imagine him hearing Seton's call for backup over the radio and telling Maggie to stay put at Idlewood while he responded.

"Should you? I'm the cop, not you. And last I checked, there are dead bodies piling up faster than I can count." He waves the gun toward a spot beside the stone wall and waits for me to move. "You should be at your aunt's house. Asleep. And far away from whatever's happening here."

Beside me, Ginger whines. Gilcrest is the only person other than Freya whom the German shepherd trusts. He could have hiked the trail here earlier, when he heard Freya shooting at targets. Maybe he watched from the cover of the forest before creeping out while Freya had her back to him, her headphones on. Maybe, for a moment, Freya was glad to see him.

He keeps the gun trained on me, eyes alert, scanning the darkness, as he crosses the grass to where Ginger sits. He offers her a hand to sniff, then retrieves a bottle of water from his coat pocket, twists the cap off with his teeth, and drizzles the water slowly enough for Ginger to lap at it thirstily. "How long has she been out here by herself?" he asks.

"You tell me," I say.

"Lose the attitude and answer the questions or I'll release her," Gilcrest says. "She'll make you tell me what the hell is going on. Where's Freya? She wouldn't leave Ginger tied up in the middle of nowhere like this."

Ginger finishes lapping at the water. Gilcrest tosses the bottle aside and strokes her between the ears. She closes her eyes, presses against his leg, and sighs. "You're okay, girl," Gilcrest says. "We'll get you off this mountain."

Gilcrest isn't here as a kidnapper or a murderer. He isn't here as a cop. He's here because of someone he cares about, someone he may love. I take a chance, and decide to trust him. "I don't know how long Ginger's been alone," I say. "I was at the farm and heard barking. Freya's truck is parked in Paul's sugarhouse. Someone stabbed my father. He's barely conscious but alive. And I couldn't find Paul anywhere."

Gilcrest takes in what I've told him. "Sounds to me like your father really did come to the Landing that night. That'll be good for the podcast."

He holsters the gun and punches a number into his phone. He gives our location and a brief synopsis of the situation. "Be fast," he says as he clicks off. "That was the chief. She's sending an ambulance to take care of your father."

I glance up the hill. "When I got here, Ginger was focused that way. There's a cabin at the summit. If Freya's anywhere nearby, we should start there."

Gilcrest surveys the trees around us, then comes close to me and places his phone in my hand. When he speaks, his voice is soft, barely a whisper. "The passcode is 0221. It's the day I met Freya. You're a runner. Take the phone. Run all the way to the trailhead, as fast as you can. If you get in trouble along the way, call the chief and tell her where you are and what you need. Otherwise, keep moving."

"What about Ginger?"

"She'll be fine. She had water, and the other cops will take care of her."

Gilcrest and I aren't competing, not anymore. "I can help you," I say.

"You'll help by getting yourself away from the scene. The less I worry about, the easier my job will be. And later, when this is all over, we'll grab a drink and work through your story. By now, I think we have enough material for a TV series." He presses his forehead to mine. "Go. Please."

I take a step backward.

"And, Charlie," Gilcrest adds, "tell Seton to hurry."

"I will," I say.

Gilcrest removes his gun from the holster as he edges along the fieldstone wall and fades into the dark, toward the cabin. Ginger watches him go, a whine beginning at the back of her throat. I toss her the last of the biscuits and give her permission to eat them. At least this time, she doesn't snarl.

"Take care," I whisper as I retreat into the trees and start to run. I've covered a few hundred yards when gunshots fill the night, followed by dead silence. I freeze in place, crouching in the shadows.

Far off in the distance, sirens scream. I picture EMTs swarming the farm as they pull my father from the back of Freya's truck. I hope he stanched the blood long enough for them to save him. Seton must have arrived by now, too. She should be jogging onto the trailhead and along the brook, cursing my name for getting myself involved. It takes me ten minutes to run from the trailhead to the summit. It'll take anyone else fifteen.

Fifteen minutes too long.

I retrace my steps to the field. Ginger faces away from me, toward the trail where Gilcrest disappeared moments ago. She's silent now, even when I whisper her name.

I keep to the shadows and make my way past the wall. As the path arcs toward the summit, I stop. The sound of my heart beating fills the night, but there, beneath it all, I find shallow, panicked breathing.

"Charlie," Gilcrest mumbles.

I crawl toward his voice. When I reach him, I feel along his coat, to his side, where my hand comes away covered in something warm and viscous, with a distinct smell of copper.

"You should be long gone," Gilcrest gasps.

"I'm not great at doing what I'm told."

I tap Gilcrest's phone. The brief light from the screen reveals blood oozing from a wound in his shoulder.

"Gunshot," he says. "Couldn't see who it was."

I put an arm around his back, forcing him to sit. "Get out of here," he says, between gritted teeth.

"I would if I could," I say, dragging him as gently as possible across the forest floor until he's propped against a tree. I reach under his coat, into the holster, but it's empty.

"Gone," he says, his head falling to the side.

"Don't close your eyes," I say. *And please don't die,* I think to myself. "Tell me anything you want. How about what you want to tell Freya when you see her next?"

"Love her," Gilcrest manages to say. "And sorry."

"I'm sorry, too," I say. "You and I, we were a couple of assholes earlier, out in Paul's driveway. But that's not the dumbest thing I've said to her. We were in bed together, and I told her she reminds me of Maude from *Harold and Maude*."

Gilcrest laughs, then winces in pain. "Smooth move, Harold."

"So, so dumb," I say. "And I'd take it back in a second if I could. I wish I had half your confidence. I don't have any game."

"Slicker than you know," Gilcrest says.

I scroll through the contacts on his phone until I find Seton's name.

"Haviland," she says when she answers, her breathing heavy. "On our way."

"It's Charlie," I whisper. "Gilcrest's been shot. He's hurt badly and needs transport off the mountain. He's about a hundred yards from the summit, near the cabin, right off the path."

"We'll be there soon," Seton says. "Ten minutes."

I fold Gilcrest's hand over the phone and put it to his ear. "Keep talking. Make sure Seton knows where you are. And whatever you do, don't close your eyes."

Ahead, up the path, a light flickers inside the hunting cabin. There, in an open window, sits Freya, her auburn hair tied in a ponytail, a gag in her mouth.

I hear Freya's voice in my ear, Gina Shock's, too, and imagine them both at that whiteboard, talking to the CBI team: *Follow the evidence.*

There's Seton's advice, too: *Go with the simplest explanation.*

Who discouraged Freya from buying the house at Burkehaven? Who wanted her to return to New York and dismiss the life she's tried to forge here? Who's known Freya for decades and had access to every aspect of her life, her every move? And who, unlike my brother, wasn't a teenager when Freya played Brenda Jackson on *Eternal Flame*?

Only one person ticks those boxes, and it's not Gilcrest, and it's certainly not my brother.

"Tell Seton to be very quiet when she gets here," I say to Gilcrest. "If she isn't, Paul will kill Freya."

Chapter Forty-Two

I leave Gilcrest with the phone and crawl through underbrush. The cabin sits twenty yards away, nestled in trees, across an expanse of granite. My hand brushes a stone large enough to fit in my palm, and I grab hold of it. I ease over the rough surface until I press my back to the cabin's timber walls and slide beneath the open window. Inside, Freya sits, bound to a chair with silver duct tape, a kerosene lantern burning beside her, her face bruised. Paul paces in front of her.

"Duncan wanted to control you," he says. "He has, ever since you met him. Hosting true crime? Singing in a local dive? You're so much better than that." Paul stops himself. "But I fixed it. And I'll fix what comes next, too."

I rise slowly over the sill. What looks like Gilcrest's gun sits beside the kerosene lamp on a wooden table. Paul's back is to me, but Freya's eyes flick my way. Paul spins around as I duck and scramble to the back of the house. Footsteps pound across the cabin floor, and light from the kerosene lamp spills into the night. "Duncan?" Paul calls. "Did you come for more? I'll shoot you again if that's what it takes."

He moves toward the corner of the cabin, the light traveling with him, the gun in hand, his shadow extending across the stony plateau. I keep to the dark, retreating as he pursues.

"Come out, come out," Paul says. "Be a man."

I stop at the next corner, the stone clenched in my palm. I'll get one chance, and one chance only. Will Paul hesitate long enough when he sees that it's me? Will he care?

He stops and turns, retracing his steps into the cabin. "What did you see?" he asks Freya.

Tape rips from her mouth, and it takes a moment before she answers. I imagine her testing her jaw and stalling for whatever time she can.

"Water," she says, her voice raspy.

"Who's here?"

"Put the gun down," Freya says. "Then water. More than a sip. After that, maybe I'll talk."

A few seconds later, I hear her gulping. Finally, she says, "Where's Duncan?"

"Dead. I shot him with his own gun."

Freya gasps. "Oh, Paul. Why?" she says.

"For you," Paul shouts. "He was stringing you along. Couldn't you see that? He had you trapped here."

I take my place beneath the window and peer over the frame. Freya's eyes are red and swollen, but this time she doesn't make the mistake of looking my way.

"This is for the best," Paul says, his voice soft. He holds a tissue to Freya's nose. "There you go. That must feel better. But Duncan's not worth these tears."

Freya closes her eyes. "You're right," she says.

In an instant, Paul has the gun in hand and thrusts it at Freya's temple. "Don't do that," he says. "Don't manipulate me. It's like earlier, when you told me you'd go back to New York. You promised. But I could tell after the others left that you were backtracking and finding an excuse to stay. You belong in New York. *We* belong in New York, without Duncan Gilcrest. And I'll keep watching out for you, no matter what it takes. I've watched out for you since the first time I saw you, since the first time I slipped into the cabin at Burkehaven while you slept."

The corners of Freya's mouth twitch up in recognition of a long-standing mystery finally solved, I imagine, though the smile doesn't reach her eyes. Paul presses the gun to her forehead and releases the safety. Freya winces. "No, no," she says. "I'm not laughing. I'm not. And come on, Paul, put that thing down. You could pull the trigger by accident. Then where would you be?"

Paul keeps the gun in place, the muscles along his arm taut.

"I'm impressed," Freya says. "That's all. Because I should have followed the evidence like Gina would have. You were the one who stole my necklace when I stayed at Burkehaven, not Isaac Haviland. You were the one who would sneak into my room in the cabin. All this time, all these years, your goal was to narrow my world, to get me to retreat and depend on you. I stopped working. I stopped seeing friends. There I was in the busiest city in the world, hiding out in my co-op, and the only person I saw regularly was my manager. You. And that was what you wanted. But I took a chance on a stupid true-crime show, one I was so embarrassed by that I kept it from you. I auditioned, and I got the role, but even though the show didn't get picked up, I met Duncan, and I told you I wanted to give New Hampshire a chance. I told you it might be time to turn a new page."

Paul lowers the gun. "You said it would be like the old days," he says, his voice breaking, "but it wouldn't have been. I'd have been alone again."

My heart almost goes out to him, and maybe it would if I weren't on a mountaintop facing down a gun-wielding maniac who's lied to me my whole life. Somehow, at some point, Paul convinced himself that Freya was the key to being loved, but he couldn't get what he wanted without controlling her.

"The stalking wasn't about scaring me *from* New York," Freya says. "It was about keeping me there, where you could have me to yourself. You were the one who kept saying Duncan wasn't prioritizing me, that he loved Nicole."

"He'd never have left her," Paul says.

"But he did leave Nicole. He just didn't hate her, which is what he kept trying to tell me. He loves his kids, and so does she, so they prioritize their family, and they make it work."

"He *loved* his kids," Paul says. "He doesn't love anyone anymore. Not even you."

"And I should have listened to him," Freya says, her voice growing cold. "Instead, I listened to my old friend. Then that old friend burned down my house. No house. No boyfriend. No reason to stay in Hero. You and I, we could go back to the way things were, and you wouldn't be by yourself."

"They were good the way they were," Paul says. "They still can be."

Out in the night, Ginger howls.

Paul moves toward the cabin door. "I should have shot that damn dog when I had a chance," he says.

"Leave her, Paul," Freya says, quickly. "She's tied up and can't get to you, and I heard sirens. The police must be at the farmhouse by now. Paul, Duncan would have called for backup."

"I know what you're doing."

"Tell me, Paul, what am I doing?"

"You're playing Gina Shock. You're mirroring my words. You're saying my name and trying to connect to me. But you don't need to do that. We've been connected for as long as we've known each other, since the first time I saw you sing at Burkehaven."

"I could sing for you now," Freya says. "What would you want to hear?"

Paul shakes his head. "Stop. You don't care about any of this. And you can play Gina as much as you want, but I know who you are. I know you're scared out of your mind."

"I am scared. I'm terrified."

"That's better," Paul says. "Why? Tell me."

"Because I care about you. You've been a friend when I've needed one. And now, I don't know how we'll get out of this without someone else getting hurt."

"I don't know if we *are* getting out of this," Paul says, retrieving a knife from the table and cutting Freya's legs free from the chair.

I duck beneath the window. Paul has no intention of leaving this mountaintop, I imagine, and he won't let Freya leave, either. I don't have time to wait for Seton to ride to the rescue. Somehow, Freya and I need to get out of this on our own.

"Move," Paul says. "And don't try anything."

Light from the lamp spills into the night as they make their way across the cabin. Freya glances toward me as she steps outside, her pale face betraying her fear.

I weigh the stone in my hand.

"Keep going," Paul says. "To the overlook."

"We can make it to my truck and leave," Freya says. "People think I'm on my way to New York."

"It's too late for that," Paul says, shoving her from behind.

Freya stumbles and rolls onto the ground. Paul reaches to yank her to her feet, and she pivots onto her hip, jabbing her foot into his groin.

"Now!" she shouts.

I charge and swing. Paul dodges, releasing the lantern so it smashes and a burst of kerosene lights up the night. He grips Freya's hair in a fist and presses the gun to her temple.

"I'll blow her brains out," he says, backing toward the cliff.

I stop, frozen in place, unable to reconcile the person I grew up with, the person who came to my parents' weekends at boarding school, with this person in front of me. Could any part of that relationship have been true, or is this person, this angry man, one of the reasons I grew up feeling so alone?

Freya meets my eyes. "We'll never be what you want, Paul," she says.

"Don't look at Charlie," he says. "After tonight, you and I will be together. Charlie won't be there. Duncan won't, either. It'll be you and me alone, the way it should have been."

"It won't, though. And it never was." Freya pauses, her gaze locked on mine. "Do you understand what I'm saying?"

I do understand. Paul needs control. It's the only way he feels connected. Now we have to make him feel alone all over again. We have to make him lose control.

I mirror his steps. "Ginger tried to rip my throat out," I say to Freya, and only her.

"That's my girl," Freya says, "but you should trust her. She likes you, more than she lets on. And she'll listen to you if you ask in the right way and show her who's boss."

"She was thirsty, but Gilcrest brought her some water," I say. "He's down the trail, hurt badly but not dead. And Seton's coming. With an army behind her."

"He's lying," Paul says.

I ignore him. "Gilcrest told me to tell you he loves you. And he's sorry."

Freya closes her eyes and whispers a silent prayer. "Thank you," she mouths.

Paul reaches the edge of the cliff. "You should have left well enough alone, Charlie. Why did you have to keep asking about Isaac? What did it matter after all this time?"

I've already established that if Paul killed Isaac, my mother would have been lying for him all these years, and why would she have chosen Paul over my father? But maybe I missed something. Maybe Paul really did kill Isaac, and my mother's concerns about Reid, the ones Hadley told me about, were unfounded, after all. The only connection I've found between Isaac and Paul is the money Paul lent out. "Isaac came to New York with a plan to rehab the Landing," I say. "He wanted you to invest."

"I refused," Paul says.

"But he left with fifty grand," I say.

"He knew too much," Paul says. "He knew about Freya, about the things I'd done. He figured out the things I was still doing."

"The night Isaac came to the West Village," Freya says, "I told him about being stalked. He must have known it was you."

"Isaac found your necklace when we were kids, the one I stole," Paul says. "He promised me it was our secret. He understood how much you meant to me. And what I'd do to keep you close."

The money Mrs. Haviland found in the ledger suddenly makes sense. "Isaac figured out you were stalking Freya and blackmailed you," I say. "That's why you gave him the money. And that's why you killed him and let my father take the fall."

Paul glances over the edge of the cliff, into the abyss. "I didn't kill Isaac," he says. "Reid did. Reid did what I told him to, right until the end."

Chapter Forty-Three

Paul holds the gun to Freya's temple as they teeter near the edge of the cliff, and his words echo in my mind: *Reid did what I told him to, right until the end.*

Reid killed Isaac Haviland. It's what I feared, and what I hoped might not be true. When I speak, my voice sounds distant, free of emotion, as though it belongs to someone else. "Why would Reid kill Isaac?" I ask.

I don't dare ask the other question, the one I've wanted the answer to since I left my brother on the dock earlier tonight: Did Reid kill my mother, too?

"You barely knew your brother or what he was capable of," Paul says. "Reid saw the way Jane acted around Isaac before anyone else noticed. He told me the way Jane touched Isaac's arm and laughed at anything he said. And Reid wanted to be a hero. He needed someone to nudge him in the right direction."

"Someone like you," Freya says.

Paul yanks her head back, his finger twitching on the trigger.

"Don't," I say, moving closer.

"Stay back," Paul says, turning the gun on me.

I raise my hands as I try to imagine what happened all those years ago, how Paul manipulated Reid—a twelve-year-old boy—into doing what he needed done. Who was at fault? The adult or the child? My mother told Hadley she feared Reid would own his choices; now I question when they became his to own, and how else Paul used those choices to control my brother into adulthood.

"You said Reid helped you to the end," I say. "Did he know about you and Freya?"

Paul laughs. "Who do you think took photos of Freya and me when we were out together? Especially during those years Reid attended NYU."

"He gave you plausible deniability," Freya said. "And I fell for it."

"You told him to steal that nail polish from Freya's apartment," I say. "And what to write on her truck."

"He made that decision on his own," Paul says. "Reid was an idiot. He thought he could escape me."

The stolen nail polish. The chase through the woods. The tiny dot of blue. I picture Reid standing in that stark, white bathroom watching the single drop of liquid splatter to the floor. "Reid brought the stalker to New Hampshire," I say, testing out a theory. "He hoped an incident up here would narrow the list of suspects enough for you to be caught. Then he'd finally be free."

"Not bad, Charlie," Paul says. "You underestimate yourself too much, unlike your brother. He thought he was smarter than he was. He was easy to manipulate, though. Back then, when I needed Isaac taken care of, I told Reid your mother was destroying your family, and someone brave had to cut out the evil before it took root."

Those are the same words Paul said to me by the firepit that night before my mother died, the same words I repeated to her later as I headed to bed. I remember how she looked at me as if she'd seen a ghost.

In a way, she had.

Off in the distance, a light appears over the lake, followed by the steady thumping of a rotor blade. The silhouette of a helicopter crosses the full moon. Maybe Seton will ride to the rescue, after all.

"They're coming, Paul," Freya says. "It's over."

I inch forward as Paul drags Freya to the very edge of the cliff. "You don't want the story to end like this," I say.

"There's no other choice," Paul says.

"You're smart," I say. "You've stayed two steps ahead of the cops for years."

"Not this time," Paul says, wrapping his arms around Freya from behind and pulling her to his chest. He glances over his shoulder, steeling himself, I imagine, for one final, magnificent act of misguided love.

"My mother," I say, quickly. "Did Reid kill her? Tell me what he did."

I'll take the answer, whatever it is, if it will delay Paul long enough for the cops to arrive.

Paul inhales the scent of Freya's hair. "You'll never know, Charlie."

The helicopter rises over the ledge, then swoops above us, a flood lamp shining across the summit. The turbulence knocks Paul off balance. Freya digs a heel into his foot and smashes a fist into his nose. She falls to the ground, rolling away from the ledge. I charge. My shoulder slams into Paul's side as the gun goes off. Freya scrambles across the granite, toward the cabin.

Seton's voice sounds over a loudspeaker. "Drop the gun, Paul. There's nowhere to hide."

The helicopter swoops low. I fall to the ground. When I look up, Paul looms over me, gun in hand.

I stand, arms raised.

"You tried to take Freya from me," he says.

"I wasn't yours for the taking, Paul," Freya shouts. "Let Charlie go. You and I can talk to the police together. They'll understand."

"One more word," Paul says, "and I'll kill your boyfriend while you watch. This time, I'll make sure to finish the job."

Above us, the helicopter circles. Down the mountain, by the shooting range, Ginger barks into the night, a rifle by her side.

"Are you sure Ginger likes me?" I ask Freya.

"She loves you," Freya says.

I back away, hands raised, drawing Paul toward me. I can make him feel alone all over again. I can make him lose control and direct his rage at me. And before this night is through, he'll answer my questions.

"Freya and I had an amazing night," I say. "A night I'll remember forever. The sex blew my mind, but afterward is what mattered. Lying beside each other, waking together the next morning. I'm so sorry things never worked out the way you wanted with her. It could have been mind-blowing for you, too. I'm sorry you've spent your life alone."

The helicopter sweeps forward. "Down!" Seton shouts over the loudspeaker.

I drop as the helicopter swoops in low. I scramble into the trees, Paul in pursuit, like I hoped he would be. A bullet ricochets off a tree. I veer from the path, sliding over the uneven terrain, not stopping until the trees open on the pasture below. I dash onto the field, through the posts topped with aluminum cans, toward the stone wall, where Ginger snarls, and the single-shot rifle waits beside her with an open box of ammunition.

I stop short when I reach the dog.

"Sit," I say, my voice shaking.

Ginger gnashes her teeth.

Behind me, Paul crashes from the trees and onto the field. "Where will you run now, Charlie?" he shouts.

I turn to face him.

He fires the gun. A bullet whizzes past me.

"Come on, Ginger," I say, reaching a hand toward her.

She barks again but doesn't bite.

"Freya says you love me," I say.

I meet the dog's eyes. She snarls. I take a step forward, then another. I haven't lost any fingers yet. "Release," I say, my voice firm.

The dog transforms, ears soft, tail wagging. I unhitch the line from her collar and dive past her, over the stone wall. "Come," I shout, as Paul shoots again.

Ginger leaps after me. I grab the rifle and a fistful of ammunition.

"Down," I say.

She goes into an active down.

My hands shake as I crack open the chamber and shove in a bullet. I rest the barrel on the wall, take aim, shoot one of the aluminum cans from its post, then fall behind the wall to reload.

"Don't make me hurt you," I shout.

I find Paul in the scope. He levels his gun in my direction. I shoot another aluminum can. "Next time," I say, "I won't be aiming at a target."

Paul pulls the trigger, firing one round after another. I duck, pressing into the stone wall and hugging Ginger to my chest as she struggles to escape the noise. Then the shooting stops. I raise my head. Across the field, Paul pulls at the trigger. The gun clicks uselessly, the clip spent.

I shoot down the final aluminum can. "There's only one target left," I shout. "You."

Paul's face blanches under the moon as the final vestige of the man who served as my surrogate father fades. He lowers his gun to the ground and raises both hands.

"Get down," I say.

He sinks to his knees.

"Tell me what you did. Say it out loud. What happened after my mother figured out what you'd done?"

"I shouldn't have come back to Idlewood to talk to you by the fire that night," Paul says. "But I wanted to stay close, to see what you'd learned, what you'd pieced together. Jane called me when I got home. I assumed she was upset about your podcast, about telling her story to the world. She told me we needed to talk, and that it couldn't wait until morning."

"You met her at Burkehaven," I say.

"In the middle of the night," Paul says.

"And what about Reid? Was he there?"

Paul takes a moment to answer, weighing what to tell me and what to hold back as a negotiating tool later, I imagine. So I load the rifle, shoot the post beside him, and reload again.

"I was alone," Paul says, shielding his face. "Reid wouldn't have hurt Jane. He loved her too much. But Jane told me she was going to the police. *I was the one who found Reid,* she said to me. *He was hunched over Isaac's body, knife in hand. My son, transformed into someone I didn't recognize.* Cut out the evil, *he kept saying.* Cut out the evil before it takes root."

I envision my mother facing off with Paul under the cover of darkness. "Reid's words have haunted me for decades," I imagine her saying. "Tell me, Paul, why would Charlie, my son who was an infant, my son who only knows what's been told to him about that awful night, why would he utter the exact same phrase twenty-five years later? The only two people on earth who should know what Reid said when he killed Isaac are Reid and me. We were the only ones there."

I wonder if Paul tried to deny what he'd done, or to rationalize, or if he simply admitted his crimes.

"Jane tried to run," Paul says, "but I smashed her head in with a two-by-four. I moved her car from Idlewood and left it in the trees a mile away. By the time I made it back to Burkehaven, the sun was up. Reid had filled the tanks for the backhoe, so there was plenty of gasoline to start the fire. Once the flames got going, I saw Andrea approaching in her boat. She's lucky you showed up when you did. Five minutes later and she'd have been dead, too."

"You attacked me," I say.

"I didn't have a choice," Paul says.

Footsteps sound in the woods behind me. Seconds later, Seton emerges from the trees, her firearm raised.

"You landed that thing," I say.

She inches closer. "Drop the rifle, Charlie."

I peer through the scope.

"He destroyed my family," I say.

He destroyed them—us—in every way, by manipulating Reid, by forcing my mother's hand, by making us live with the cruelty of the unspoken. I spent my life feeling as if I didn't know anyone in my family, and now I never will.

"Everything . . ." Paul begins. "Everything got out of hand. I'm sorry, Charlie. I'm so, so sorry."

"Tell Seton what you did," I say.

"I killed Jane and burned down the house," Paul says. "I drowned Reid, too. He knew I'd killed your mother and threatened to come clean about what he'd done, about what I'd been doing to Freya. I killed them both."

I doubt a coerced confession will matter much, let alone hold up in court, but it's what I needed to hear. There are other pieces to the story, though, and once we're off this mountain, Paul will remember how lawyers evade answers. "The detective?" I ask. "Wendy Burrows?"

"What does it matter?" Paul asks.

I pull back the hammer to release the safety.

"Don't, Charlie," Seton says, edging toward me.

"Wendy got close to solving the case," Paul says, quickly. "But she was a drunk. I found her passed out behind the wheel over on Foss Hill with an empty fifth of vodka on the seat next to her. She went there after most of her shifts. I put the car in neutral and let it roll off the ledge and into the lake."

"And my father?" I say. "You knew he was alive all this time?"

"Not until tonight," Paul says. "Your father found me at the farmhouse, after Reid died. I hadn't had a chance to change out of my wet clothes. As soon as Mark saw me, he knew what I'd done."

I feel the cold steel of the trigger against my finger and picture my father in that photo I have hidden in the thesaurus, at the beginning of a long line of choices and an unimaginable future. Shooting Paul would be so easy. I could call it self-defense, and maybe Seton would back up my story. But then that imaginary wall between us would turn to solid brick, and we'd never manage to get through it. And I'd spend the rest of my life knowing what I'd done, living with another secret, this one of my own making.

"Put the rifle down, Charlie," Seton says.

I can't give Paul any more power. I let the rifle clatter to the ground and hold my hands in the air. "For you, Seton," I say, "anything."

Two weeks later

Chapter Forty-Four

Andrea Haviland pulls the boat around in an arc while I hold the handle in both hands. When the line goes taut, I give the signal, she revs the engine, and I lift out of the water on both skis. I kick one ski off and balance on the other as I angle in and out of the wake.

In the last two weeks, I've learned more about Isaac Haviland's murder, and that not much of what I've assumed or been told for most of my life was true. My parents didn't have cocktails with Paul on the dock, though my mother asked him to tell the police they had because it supported her narrative. What really happened was that my parents got into an argument that afternoon while my father prepped the Bolognese. After he stormed off the island and drove away in the Volvo, my mother finished cooking and went to look for him in her own car, with me strapped into my car seat.

Sometime after she left, Mr. Haviland came to the island, where Reid was working on his homework. No one knows what happened between them, but Reid used a chef's knife to kill Mr. Haviland. My mother returned to Idlewood and found Reid, and when she tried to take the knife from him, they struggled, and Reid stabbed her. He took me from the car and fled in the rowboat, while my mother dragged herself through the woods to escape.

Much of this we've learned from Paul, who, once he began to tell his story, couldn't stop, no matter what his own lawyer advised. It was as though telling the story helped cleanse him of his sins.

As a teenager, Paul became fixated on Freya, a secret he shared with Isaac only after Isaac found the necklace he had stolen. Paul was the one who followed Freya to that Westchester mall when she was on *Eternal Flame* and left his first message on her windshield. He became addicted to the power that came from terrifying her. He even leaked compromising photos to a tabloid of Freya's husband with another woman, which led to the end of Freya's marriage.

Once Freya told Isaac about being stalked, it didn't take much for him to connect Paul to the incidents. He used that information to blackmail Paul into financing the Landing, but when Paul found out about my mother's affair with Isaac, he convinced Reid that the only way to save his family was to remove Isaac as a threat.

To cut out the darkness.

Reid was twelve years old when he killed Isaac, and Isaac was strong and in shape, so I suspect Paul helped, though he hasn't admitted that part to the police yet. Maybe he will, eventually.

Mrs. Haviland makes a sharp turn, the boat careening across the water. I ride the wake, flying up in the air, but miss the landing as I release the handle and sink into the cool water. I lie on my back and face the sky, letting the life jacket do the work of keeping me afloat until Mrs. Haviland pulls up beside me and we swap places. I take the helm and wait for her to signal with a thumbs-up before pushing the throttle forward.

After she finishes her turn, I say, "I should get back, unless you want to go again."

"Another day," she says, handing me the ski and hauling herself out of the water. We pull in the line and pick up the second ski. Before Mrs. Haviland can rev the engine for the return trip, I touch her arm. "Did you see my father at that soccer game?" I ask.

"Way back when?" she says. "I didn't, though I wish I had. All these years, I believed your father was dead."

"You didn't drive him to the White Mountains or help him escape."

"Nothing like that," she says. "Are you recording?"

"No," I say.

"Well, here's my secret, and I'll deny this if you repeat it to anyone, but I'm lucky I missed that one camera at Burkehaven when I smashed the other ones with a sledgehammer. If I hadn't, I might be in jail right now." She glances at me out of the corner of her eye, waiting for my reaction.

"You said you didn't do it," I say, shoving her shoulder. With all the lies and omissions I've sorted through recently, this one should hardly register, but it feels personal. "I defended you!"

"That's why I'm telling you now. I don't want a secret hanging between us."

"Fine," I say. "I suppose I'll give you this one. Were you planning something for Burkehaven like you did with Rocky Nook? Were you going to block the development?"

Mrs. Haviland considers the question for a moment. "People think I'm a crazy old lady," she says. "But I can still water-ski, and I get my own way most of the time. I'd have figured out how to stop that project." She stows the skis in the keel and sits behind the steering wheel. "There's something else I should tell you: I found those payments from Paul in Isaac's ledgers a few weeks after Isaac died and assumed they were loans."

"You already told me that," I say. "You found the loans and paid them back."

"There's more, though. I didn't have the fifty grand to pay Paul. I didn't have fifty cents, for that matter, but I had a one-year-old child and a business to run. There were six deposits in total, all under ten thousand dollars, right below the amount that would trigger the IRS. The deposits were suspicious enough that when Paul brought up the loan, I told him his secret was safe with me. That's all I said. Nothing else. He never mentioned the money again." The lines around Mrs. Haviland's eyes crease into a smile. "That's why Paul couldn't stand me. He thought I knew something I didn't. He thought I knew what had happened on the lake." She shoves the throttle forward, and we shoot across the water. "I'm lucky to be alive."

◆ ◆ ◆

At the marina, I help Mrs. Haviland unload and cover the boat and then follow her up the ramp toward the Landing.

"You coming in for breakfast?" she asks.

"Is he here?"

"Probably."

The bells over the door ring. Groups of friends gather at tables and line up to place orders. Blancy works the counter and acknowledges me with a nod, while Mrs. Haviland kisses my cheek and makes me promise to go water-skiing again soon. Then she says hello to my father and retreats to the kitchen.

Mark Kilgore perches at the counter, on the same stool where he sat weeks earlier, when he traveled to Hero, concerned because my mother hadn't met him in Finstock. They'd spent years keeping in contact with burner phones and meeting up when they could. My father lived off the grid in a tiny house on a piece of property long forgotten after it was seized by eminent domain from Reid Construction for a failed highway project. My mother provided cash for him to live on by skimming profits from the firm.

Now I slide onto the stool beside him, as I have most mornings in the week since he was released from the hospital. He wears the same glasses, but a neat crew cut has replaced the ponytail. "You're here," he says.

"Where else would I be?" I say as Blancy brings me a mug of coffee.

"What about work?" he asks. "They must want you at the radio station."

I took another two-week leave after what happened. Technically I'm due in the office next week, but I won't trust Julian after he unleashed the podcast on the world, and I have the estate to sort out and the construction firm to run. I have to untangle the finances to see who's owed what, and who I can hold off for a bit longer. As Reid told me, it's a shell game, one I suspect I can make work.

My father and I are feeling each other out. I haven't referred to him as anything yet, not sure whether I should call him Mark or Dad or something else. Most mornings, we pick up our conversation exactly where we left off the day before. He's already told me about returning to Idlewood on the evening Isaac Haviland was killed. He found my mother slumped on the road halfway to the bungalow, bleeding from the knife wound. "I started the argument with her," he told me. "I couldn't let go of the affair, or how betrayed I felt, which wasn't fair to Jane, not by a long run, not after the things I'd done. I left to cool off. By the time I returned—"

He didn't complete the thought. "I couldn't turn Reid in," he said. "I couldn't let his whole life be ruined because of his parents' mistakes. So I ran and took the blame."

Yesterday, my father told me he came to Idlewood the night Reid drowned to talk to him—to confront him, really.

"I worried he'd killed your mother," my father said, staring at the counter as he spoke. "But Reid was dead when I got there. You showed up a few moments after I did, and I didn't know what to do. I came to the Landing first to find Andrea, but I saw her working in the kitchen and realized I'd already done her enough harm. After I talked to Blancy, I went to Burkehaven Farm. Living off the grid was tolerable when your mother came to visit, when there was something to look forward to, but after Jane died . . . I couldn't face being on my own. I might as well have been in prison. I was ready to turn myself in and thought Paul could help. When I got to the farmhouse, Paul was in the kitchen, sopping wet."

Something clicked for my father in that moment. The players had been cut away one by one—first my mother, then Reid, until only Paul remained. "I confronted him," my father said. "It didn't take him long to confess. Or to pull a knife on me."

Today, I take a long sip of my coffee. "What if you'd let Reid take the blame for his choices?"

"We'd have had a different life," my father says. "All of us. I can't tell you what that life would have been, better or worse, but it would have been different. I made the choices I made. So did your mother. And so did Reid. That's all we can know."

"Very Zen," I say.

"Try spending twenty-five years mostly by yourself," he says. "You'll find your Zen, too."

Behind me, the bells over the door ring. A second later, something cold and wet nudges my hand. Ginger stands by my stool, tail wagging, Freya beside her. "Harold," she says. "Mark, it's good to see you up and about."

My father nods hello, like someone not yet used to engaging with the public.

"Maude," I say.

"That's a bridge too far," Freya says. "I may sic Ginger on you."

"Or she can be a dog now."

"You mean no more killing machine?" Freya asks. "She probably has it in her to change, like we all do. And now that the stalker's been caught, let's hope he doesn't make a return appearance for Sweeps Week."

"Let's hope," I say.

"I was at Burkehaven this morning," she says. "The new construction is looking good. I like seeing you take charge."

Freya's opted to stay in Hero for the time being, though she's not giving up the co-op in New York. After confessing, Paul took a plea deal that kept him from facing federal charges. Freya agreed to buy the lot of land at the end of the point if he'd put the rest of the lots in conservation. Soon, the town will set about replanting the shoreline to restore Burkehaven to what it used to be.

"Maybe construction is your calling, Charlie," my father says.

I'm not sure what my calling is. The firm is mired in debt, but if I can turn things around, it could be worth some money. I also have the recordings I made, and a lurid story, one that's mostly mine to tell. My father's reappearance and Paul's arrest garnered attention in the media, but for all the gossip and small-town whispering, the people in Hero protect their own. They closed ranks and froze out the reporters, so that a week after the story blew up, it fizzled away on its own.

The bells over the door ring. This time, Duncan Gilcrest enters. I haven't seen him since the EMTs lifted him onto a gurney and wheeled him down the mountain. Now, two weeks later, he's as handsome and charismatic as ever.

"He really is ridiculous," Freya says as Gilcrest talks to anyone who will listen. "But he's also been working with Lisa Lawson, Wendy Burrows's widow, to see if she can qualify for survivor's benefits now that we know Wendy died on duty. He's a lot more good than bad."

"What about Gilcrest's wife?" I ask.

"Near-death experiences bring clarity. For everyone," Freya says, in a way that tells me she not only likes every inch of that ridiculous detective but has found her own clarity.

"I'm glad," I say.

"Come out tonight," she says, then kisses my cheek. "I have a show at seven. We can have a drink afterward."

"I'll see you then," I say.

She joins Gilcrest and clasps his hand in hers, dragging him toward the door. He catches my eye. "Charlie Kilgore," he shouts. "My man!"

I hate to admit it, but something tells me Gilcrest and I might wind up being friends.

My father pats my back. "Freya's like me," he says. "In the third act, looking backward, wondering what she could have done differently, asking what she still has time to accomplish. You have your whole life in front of you, with plenty of room to make mistakes. Find someone to make those mistakes with."

It takes a moment for me to realize my father's offering advice on my love life, that he thinks Freya's left me brokenhearted. I don't correct him. There's a comfort in his offer. The advice feels fatherly and honest, as though we're both on the inside being seen.

I could get used to this.

◆ ◆ ◆

When I get home to Idlewood, Seton waits for me in one of the Adirondack chairs on the dock. She wears that same boxy uniform I saw her in the first day I drove into town. I slide onto the chair next to her.

"Want a drink?" I ask, resting a hand over hers.

"I'm on duty, you idiot," she says, but she doesn't take her hand from mine.

"Are you here to arrest me?" I ask.

"Consider this a wellness check. You're out here all by yourself. Why not ask your dad to stay with you?"

"Soon," I say. "Once we know each other better."

Seton scans the cove. "What will you do with Idlewood now?" she asks.

"I can't afford to keep it."

"You're selling?"

"Not in a million years. I'm donating it to the town. I'll hang on to this dock so I have a place to keep the boat, and enough property to, I don't know, have a firepit. Otherwise, I'll stay in the bungalow."

"It's not a bungalow!" Seton says. "And that's a lot of money to pass on."

"Who needs money?"

Seton squeezes my hand. "I'm glad you figured out what happened to my dad. I didn't realize I needed closure till I had it. The whole thing has been healing, in a way I never could have imagined. Thanks for pushing when I told you not to."

In the two weeks since Paul's arrest, that imaginary wall between us has begun to dissolve. What's on the other side is taking shape, but I'm looking forward to finding out what's there. For that to happen, I need to be honest about the side of myself I saw on that mountaintop, a side that scared me. "I almost shot Paul that night," I say.

"You didn't, though," Seton says.

"If you hadn't shown up—"

She takes my hand to her mouth and kisses my fingers. "Do you mind?" she asks.

I close my eyes and rest my forehead on hers. Our lips nearly brush. "Not at all," I say.

"I did show up, though," she says, her voice soft, "and once I was there, I'd have shot you in the leg before I'd have let you do anything to ruin your life. But I didn't need to be there to save you. There's a difference between wanting to kill someone and following through. I want to shoot my mom ten times a day, but I wouldn't do it. You wouldn't kill anyone, either. You don't have it in you."

The radio on her shoulder chirps, something about two free-roaming Rhodesian ridgebacks out on Sheridan Road. "That's Juna and Autumn," she says. "Off on an adventure."

I take her hand to my lips and kiss each of her fingers. "You should probably find out where they went."

"I should," Seton says without moving, but I sense her pulling away.

"Are we back to the friend zone?" I ask.

She turns to face the water, her body hunched forward. "I came here for another reason. I had the DNA from the pint glass tested."

"Let me guess," I say. "It was my father's DNA."

"It was," she says, and I can tell she's weighing what to say next.

"If there's more to it, tell me. I'm done with secrets."

Seton bites her lip. "I don't want to make a mistake."

Her fingers tighten on my hand, and I suddenly don't know whether she's talking about the DNA test or something much more important—the two of us. In my mind I flash forward fifty years. We sit in this same spot on another summer day like this one, our hair white, our joints creaky. I wonder how many tattoos Seton will have by then, or what we'll be planning to accomplish in our own third acts. It's a life I want, and one that's anything but a mistake.

"Tell me whatever you need to," I say.

◆ ◆ ◆

Hadley's head bobs among the daisies in the perennial garden beside the bungalow. As I approach, she glances up from under her sun hat. "Good thing you're here," she says to me. "I need some muscle."

I flex my arm. "You'll have to look elsewhere."

"Fill that wheelbarrow with mulch. I'm heading out to Port-au-Prince later this week. You can help me get these beds ready before I leave."

I roll up the sleeves on my shirt and shovel mulch into a wheelbarrow.

"I'll be gone for most of the summer," Hadley says. "But you can call, no matter what it's about. You know that, right? I'll always be here for you." She crouches in a second bed and yanks at a patch of clover. "Weeds are insidious. And hard work helps keep your mind off things, things that maybe you don't want to think about otherwise. It does for me."

Behind us, the kitchen door opens, and someone with a thick Australian accent says Hadley's name. She pops her head over the daisies to where Lee, the helicopter pilot, stands in the doorway, shirtless. "Charlie and I are talking," she says to him. "We'll be done in a bit."

Lee gives me a wave, calls me *mate*, and retreats into the house.

"Looks like you have an ample supply of muscle," I say.

To her credit, Hadley blushes. "Lee and I, we've run into each other around the world. Now we're running into each other here."

I dump the load of mulch onto the bed. "That morning I shouted your name, when I called 9-1-1—" I begin.

"I was on my way back from Lee's place," Hadley says. "That's why I wasn't home."

"Why didn't you tell me?"

"You didn't ask," Hadley says. "And a girl's gotta have a few secrets."

"Secrets," I say, spreading the mulch with a rake. "There are secrets everywhere. I was talking to my father this morning—"

"I haven't seen him yet," Hadley says, cutting me off. "And I'm not sure what I'll say when I do. But your mother didn't tell me he was alive, if that's what you're asking. Jane knew secrets had to be controlled. If they get out into the world, they aren't yours anymore. She also knew I had feelings for your father, that I'd had them for a long time, and that I might do something stupid if I knew too much."

I kneel beside her, still processing what Seton told me out on the dock, weighing how much I want to share with Hadley, how much I want her to know that I know.

"I had the pint glass tested against your DNA," Seton said to me, *"but I also had your DNA tested against your mother's. The results weren't what I expected."*

I touch Hadley's hand. "You and my father," I start to say. "The two of you—"

Hadley cuts me off. "Your mother was your mother, and I'm your aunt. Your favorite aunt."

"My only aunt," I say.

"Your favorite. And nothing will change any of that, ever. Jane loved you in a way I couldn't have, in a way I didn't want to. She was right about a lot of things, and one is that I'm selfish. I mean, look, I'm flying to Port-au-Prince when I should be staying here and offering support, but I like things my way, and I don't compromise, no matter who's asking."

"Why didn't you tell me before?" I ask.

Hadley sits cross-legged on the pile of mulch. "My father cut me out of his will, and I was angry, much angrier than I've ever admitted. I took that anger out on your mother. Your father and I . . . we had feelings for each other, even after years apart. And one night, we got drunk, and it went too far, and you showed up nine months later. That indiscretion is what led Jane into having an affair with Isaac. It was the catalyst to all of this, and I've spent a lifetime wondering what would have happened if I'd left well enough alone."

She grips a tiny maple sapling in her fist. "See this. It's got to go because we don't want a maple tree growing in the middle of the cutting garden. Those are the choices you make, right? And you don't look back, no matter what. The only thing you need to know is that your mother loved you more than life itself, and more than anyone else ever could have. She felt that way from the moment I handed you to her. And she never, ever stopped."

I place my hand over Hadley's and try to picture the two of us, traveling the world, far from Idlewood, but the images don't come into focus. As my father said over breakfast this morning, the only thing I know about that imaginary life, better or worse, is it would have been different from the one I've already lived.

We yank the tree from the ground. "You *are* my favorite aunt," I say.

"Don't ever forget it," Hadley says.

◆ ◆ ◆

Later, after we finish mulching, I change into sneakers and start to run, up the road, past Burkehaven Farm, onto the trailhead.

When I reach the summit, I sit on the granite outcropping, where the lake stretches to the horizon. These last few weeks could have broken me. Instead, I feel as though I've started on a path toward discovering who I might be, and I can't wait to learn more about that person.

Still, I can't forget what I've lost.

I take out my phone and delete each of the audio files from the cloud, all but the last conversation with my mother. I listen, her voice floating over me: *You have a right to know your story and to understand who your father was,* she says toward the end of the recording. *I should have told you about him a long time ago.*

"I love you, Mom," I say, my chest tight. "Always and forever."

That, I know, will never change.

I move the recording from the cloud and save it in a place where only I will ever be able to find it.

I don't owe Julian, but I'll make sure he understands the podcast is off when I hand in my resignation at the radio station. I'll also tell Gilcrest we aren't writing a book or making a TV series. Right now, I want to give Hero a chance. I want to water-ski with Mrs. Haviland, and learn more about my father, and explore a friendship with Freya and Gilcrest, and be here when Hadley returns from her trip to see what else she might reveal. Mostly, I want to spend a lot of time with Seton.

This story is mine, and mine alone. I'll pack it away and keep it for myself. I'm pretty certain that's where it belongs.

Acknowledgments

This book is dedicated to my father, Jack Hill, who died in 2023. He was a kind, generous person who made the world, and my life, better in so many ways.

For anyone who'd like to visit Hero, New Hampshire, you can find pieces of it in the lake towns of Sandwich, Sunapee, Holderness, and Wolfeboro. I'm grateful to the Foothills Café in Sandwich and the Anchorage in Sunapee for providing inspiration for the Landing. The rest, particularly the residents, I made up.

A special thanks to my longtime agent, Robert Guinsler, for guiding this novel to publication. I couldn't do this without you.

To all the people who helped make this novel a reality:

To Laura Van Der Veer for taking a chance on this story; to Laura and Charlotte Herscher for making the story stronger; and to Miranda Gardner and her team for guiding this novel through the bookmaking process. I'm excited to join the Thomas & Mercer team!

To Will Watkins for navigating the world of film and television.

To Cornell Charles Stamoran for donating some cash to the Sisters in Crime auction for the Innocence Project and lending his name to Duncan Gilcrest's partner in law enforcement.

To Maggie Barbieri, Jenna Blum, Mark Cecil, John Ferrall, Dana Isaacson, Joseph Moldover, Chris Sharp, Alex Sunshine, and Jess Zeidman for being tough editors and readers and making this novel so much better.

To anyone involved in any version of *Law & Order*.

To Michael Starr, Edith Ann, Betty Hill, Christine Hill, and Chester (we miss you!); and all the Hills, Rowells, Starrs, Miraldas, and Sullivans.

To librarians and booksellers everywhere.

I like to keep a running list of the people and organizations who have helped me out in my writing journey. After six novels, the list is long! Larissa Ackerman, Michelle Addo-Chajet, Samantha M. Bailey, Lou Berney, Trisha Blanchet, Bookstock, Peter Cannon, Hillary Cassavant, Bruce Robert Coffin, Oline Cogdill, Liv Constantine, John Copenhaver, Crime Bake, Karen Dionne, Sara DiVello, Charlie Donlea, Emerson College, First Clue Review, Daniel Ford, Stephanie Ford, Charles Garabedian, Julie Gerstenblatt, Mario Giordano, Connie Johnson Hambley, Julie Hennrikus, Femi Kayode, John Keyse-Walker, Sonya Larson, Dru Ann Love, Kimberly Hensle Lowrance, Bracken MacLeod, Malice Domestic, Missy Stockwell Martin, Hannah Mary McKinnon, Louise Miller, Scott Montgomery, Paula Munier, Mystery Writers of America, Carla Neggers, Newburyport Literary Festival, New Hampshire Book Festival, August Norman, Karen Odden, Ohlinger Studios, Hank Phillippi Ryan, Salem Lit Fest, Joanna Schaffhausen, Whitney Scharer, John Scognamiglio, Alex Segura, Shawn Reilly Simmons, Sisters in Crime, Adam Stumacher, Peter Swanson, Jessica Treadway, John Valeri, Gabriel Valjan, Tessa Wegert, Steven Zacharius, Kristopher Zgorski.

And most of all, thanks to you for taking a chance on this novel. You can find more information about my upcoming projects at www.edwin-hill.com or on Facebook, Bluesky, and Instagram @edwinhillauthor. Please stay in touch!

About the Author

Photo © 2018 Thomas Bollinger

Edwin Hill is the Edgar and Agatha Award–nominated author of the stand-alone thrillers *Who to Believe* and *The Secrets We Share*, as well as *Little Comfort*, *The Missing Ones*, and *Watch Her* in the Hester Thursby series. He has been featured in *Us Weekly*; received starred reviews in *Publishers Weekly*, *Kirkus Reviews*, *Booklist*, and *Library Journal*; and was recognized as one of Six Crime Writers to Watch in *Mystery Scene* magazine. Edwin lives in Roslindale, Massachusetts, with his partner, Michael, and his favorite reviewer, their Lab Edith Ann, who likes Edwin's first drafts enough to eat them. For more information, visit www.edwin-hill.com.